# JAKES BURN

_Diane — Thanks for your support !!_

_R²_

# JAKE'S BURN
## by Randy Rawls

_Randy 5/2/04_

Quiet Storm Publishing • Martinsburg, WV

Published by  Quiet Storm Publishing
PO BOX 1666
Martinsburg, WV  25402

www.quietstormpublishing.com

Cover by : Dustin Evans

ISBN: 0-9749608-1-0

Library of Congress Control Number:  2004101802

Printed in the United States of America

This book is dedicated to Sue Hartigan, a dear friend who saw potential in me that others missed.  Without Sue, there would be no *Jake's Burn* as we see it today, and no Randy Rawls with **Quiet Storm Publishing**.  Without Sue, my career would not be.

Thank you, Sue.  And thank you, Clint, for listening to Sue.

# PROLOGUE

He tore two matches loose. The small print below a local bar's slogan said, *Close Cover Before Striking.* He complied.

From his position in the entryway, the crystal chandelier reflected in his eyes. A deep sigh escaped as he blinked rapidly, fighting tears. His attention turned upward, up the winding staircase to the second floor balcony and he frowned. His head slowly rotated toward the study as his face evidenced sadness and regret.

He stared at the matches. It had to be done, and it had to be done now. But still he hesitated, studying the lines of dampness running from him into the study, up the stairs, and over the sofa and the drapes. His eyes watered from the gasoline fumes that filled the room. With a shrug and a half-grimace, he struck the matches and tossed them onto the wet Persian rug, an original.

The whoosh and tongues of flame startled him as he stooped to pick up the cans. He spun, his heart racing. The flames leapt upward, grabbing at the furniture, the drapes, the walls, everything in its path.

Randy Rawls

Spurred by the fierce heat, he ran from the house, intent only on escape. A tree root snaked upward in the darkness and grabbed him, sending him into a forward sprawl, the cans flying in different directions.

The force of an explosion forced him forward. He caught himself, then whirled toward the blazing inferno. The flames curled from the second floor windows greedily reaching for the third. Glass tinkled to the ground from exploding windows. The shrubbery withered, then burst into flame. The fire appeared bright enough to alert all of Eastland County.

*Gotta get out of here.* That primary thought dominated the top layer of his consciousness. Fear, fear of the fire and fear of retribution occupied the second level. There was no third.

His pickup truck loomed before him and he yanked the door and jumped in. A second later, he sped from the inferno he'd created.

Only when he reached the outskirts of Cisco did he relax and breathe normally. He slowed and looked over his shoulder. The glow from the burning house atop the distant hill filled his mind.

## CHAPTER ONE

My ears screamed that a phone rang while my brain refused to acknowledge it. I turned my head and squinted at the clock. Right brain yelled, *I don't want to be called at three in the morning.* I rolled toward the lamp but a heavy lump in the middle of my chest slowed me—Striker. Anytime I sleep on my back, he thinks I'm a kitty-bed.

My ears alerted again and Striker hissed quietly plunging his claws through the blanket into my chest. That sped my waking process. Who could it be? And, where's Sweeper? My mind cleared enough for me to curse and vow not to answer.

On the next ring, other senses yelled at me to do something to stop that nerve-scraping sound. Was it my imagination or were the rings longer and louder? Although it could cost me, I decided to let the answering machine get it. Besides, most of my business calls came during the morning after the wife found lipstick on her husband's collar.

I grabbed my blanket and rolled to my right, away from the phone. That's when I discovered Sweeper. How

3

can a twelve-pound cat be so heavy and fill so much space when he's asleep? One of those quirks of nature, I suppose. I gave up on the blanket and rolled without it. Striker rode with me and ended the move sitting on my side, firmly anchored to the bed covers.

Finally, the fourth ring. Time for the answering machine. In spite of my desire to sleep, I wondered who it was. Figured I'd listen to see if he, or maybe she, left a message. Nope, not much chance of a she. I was between shes and didn't know any who would call me any time. Well, maybe my ex-wife, but I didn't need to hear from her.

The answering machine kicked on with the cute message I'd recorded. It started with the theme from *Dragnet*.

> Dum, de dum, dum. Edwards here, Ace
> Edwards, Private Investigator. I can't
> take your call right now. Give me your
> name, number and a message. I'll get
> back to you because I'm Ace Edwards,
> Private Eye. Dum, de dum, dum.

It seemed humorous when I recorded it, but at three in the morning, it only sounded stupid.

"Arty, wake up. I know you're there."

That woke me. Arty! Only one guy called me that, and he only did it to get my goat. I reached over, dislodging my cats, and switched on the bedside lamp.

Striker complained, "Meow."

Sweeper woke and scowled at me as he stretched. I suppose his curiosity overcame his natural inclination to sleep through anything. Well, if curiosity killed cats, I'd have lost him long ago.

"Okay, you're ignoring me," the speaker phone said. "Won't work, I know you're there. Here's some blue grass for your machine."

Fiddle-sawing in an up-tempo number raked across my nerve endings. Sweeper and Striker jumped from the bed and ran underneath. They share my tastes in music, and that does not include fiddle mutilation.

I snatched up the phone. "Jake, you son-of-a-bitch, what do you want?"

"Why Arty, is that any way to talk to an old friend? I'm sitting here watching my house smoke and thought of you."

"Don't call me Arty." I was set to give him hell when I realized what he'd said. "What do you mean, watching your house smoke?"

"Just what I said. I got a call from the Eastland County Sheriff's office about two hours ago. Said my house was burning." He hesitated, then continued in a softer voice. "By the time I got here, it was gone. Nothing left but the chimneys, and smoking ashes."

I heard passion in his voice and hoped he wouldn't cry. That I could not handle at three in the morning.

"Wait a minute. Are you telling me your house burned?"

"That's why I like you, Arty. You're really quick."

I resisted the impulse to pull the cord from the wall and throw the phone across the room. "Jake," I growled through clenched teeth, "it's three o'clock. Start over and tell me what happened. And cut off that damn blue grass. It's stunting my cats' growth."

He said something, but I interrupted. "House? What house? Last I heard, you live in a penthouse in Fort Worth."

5

Jake let out something between a laugh and a sob, but the music stopped. "I'll keep it simple," he said. "One, my house—the one Sheila took from me. Like I said, the sheriff's department called and told me it was on fire. Two, I drove over here. Three, it's gone. Four, I'm sitting here watching it smoke. Five, I need an investigator. Six, you have a license, and you're hired. Is that simple enough?"

"Yeah. What about Sheila? Is she okay?"

"Don't know, haven't seen her, don't give a damn. She's probably out with her latest stud. Hell, she might have torched the place herself. But if you're so hot to know, you can find out while you're investigating."

Jake is one of my oldest friends, although friend might be too strong a word. We grew up in Cisco in different neighborhoods. You might even say, different sides of the tracks. Not that I grew up poor, his family was just so damned rich.

We met in school, but became friends on the football field. He was the star quarterback and I was a substitute running back. Glory washed over him while my body collected bruises on the back-up team in practice and splinters during games, except for a few carries coach gave me occasionally.

Jake contacted me three years ago, before he went to court for his divorce. He hired me to investigate Sheila, his ex-wife. What I found wasn't pretty, and Jake's lawyer used it. Based on her proven poor character, the judge cut her share to only forty percent of everything Jake had. Of course, that was enough to finance a coup in a Third World country.

That was the last time I talked to him, and now he was on the phone at three in the morning acting like we'd spoken yesterday.

"Hey, Arty. You still there?"

I snapped out of my reverie. "Yeah, I'm here. Just remembering when we were in high school, and how much I loved knocking you on your butt."

"Yeah, in your dreams." Jake's chuckle filled me with memories of his racing past as I snatched air.

"What do you mean, when I start my investigation?" The fog of sleep had almost lifted, and I didn't know if I liked what I'd heard.

"Oh, I thought you understood, Arty. I hired you to find out who torched my house."

He said it as if he were talking about washing his car, not that he ever had. He'd always had too much money to get wet himself.

"Whoa, Jake. Hold on there. You're galloping off like a half-broke mustang. First, don't call me Arty. Second, you haven't hired me. I might not want the job. Third, it's not your house, it's Sheila's. You just get to pay for it. And fourth, what makes you think someone torched it? What makes you think I even want your case?"

"Hmmm. Haven't had a chance to think you might not take the case. Like I said, I'm watching ashes." He paused. "Not take the case? Nah, you're hired at twice your daily rate. I'm not going to let you out of it. No matter how hard I try to spend Dad's money, it keeps multiplying. Hell, it almost recovered from the chunk Sheila took. You're another tax dodge. A fresh one's always nice."

I had no doubt he spoke the truth.

7

"Now, what was second? Oh yes, the house." Jake kept talking without breathing, or so it seemed. "It'll always be my house. I was waiting to buy it back from Sheila. She'd have sold. Third, oh shit, what was third?"

I don't know if all rich guys are so blasé about money, but Jake had always been this way—not arrogant, mind you, just blasé. "Third was what makes you think someone torched your house?"

"One of the firemen said arson. He's coming back to investigate. I told him I knew the best, and I'd hire him."

"Oh, thanks a lot," I replied, picturing the greeting I'd get from the firemen.

"They're expecting you. Check in at the fire station, and they'll take you out to the house. You'd better get moving. They start early in the country. Is a thousand a day enough?"

I almost choked. "A thou a day?" Four hundred a day was the best I'd ever made, and that was from Jake.

Striker and Sweeper came from under the bed and stared at me, their green eyes slitted as if daring me to turn down the money.

"Sorry, Arty, that's probably not enough. I know you have other cases, but I need priority. Tell you what. Get on the phone and cancel your other commitments for the next two weeks."

I could do that with one phone call. On Friday, I had an appointment to have the oil changed in my Chrysler convertible. I didn't tell Jake.

He prattled on. "Let me see. I don't want you losing money so I'll go to fifteen hundred a day if you promise me exclusivity for at least two weeks."

At this point, my memory gets foggy. I don't remember what I said but I hope it was something intelligent. I was too busy trying to digest fifteen hundred bucks a day to remember anything. Fifteen hundred times fourteen days was . . . was . . . Hell, it was too much for me to figure although I remembered from some dark recess in my mind that fifteen squared was two-twenty-five. Did that mean Jake was talking about twenty thousand for two weeks' work? I decided I'd put the math off until I found my calculator.

Whatever I said attracted the cats' attention. Both jumped onto my lap and stared into my face, pleading with me to accept Jake's offer, or so it seemed.

Sweeper rubbed his back underneath my chin with his purring volume cranked to about fifty decibels. Obviously, he thought the rate was adequate. I heard myself saying, "Yeah, fifteen will do it—plus expenses."

"Of course, Arty."

I skipped telling him not to call me Arty. "What happened to your house?"

"Don't know any more. I think somebody torched it and Sam agrees. Said he'd be here at first light to get started. You'd better get some rest. You remember where the fire station is, don't you?"

"Yeah, Jake, I remember. You didn't really tell them I'm an expert, did you? Who's Sam?"

"Sure did. Said you're a high-priced private eye now, but you used to be the backbone of the Dallas Police Department. Sam's looking forward to meeting you."

"I'll just bet he is," I said as he hung up.

I sat for a moment stroking the cats and staring into the mirror. The clock's reflection read three-thirty. "Guess I'd better hit the shower, boys. Wanna join me?"

"Meow." Sweeper asked.

"Meow." Striker echoed.

## CHAPTER TWO

Cisco has a population of roughly three thousand people and is about halfway between Fort Worth and Abilene. The population hasn't changed in a long time, and not much of anything else has either. It has a varied history but is now simply one of the many rest stops along Interstate 20.

I rolled into town at seven-fifteen and drove to the fire station. There's only one in Cisco. It's been in the same spot since I was a kid, and probably long before. After parking, I crossed and walked through the big door.

A young man wearing a dark blue T-shirt with Cisco Fire Department written over the left breast threw a bag into a four-by-four. He looked young, and I assumed he was a teen-age volunteer. "Excuse me, young man."

He turned toward me, smiled, and walked in my direction. "Can I help you, sir?"

I could have lived without the sir, a clear indicator of what he thought of my age. "This is a wonderful old building and I don't think it's changed a bit since I grew

11

up here," I said, looking around the area where I'd spent many hours as a kid.

"Not sure about wonderful but it does have character, although it could use some modernizing, especially the bathrooms." He chuckled and pointed toward two doors that showed the ravages of age. "We could use new equipment, too. Are you in town for a visit?"

"No," I replied, "business. I'm looking for the arson investigator. Is he here?"

He eyed me before saying, "Arson investigator? What'd you do, come in blindfolded? This burg can't afford an arson investigator. Heck, we can't even afford full time firefighters."

That changed my approach. "How about the fire chief? Is he here?"

That produced another suspicious look. "Why do you want to see him? Who are you?"

I looked at him again, and saw I had misjudged his age. He wasn't a teenager, although he couldn't have been out of his formative years for long. Helping me figure it out was the fact he was about six inches taller and forty pounds heavier than I. He looked about six-two and over two hundred pounds. He had to be around more than nineteen years to get that big.

I stuck out my hand. "I'm Arthur Conan Edwards. My friends call me Ace."

Ignoring my offer to shake, he responded, "Whuy Mistah Edwards, mah name is Sam'ul Raleigh, and ah'm jist so impressed to meetcha."

The change that came over him told me my guess about my reception had been correct. At least I'd learned who Sam was—and Sam wasn't happy. Thanks a lot, Jake.

"Ah'm the countr' boy what runs this-here far station. Shucks, ah ain't never worked in no big city. Ah been right here since I gratiated high school. Course ah been hangin' 'round th' station since I wuz fourteen. You kin call me Mustah Raleigh, Fire Chief."

He still hadn't offered to shake hands, and I got the impression it was not an oversight. He walked away, then turned and said back over his shoulder, "You kin jist follow me over heah. We're gittin' ready to go out to the house whut burnt last night."

Wow. I knew how a postman feels when he enters a strange yard and is attacked by the family pooch. I'd gotten off to such a bad start with Sam, I punched my humility button. "Hold it a minute, Mr. Raleigh. I don't know what you've heard, but I'm not a hotshot arson investigator. It's true Jake Adams hired me but he exaggerates. I'll need your help all the way. Now, what say you knock off that country bumpkin accent and let's start over?" I stuck out my hand, offering again to shake.

He slowly turned, facing me, no smile on his face.

By now, I figured he knew my features well enough to paint me in oil. His attitude said he'd prefer to boil me in oil.

"Okay. Maybe what I heard was Mr. Adams' bluster." He reached and shook my hand, squeezing hard. "But you can still call me Mr. Raleigh, or Chief."

I thought I saw a small grin after the last remark but I couldn't be sure. I was too busy pretending he hadn't crushed my hand.

A second fireman entered and spoke to Sam. "I'll be ready as soon as I grab a doughnut." He turned toward me. "Are you the hotshot they sent in to show us our job?"

Sam answered before I could. "Yeah. Ace Edwards, P-I-E. That's Private Investigator, Extraordinaire. Get your doughnut and let's roll, we're burning daylight."

While he spoke to the other fireman, I surreptitiously counted my fingers. Yeah, he'd left five, although two were still numb.

"That's Al, one of our EMTs," Sam told me as Al ducked back into the office. "He has his bachelor's from UT. Of course, like me, he doesn't have a big city reputation to throw around."

There was a cold wind blowing through Cisco, Texas that morning and I stood in the middle of it. My first impulse was to kiss it off and head back to Dallas, but that was replaced by dollar signs—fifteen hundred of them a day. I'd be able to pay my mortgage without raping my bank account.

Al re-entered the bay with a doughnut in each hand, saving me from the cold shoulder Sam threw my way. "Okay, I'm ready." He took a bite from a jelly doughnut.

Sam smiled, grinned, then laughed. "Al, no damn wonder you're overweight. You drink diet colas and eat doughnuts all day. It'll never work."

I was glad to learn Sam could be something other than dour. I took a closer look at the four-by-four. It would be a contest to judge which was older, Sam or the vehicle. "Why don't we take my car? We can drop the top and air it out." Getting stranded in Eastland County was not high on my list of things to do.

"We'll need the equipment at the house, but we can go in your car," Sam said. "That'll give me a chance to absorb some big city modus operandi. At my tender young age, and with my lack of experience, I'm always looking to learn from the best."

Before I could reply, he turned to Al. "Follow us in the four-by-four. I'm ridin' with Mustah Edwards. We's gonna put the top down."

I looked at the concrete at his feet expecting to see a puddle of sarcasm. It sure dripped from his words.

As I watched the four-by-four laboring to start and warm up enough to move under its own power, I decided to talk to Jake. I'd tell him he needed to take a civic-minded attitude toward his hometown and donate a new utility vehicle to the fire department. I supposed he knew a museum somewhere that would welcome the old one.

We drove out of Cisco followed by the four-by-four, and worked our way to where Jake's house had stood. From a mile away I saw the house, but not as I remembered it. Today, all I saw were three chimneys reaching into the sky like sentinels. They would have been impressive but I had seen them before. The house had stood at the peak of one of the highest hills near Cisco, dominating the landscape as buffalo once had. The chimneys were part of what had been the most beautiful home in the area, a home constructed by the best craftsmen Jake could hire.

We pulled into the long circular driveway and I searched our back trail. Sparse vegetation, sagebrush and mesquite—no buildings, only a few cattle. Jake picked the best site in the Cisco area for his home, also one of the most isolated.

When I looked toward the hill again, the devastation made me sad. An occasional swirl of smoke escaped from the burned timbers. I could now see that in addition to the chimneys, a sink from an upper floor bathroom survived, hanging precariously, swinging in the slight breeze, the pipes anchored to the center chimney.

"Pull over here, Edwards. This is as far as we need to go." Sam seemed to have grown another few inches and his confidence appeared to soar. We'd reached an area where he was the expert, and it showed.

I pulled over and Al parked behind me. When he killed the engine, it refused to die, run-on they call it. It sounded more like it'd never run again, on or off.

Sam and Al whispered for a moment then turned toward me. "All right," Sam said. "Let's move out. Edwards, you walk behind us, and try not to step on my heels. From this point in, anything can be important."

"Why are we starting out here?" I asked. We were about fifty yards from the house. "The fire was up there." I pointed toward the remains.

Raleigh looked at me as if I'd cut wind in church. "Look, Edwards, I don't have time to explain everything to you. Try to keep up, and don't get in the way."

I could tell I was still low in Sam's estimation. I figured I'd play his game. I've learned that by playing dumb, I often learn more than if I let others know the breadth of my knowledge. "Okay, you're the boss. I'm here to learn."

Sam and Al started walking and I fell in behind them. They paced a circular route around the house, their heads swinging back and forth, examining the ground and the vegetation. We walked around the house, and around the house, and around the house until I wondered if one of Sam's legs was shorter than the other. But we did cut the diameter of the circle each time.

About thirty yards from the house, Jake had put in a rose garden. He claimed they would save money on florists—he'd pick a dozen roses for Sheila. The only one who ever cut roses was the gardener.

The area was in disarray now. Obviously, Sheila had given it a low priority. The automatic sprinklers kept the roses alive and encouraged every weed found in Texas.

Al probed with a stick. Sam seemed intent on studying the ground, looking for footprints, I supposed. I heard Al say, "Sam, over here. I think we've got something."

Sam and I walked to where Al peered into the weedy rose garden. "What is it?" Sam asked.

"Looks like a jerry can."

I peeked over Al's shoulder and saw a five-gallon gas can, or a jerry can as they're called in the military, laying on edge, leaning against one of the rose bushes. Weeds were crushed under it, indicating it had been thrown there recently. The cap was off, dangling from its chain.

Al reached with his stick, hooked the can, lifted it out, and sat it on the ground. He headed toward the utility truck.

Sam sniffed the can. "Gasoline. No doubt about it. Might be the accelerant. The way this baby went up, there could be others."

Al returned with a large paper bag. It had handles like a shopping bag, and Sam used the stick to place the can inside.

"Gas?" Al asked.

"My guess," Sam replied, "but the lab boys will have to give us the legal answer."

We went back to circling and probing. I got into the mood of the day and picked up a stick. Before we reached the edge of the house, we found two other jerry cans that Sam declared had held gasoline. Al put them in paper bags like the other. We accepted that gasoline was the accelerant.

As we approached the foundation of the house, I kept a wary eye on the sink swinging in the breeze. I figured it represented all that was left of a third floor bathroom. As I worried about its position, I pictured my tombstone. *Killed by the kitchen sink.* Okay, bathroom sink. In any case, I wasn't eager to have it fall on me.

Bricks lay everywhere, some still so hot they steamed from the water poured on them during the night. Burned timbers lay about, tendrils of smoke rising in the air. We stepped into the chaos. I envied Sam and Al. They wore sturdy work boots. Me, I wore my Dan Post western boots.

Sam and Al were more intent with their searching now. I watched my boots turn black, and that swinging sink while my brain swirled with the knowledge that Jake was right. This looked like a torch job. The gas cans supported him.

Al was a few paces ahead. He probed a charred pile of rubble. "Oh shit, you guys better see this."

Sam and I stepped to where Al held up what appeared to have been wallboard. Sam blocked my view as he knelt to get a closer look.

"What do you think, Al?"

"Same as you."

I still couldn't see what they saw. "Hey, guys, clue me in. What's down there?"

Sam looked over his shoulder, then leaned aside. I saw a body, or what was left of one. As I knelt to get a better look, the wind shifted and blew the stench of charred meat into my face. My stomach rolled over as I scrambled to my feet. I'd seen enough. A human had died there, a person who'd fallen on his or her back and been consumed by the fire. I muttered, "That's a body, a human body. Who, who could it be?"

Sam gave me a look. "Yeah, it's a body but we can't tell who it was. Looks like another job for the lab boys. Al, get the sheriff up here. It's his game now."

Al headed toward the four-by-four and Sam marked the spot where the body lay. He began to search again and I walked beside him, combing the rubble as conscientiously as he. The sink wagging in the breeze and the condition of my boots were no longer on my mind. I'd dropped my bumpkin façade and gotten serious about the investigation. The body changed the whole picture.

Al brought the four-by-four up to the house and rejoined us. We continued moving through the rubble, searching and hoping, at least I was, that we found no more bodies.

A police cruiser pulled up the driveway about ten minutes later, and Sam went to meet it. Al and I continued, closing on the center of the circle.

I stopped and looked to where Sam spoke to a deputy sheriff. I couldn't hear what he said, but I saw him point toward the house. I glanced at Al and saw he had almost completed the search. I moved toward Sam, thinking I'd find out what he reported. I was more in tune with policemen than firemen. I wanted to know the deputy's reaction.

19

"Ah, shit."

I turned toward Al and saw him probing another pile of rubble. "Dammit all to hell, another one," he said.

"Not another body?"

"Yeah, get Sam."

A few minutes later, the four of us stared at the remains of a second body, burned like the first. All the flesh was gone, leaving bones charred black by the heat and fire. Sam and the deputy went to the patrol car to call the coroner, leaving Al and me standing in the middle of the residue of Jake's home.

"What a damn shame," Al said, kneeling beside the remains. "Ms. Adams might have led a wild life but she didn't deserve to die like this."

I spun toward him. "Sheila? What makes you think it was Sheila?"

"Makes sense to me. Two people dead in her home. Stands to reason one was her."

My subconscious knew he had to be right but my conscious mind wanted to deny it. "Might have been anybody. There's no way to tell. All I see are bones."

"Yeah, and I hope you know more than I do, but until I hear different, I'll guess one was Ms. Adams."

## CHAPTER THREE

That afternoon, I drove to Jake's office building in Fort Worth, hoping to catch him without a heavy schedule. I walked into the foyer and was greeted by a thin, gray-haired lady whose desk sign said she was Matilda.

"May I help you?" she asked in a squeaky voice.

Since I hadn't been to see Jake in three years, I replied, "Yes, where is Mr. Adams' office? I'm headed in to see him."

Matilda turned to her computer. "Do you have an appointment, young man? What is your name?"

I sensed I was in trouble. Nobody had called me young man in many years. "Ace Edwards. You won't find me in there though, I'm just dropping in on him."

She bristled, and her look was from a different generation. "Young man, nobody visits Mr. Adams without an appointment. If you tell me—"

"Edwards, Ace Edwards."

"Yes, my hearing's fine." She scrolled through a list on the computer. "As I said, tell me when you'd like to see Mr. Adams, sometime next week or the week after, and I'll see if there's an opening." The tone of her voice

21

and her glare said I'd better not interrupt again. "Will fifteen minutes be long enough?"

My mouth must have hung open because she continued, "What's the matter with you, young man, and why are you dirty? Didn't your mama make you take a bath when you were a little boy?"

She had me there. I was sooty from one end to the other, and although I hadn't checked, I'd bet my face looked like something from vaudeville. "Ah, excuse me, ma'am. Let me be more specific. My name is Ace Edwards. I'm a private investigator. Mr. Adams is not only an old friend, but he hired me to investigate the arson of his house last night. I'm dirty because I walked through the ruins. There's nothing left. Now, either get him on the phone, or tell me how to get to his office."

I rocked back on my heels, scowled at her, then turned on my sexiest smile. "It's important I see him."

She looked at me again, and patted her hair. I guess she sensed one strand had escaped the hair spray. "Why Mr. Edwards, why didn't you tell me who you are? Mr. Adams said you might come by, and I should point you to his office. His suite is 901 through 907. Enter through 905. I'll be happy to show you the way."

She gave me a big toothy grin, convincing me she either had an excellent dentist or a great set of dentures. The sudden change that had come over her was unnerving, to say the least. I mumbled, "No, I see the elevators. I'll find my own way."

"Fine, Mr. Edwards, I'll let him know you're on the way up. Next time, don't be timid. Just tell me who you are. You'll find I'm easy to get along with."

I kept an eye on her as I walked toward the elevators. If she morphed again, I didn't want to miss it.

I punched the elevator button and waited. My mind drifted back to what I knew about Jake. His grandfather had owned several sections of land in Eastland County. When McClesky Number One in Ranger spouted oil in 1917, and the oil boom took off, his modest fortune soared, and he became one of the richest men in the area. He and almost everybody else who owned land pumped oil and rolled in dough. However, there was one big difference between him and his neighbors. Jake's granddad saw the end coming and sold his oil rights in '21, before the black gold petered out. He walked away with more money than he could count, and still had the land he started with. He was the kind of granddad every youngster should have.

The elevator dinged and the doors opened. I stepped forward but changed my mind when a gorgeous blonde exited. She smiled, I smiled, and she walked by. I almost missed the elevator as I watched the swish, swish, swish of her skirt. Coming or going, I always enjoyed the artistry of a beautiful woman.

As the elevator soared upward, my thoughts returned to Jake. His dad had been an only child, and after serving in the Korean Conflict, he came home to a General Motors dealership that rolled Cadillacs out the front door as fast as Detroit could deliver them through the back. He was the sole heir to his father's fortune. He added to it.

Jake and I attended college together. He with a full ride on a football scholarship while I worked my way through. My parents helped as much as they could but Dad emphasized that if it was worth having, it was worth working for. He set values development before anything else. Today, I agree with him.

23

I fell in love with the game of soccer in college, and played as much as I could. Jake rode the bench on the football team and wished he could play intramural sports. The football coach vetoed him every time he asked to play soccer. I've noticed football coaches aren't eager to see their players involved in anything other than football.

College blew by in a blur, ending far too soon. After graduation, we kept in touch for a while as we moved in different directions and began our lives. Jake returned to Cisco to a ton of money, and launched a career spending it. Some said he bought a front-end loader to move it around. Eventually, he moved to Ft Worth and opened the offices I now visited.

The elevator jolted to a stop and the doors slid open. I stepped out and stopped dead in my tracks. Someday I hope I'll have a rug in my house as plush as the one leading to his office door. It was a dark, rich red with a nap so deep it lapped over my boots. Each step I took left a sooty footprint behind.

The door opened. "Mr. Edwards. Please come in and have a seat. I'm filling in for Kathy. Mr. Adams said he'll be with you in a few minutes."

She looked like she could be the daughter of the receptionist so I wasted no charm on her. I still grappled with my memories of Jake.

He married Sheila right after graduation from college. She was the head cheerleader, one of the most beautiful women on campus. They became the local high-profile couple, always in the news, hits on the Fort Worth social scene. Everyone said they would have the perfect marriage if they had two children, a boy and a girl. There were no children.

Four years ago, Sheila walked out with her combination chauffeur-bodyguard-personal trainer, a man several years her junior. Fort Worth was aghast, and the news media jumped all over it with story after story. The rumor biddies couldn't stop talking. Jake took the obvious route—filed for divorce.

Me, I moved to Dallas after college, and joined the police force. Janice, a sweet, spoiled, beautiful young woman I'd met in college, became my wife. It took her three years to get tired of me, which made her smarter than I thought. She walked out and moved to Fort Worth. I wished her luck and waited for her to file for divorce. Since we didn't have much, and she made more money than I, it was an even divorce with neither owing the other anything.

I invested seven more years in the police force before I got the cockeyed idea I could make more money as a private eye. After cashing in my small retirement fund, I started a one-man private detective agency, and that's where I've been for the past ten years.

I haven't heard from Janice for five years, and that's good. I still have painful memories there. My agency brings in enough for the cats and me to live, nothing more. I keep hoping to hit a big case that will allow me to put money away for retirement, even as I sweat paying my mortgage each month.

I looked up as an inner door opened. A distinguished looking man came out, then turned back to shake Jake's hand. I compared my appearance to Jake's. I lost—even in my best duds, I'd have lost. That told me how far apart we were on the success strata.

Jake looked great, tan and athletic. As his visitor left, Jake smiled. "Arty, come in. You're looking grubby, as usual."

I followed him in, thinking, Thanks Jake. I settled into the deepest wingback chair I've ever seen, and knocked soot off my boots onto his beige rug. I hoped my sooty jeans were leaving smudges on the buffed leather that caressed my rear. I'm short, but usually my feet can at least scrape the floor. However, the chair fit his office perfectly.

I hadn't been there since I reported the results of my pre-divorce investigation. The office was as big as ever, huge better describes it, but he'd remodeled and had cut no corners. I wondered if he'd found a way to write it off his taxes as I took in the dark mahogany paneling, the surface so reflective it could be used as a mirror. The carpet was thick and plush and looked soft enough to sleep on. The paintings on the walls reminded me of art museum. Any other day I would have been impressed with his extravagance. However, the morning's findings had dampened my enthusiasm for Jake's use of money.

"So, Arty, how's life been treating you? Cigar?" He opened a silver case and pushed it toward me. I had no doubt the cigars violated the trade embargo on Cuba.

I looked at him sitting behind his massive desk and the only word that describes how I felt is jealous. I know it's petty but there he sat, same age as me. I'm losing my hair, but his thick black hair had gray sprinkled through the temples, giving him a distinguished look most men have to pay for, and women find attractive. I knew he stood six-foot-two, towering over me. Women describe him as handsome. I doubt many use that word for me. The suit he wore would go for at least seven hundred.

My jeans were worn although they were only three years old. That was a reminder. I needed to watch for a sale on jeans.

"No, no cigar," I said. "Haven't you heard, the Surgeon General says smoking is detrimental to your health?"

"Maybe." Jake selected a cigar and closed the case. "What did you find?"

"Two bodies, Jake. Two people died. Do you know who they were?"

"No, I guess one of them might have been Sheila. As far as I know, she was home last night. The second one—I don't have a clue." He fiddled with the cigar, clipping the end and taking his time lighting it.

"Bullshit, I can't buy that. What the hell's wrong with you? Sheila was your wife, your best friend for a long time. Don't try that cavalier attitude on me. I know you too well."

Jake looked at me, laid the cigar in an ashtray, then switched his concentration to his manicured fingernails. A flush rose from his throat flowing over his face.

I waited, determined to force him to comment.

"Okay, Arty. To tell the truth, I don't know how I feel. I've been mad with her so long, I don't know how to react. She made her decision when she took off with Bubba, and I buried my feelings under anger ever since. I had no clue how much I loved her until I lost her."

He hesitated, then sighed. "You remember, Sheila made a big fuss about our home during the divorce so the Judge gave it to her. No one but me knows how bad that hurt."

I remembered. In a perfect example of divorce court justice, the judge handed the keys to Sheila and returned the payment book to Jake. One of those things I can never figure out. That was one of the reasons I quit the police department—judges who ignore facts and reward or refuse to punish the guilty.

"The house went to Sheila, but I had to pay the bills. I even had to pay for the hired help—gardeners, butler, upstairs maids, downstairs maids, cooks, all of them."

I knew his memory had slipped. He refused to pay for the chauffeur-bodyguard-personal trainer, the one Sheila walked out with.

He stopped and examined his nails again. I wondered if his manicure had chipped.

He gave me a straight look—eyeball to eyeball. "I could never wish her dead though."

As our eyes stayed locked together, I made a judgment call. I believed him. But that didn't change what I had to do. "I gotta ask you this. Where were you last night? Did you torch the house?"

"Arty, I'm going—"

"Dammit, Jake. Don't call me Arty. How many times—"

"You asked a question, Arty." Jake returned my interruption. "At least let me answer it. As I was saying, I'm going to assume you had to ask me if I burned my house. No, I did not. I loved that house. I designed it. I oversaw the laying of every brick, the nailing of every timber. I wanted that house back, not burned to the ground. I hoped Sheila would sell it to me if I left her alone and didn't fight the judge's orders. No, Arty, I did not burn my house."

I squirmed forward, trying to touch the floor with my boots. "Okay, suppose I buy everything you say.

Everything except calling me Arty. Do you know who might have a grudge against Sheila, who might kill her and burn the house?"

Jake had a faraway look in his eyes. He ignored my question, rose and walked to the far end of his office. "Come here, Arty, and look at this."

I fought my way out of the parasitic wingback chair and joined him.

"Look at that." He pointed at a photograph on the wall, a twenty by twenty-four of the house. "It's the most beautiful home ever built in Eastland County, perhaps all of Texas. You know the area, you know the view from there. I'm going to rebuild it, like it was before some son-of-a-bitch burned it to the ground."

"Jake, wake up, dammit. Quit crying about the house. Sheila may have died in that fire. Don't you have any feelings for her?"

"No. Absolutely not. You'll never understand how she hurt me when she took up with Bubba. For God's sake, Arty, Bubba was her damn chauffeur—a high school dropout. You want me to feel sorry for her? I can't. I don't feel a damn thing for her. She knew what I loved and took it from me. She didn't give a hoot for the house."

The bitterness in his voice surprised me. In all the years I'd known him, there had never been an occasion when he voiced anything close to what I'd heard. All I could think to say was, "You gotta get over it. If you don't, it'll eat you alive."

"Yeah, I know. I'm in therapy. I'm coming together with the fact I left her alone too many times, and was away too often. My shrink says I set up the crash—it had

29

to happen. Maybe someday, I'll accept my guilt, but for now, I hurt."

I saw the pain in his eyes, but as I looked, they changed. The old Jake rose to the surface. "Now, look at the plans of the house. It was fantastic."

Jake walked behind his desk while I circled to the front of it. I couldn't help but wonder what great oak had surrendered its life for him to have such a desk. It was solid oak—well, looked like oak—and was about six by twelve feet. It must have taken a team of weight lifters to bring it into the office. Either that, or it was assembled in place. The finish on it was beyond my vocabulary, something you see few times in your life.

He dropped into his chair and scooted to one end of his desk where he opened the bottom drawer. I wondered why he didn't have a motorized office chair to move from one end to the other. He pulled out a tube and withdrew a roll of papers. "Come over here." He stood and walked to a small conference table at the other end of the office.

Since I'd stayed away from the wingback chair, I was able to follow him without exerting myself. He spread the plans and we spent about thirty minutes examining them while Jake explained each line.

He slowed and I seized the opportunity. "This is all great, and I understand how much you loved that house, but I'm no closer to figuring out who torched it. That's why you hired me, but I need help. To find the arsonist, I have to backtrack on Sheila's life after you two split. Who were her friends? Who did she run with? Did Bubba still live with her?"

Jake looked at me, then walked to his desk. He opened another drawer and pulled out a brown folder, flipped it open and studied it for a moment. "Now Arty, I hope you won't be upset with me, but . . ."

He stopped and flicked his eyes over me before looking back at the folder, then continued, "I hired another PI to follow her. I wanted to know who she was spending my money on. I knew you were too busy for small stuff."

Now, that did hurt my feelings. I didn't tell him not to call me Arty. I wondered how much he'd paid the guy, and thought about how hard up for money I'd been. I said, "What'd he get? Anything I can use?"

He took out a sheet of paper and handed it to me. It was a list of names, dates and locations. I studied the list. "I recognize some of these as the group she ran with before the divorce, but the others mean nothing to me. Some of the last names look familiar, same as people we grew up with. Are all these from around Cisco?"

"More or less, and I'm not surprised you don't recognize them. Some moved there after you left, and some were conceived when we were in college. Here's some pictures."

I laid the list aside and took the pictures. They showed young people in their twenties and thirties. I looked at Jake. "Are you telling me Sheila ran with a group this young?"

"Yep, that's it. She had this problem with age. It wrecked our marriage. When she passed thirty, she went nuts. She couldn't stand the thought of the years passing her by. Remember, she was thirty-five when she took off with Bubba. He was twenty-eight. These people are all Bubba's followers, his group. The guy I hired said she tried about every one of the men."

31

Jake stopped and looked at his desk. His voice dropped to barely above a whisper. "In fact, she might've tried the women, too. Seems like it's a pretty versatile group."

I sat there, feeling Jake's embarrassment and pain, not knowing what to say. I've learned that sometimes it's best to keep your mouth shut.

The alarm on Jake's Rolex sounded, telling us it was two o'clock. I looked at my Timex. Yep, two o'clock. "Well, what's the chances one of these characters did her and burned the house?"

"That's what I'm paying you to find out. But, be careful. They're a pretty rough group—sex, booze and drugs. The investigator said they do it all."

I looked back at the photos. The women were attractive and didn't need a lot of fancy makeup. The guys were grubby looking in that way women find handsome. Some had shaved heads and faces, a few had long, stringy hair and scruffy beards, and a few had combinations of each. The women wore clothing that emphasized their physical attributes. The men dressed in jeans, plaid shirts and boots. The women's clothing was clean and carefully chosen. The men looked like they had come from work.

Sheila stood out, the most beautiful woman among beautiful women—a beauty pageant collection. She was also the most mature, or I could say, the oldest.

I laid the pictures aside. "Back to the fire. We have to assume one of the bodies was Sheila's. Any ideas on who the other might have been?"

"No, not really. Could have been anybody or nobody. I don't know who she's been with recently." He reflected for a moment, then asked, "How long until they I.D. the bodies?"

"Not sure," I replied. "They'll probably have to get help from the state. There's not much to work with. I hope it's soon though. The solution might be in the second body."

## CHAPTER FOUR

"Yeah, I remember you. You're that asshole cop that went private. Adams' private dick, digger of dirt, and all round sonofabitch."

I had come to interview Bubba, and we stood in the living room of his apartment. He was so involved in abusing me he'd forgotten to offer me a chair. I took his insults, hoping he'd slow so I could get in a couple of questions. After several minutes, I decided, screw him and his lack of manners. I walked to his couch and sat. When he stopped to inhale, I jumped in. "When'd you see Sheila last?"

Bubba stepped toward me with both fists clenched. "You bastard! Don't mention her name. She was the most perfect human being ever born. You helped that scumbag ex of hers. You bastards made up a bunch of lies to hurt her at the divorce. She told me about it."

I'll bet she did, I thought, while you two played hide the weenie in Jake's bed.

All you macho folks might wonder why I tolerated his insults. Simple. The name Bubba fit like an expensive glove. His real name is John Wayne Hudson and that fit too. He stood six-foot-four, and his muscles had muscles on their muscles. I always assumed one of the reasons he became a chauffeur was because he didn't need a jack to change a tire. He could pick the car up, jerk the flat off, and jam on a good one. Jake told me one time they were out and the car died. Bubba didn't call Triple A. He towed it himself.

Nevertheless, I needed answers. Maybe I could turn the tables on him. "'Scuse me, Bubba. You might find this odd, but I think Sheila was a very nice person. But you know, a job's a job, and right now, Sheila's my job. I know how broken up you must be, losing someone as sweet as she was."

It was enough to stop him from cursing. He gave me one of those looks somewhere between I wanna beat the shit out of you and I'd like to buy you a beer. "Huh, you mean you liked Sheila, too?"

"Of course. I knew her in college before she married Jake. We go way back together. I always respected her. I thought she was a perfect lady."

Bubba stared at me, and I sensed that in his cobwebby space where most humans store a brain, rusty gears engaged. I pictured an old gristmill with the millstone slowly turning.

"Well, why'd you tell all them lies?" His expression told me he wasn't convinced, and my health was still in jeopardy.

"Listen to me. Didn't she get the house? Didn't she get more money than you guys could spend in a hundred years? Didn't Jake have to pay her bills? Didn't you two leave the courthouse laughing at Jake and the judge?" I leaned back on the couch like I didn't have a care in the world.

The millstone made another revolution. Bubba walked over and dropped into a recliner. "Yeah, I guess she kinda did. But you didn't plan for her to get nothing."

"Of course I did." I could see a ray of sunshine beginning to show—right through his ears. I didn't say anymore. I didn't move. I wanted to give him every opportunity to think, and I figured any small distraction would be like a volcano erupting on a small ocean island.

"Maybe you ain't so bad after all." He stood, sticking out a hand the size of a country ham. I reached and watched my hand disappear up to the elbow, or so it seemed. The thought crossed my mind that if he wanted, he could send me looking for a prosthetic device. I was lucky. He only jerked it up and down several times like priming a pump. He almost lifted me off the couch with each motion.

"You're all right. I like you." I was relieved he'd turned me loose. I surreptitiously counted my fingers, something I'd been doing a lot recently. They were still tender from shaking hands with Sam Raleigh. I was glad to find Bubba had also left five.

"I want to find out who killed her, and I want to find out who burned the house. I need your help."

Bubba shook his head, saying, "You think somebody killed her? Naw, everybody loved Sheila." He settled back into his chair.

"I know she was special. But somebody doused the house with enough gasoline to fuel the Indianapolis 500. Now, if they did that, I'm betting they killed Sheila first." I stopped because Bubba's face was turning ugly.

He bounced out of his chair, stretching up even taller—seemed like about ten feet—and said, "I'll kill the sonofabitch. You find'm, and I'll rip his head off. He shouldn't have hurt my Sheila." Then he collapsed in his chair, crying.

Any doubts I'd had about Bubba's innocence washed away with his tears. He cried like a three-year old. If he hadn't been so big, I might have put my arm around his shoulder to comfort him, but I wasn't going to take any chances he might misinterpret my empathy.

He cried about five minutes while I let my eyes roam his apartment. It was obvious Sheila hadn't bought him any expensive presents, or if she had, he didn't keep them here. I didn't spot anything beyond a chauffeur's wages, or a yard sale.

"Okay, what're we gonna do? You tell me what to do and I'll do it." He wiped his eyes, blew his nose in a red bandanna and stood. "Get up. We got work to do. We gotta find Sheila's killer. I'm gonna hire you, and when you find him, I'm gonna kill him."

I tried to explain I was working for Jake, and I could only have one client at a time, but it didn't work. He'd used up his quota of brains for the day. After three tries, I gave up. "You wanna hire me, it's going to cost you two bills a day." I figured he'd say it was too much. That way, I could scoot out by refusing to charge less.

He didn't hesitate. "Two hundred a day? You're hired. Do I start paying today or tomorrow?"

"Tomorrow," I squeaked.

# CHAPTER FIVE

I approached the door with trepidation. I hate going through doors not knowing what's on the other side. There have been too many surprises, too many times when I wish I'd stayed out. I fitted the key into the lock and turned it. A quiet click as the tumblers fell into position was the only sound. The deadbolt slipped backward noiselessly. I sighed. Gently, I turned the knob and pushed the front door inward. The heavy wooden door swung on its brass hinges, easing its way open until there was almost enough space for me to squeeze through. Then, a telltale squeak, a shriek of protest from a hinge not properly oiled. I froze, not daring to move. Maybe the sound went unheard. Maybe my luck would be good for a change. I held my breath until my lungs protested, forcing me to exhale. I sucked in fresh air, congratulating myself, thinking I had made it. There was no noise, no sounds indicating the squeak had been heard. As soon as the slit was large enough to accommodate me, I stepped through. I turned to close the door, and a force shoved me into the wall.

I fell, a heavy weight riding my shoulders. Sweeper had again won our game. I rolled over laughing.

Sweeper moved with me, ending on my chest. It was dark in the house, but enough moonlight sneaked though the curtains for me to see his eyes. I swear he was smirking, as if saying, "Ha, gotcha again." Once more, I congratulated myself for giving him the right name. Nothing gets past a good sweeper on a soccer team, and nothing gets by my Sweeper.

"Okay, you old tomcat," I said, as I gave his ears a scratching. "One of these days, I'm gonna sneak in and surprise you. Where's Striker, ghosting again?"

I climbed to my feet, holding Sweeper in my arm, and hit the light switch. I saw what I expected. The living room was a mess. The lamp that usually stood on the table by the couch lay on its side. The tops of the tables were bare. My boys are excellent at demonstrating their displeasure at being left alone, and they never fail to welcome me home by clearing all the tables.

I sat Sweeper down. He flipped his tail, raised his nose and walked toward the kitchen. His message was clear.

"Striker," I called. "You can come out now. It's me." There was no use looking. He's an expert at hiding.

When they were kittens, I hired someone to come in and check on them when I was away. The first two trips ended with my returning home after a frantic call from my cat-sitter. The message was the same each time although a different person delivered it. "Striker's gone. I can't find him anywhere. He must have run out when I opened the door. I'm sorry, so sorry."

I rushed home expecting the worst—Striker dead, crushed under the wheels of a car. But to my surprise, when I opened the door, he greeted me. Three more times I received panicky phone calls from a sitter. After those episodes, I gave up and left them alone. Two bowls of food and water a day would keep their appetites sated. As for bathroom facilities, I had several litter boxes, and tonight, the house smelled like it.

My first item of business was to haul the litter out and dump it in my neighbor's compost pile. My trips, four of them, were made in haste and I hardly looked right or left. Oh, in case you're wondering, my neighbor asked me to put it in his compost pile. He said it helped the compost cook faster. I thought he was nuts, but it helped me get rid of the boys' litter.

I sprayed each room with air freshener, then looked for candles and matches. I was lighting candles in the cats' bathroom when a vision hit me. Had I seen something as I dashed from house to compost pile and back?

I walked to the front room to peek out the window. Striker and Sweeper were there, noses pressed against the panes, staring out. Their tails were double their normal size with the hair standing tall. Low growls and snarls came from their throats. I killed the lights and edged my way to the window. My night vision was shot but I hoped there'd be enough moonlight to allow me to see.

I peeked out. "What is it, boys? What do you see?" I thought I saw a car creeping along the curb. If there was, it was under the moon shadow of the trees growing alongside the street. The cats' throaty growls were non-stop. Also, there was movement in my front yard, sneaking closer to the house, blending into the darkness. I saw a head swinging right and left, and a tail swishing—a dog.

"Thanks, guys. You scared the hell out of me to let me know a dog was passing though. Some watch-cats you are." As I berated the boys, I heard an engine start. Looking at the street, I saw a car accelerating away, its lights flicking on as it gained speed.

Thirty minutes later, I still paced the floor, trying to piece it together. Why had the cats been growling? Did I see a car creeping down the street with its lights off? Was it the same car I saw down the block turning on its lights as it drove off? Was I getting too old for this business?

"Okay, boys, family meeting." I dropped into my recliner and Striker took his customary position in my lap while Sweeper claimed the arm of the chair. "I'll fill you in on our current case." I told them the details, including the people I'd met. "Got any clues for me?"

Sweeper jumped to the floor and disappeared from the room. I scratched Striker behind the ears. "At least one of you guys is loyal and will tolerate my stories."

Sweeper bounded into the room in hot pursuit of their favorite toy, a miniature soccer ball. The two of them play with it for hours, contesting every touch. This time though, Striker stayed in my lap.

Sweeper dribbled around my chair several times then launched an accurate shot at the corner. Once he'd followed up, he stared at me.

"Very good, Sweeper. Again, you prove your name to be a good one. Now, it's time for bed."

Before heading for the bedroom, the boys and I checked the windows, doors, and locks. I found my Beretta, checked the magazine, and laid it on the nightstand. I might be getting old, but I wasn't taking any chances. When I crawled into bed and pulled the

41

covers up, the boys were underneath. They usually sleep on top.

## CHAPTER SIX

I returned to Cisco where I picked up Bubba. We were in my car, heading for the Down Home Bar. He said Sheila's friends hung out there.

"Bubba, where were you the night Sheila's house burned?" I'd put off asking, afraid Bubba might take offense.

"You got a nice car here. Someday, I'd like a convertible like this."

"Thank you, but you didn't answer my question. Where were you when Sheila's house burned?"

"I was kinda hoping you wouldn't ask again. Now that you work for me, you ask other people things like that, not me."

"If you don't talk to me, I'll not work for you. I don't work for anybody unless I'm sure they're innocent." I hoped he would connect the dots and give me an answer.

"Yeah. That mean you think Adams is innocent?"

I wondered about Jake. I didn't want to believe he had anything to do with Sheila's death, but he had good reasons to be happy. Bubba waited for an answer. I lied. "That's what it means. I don't think Jake did it."

43

"Humph, maybe you're not so smart, after all."

"Bubba, you hired me. If you change your mind, just say so. I'll let you out of our contract."

"Nah, you're still on the payroll. But, I don't think you oughtta write Adams off. You ain't heard all the things I have."

"You're right, I haven't. However, that still doesn't answer my question. Where were you the night Sheila died?"

"You ain't gonna quit askin', are you?"

"Nope."

He inhaled deeply, then blew it out. "Okay. We had a fight. She said she had plans for the night, and she didn't want me around. I knew what that meant. It meant she had a guy coming by. She was . . . ah . . . she liked . . . ah hell, she liked a new guy whenever she could find one." Bubba's head hung, his expression like a whipped dog.

"I understand. Remember, she did the same thing to Jake."

His head jerked up and he glared at me with an intensity that made me wish I hadn't said that. "All right, Mistah Cop. You think I don't know—don't think I know I took a man's wife away—don't have no conscience. I knowed I shouldn'ta done it, but I loved her so much. I still love her." Tears streaked his cheeks.

I watched him, wondering if I'd ever met a grown man with so many tears. We had reached the Down Home Bar. I pulled to the back of the parking lot where it was darkest. I sat, giving Bubba time to recover.

After a few minutes, Bubba blew his nose in his red bandanna then continued where he'd left off. "She told me to get lost for the night and don't come back 'til tomorrow afternoon. I argued with her, told her I loved her. She laughed at me. She said I was her stud, but tonight she had other plans. She told me not to worry, she'd be using my services a lot more times."

Bubba stopped talking and I whispered, "That must have hurt."

"That's not all she said. She said I'd be there anytime she needed me. She said all she had to do was pop her thighs and I'd come running like a puppy. I was so mad I just hadda bend something. I charged out—and, and, never saw her again. She's dead, ain't she?" The creases on Bubba's face showed the depth of his despair.

I looked at him, wondering how it would feel to love someone so completely, so deeply. As I sat there watching a man twice my size cry his heart out because he dared to love, I wondered if that was why Janice left me. Maybe that was how love was supposed to be. Maybe I didn't have the capacity to love her enough.

I wanted to give him time to settle down, but after several minutes, I interrupted. "Where did you go? What did you do?"

He wiped his eyes and sniffed. "I drove down to the tree farm. You know, the one Adams kept so he'd always have hardwood for his fireplace. Sheila got it in the divorce. I cut down trees, sawed them to fireplace length, and split them. I musta cut and stacked about a cord that night. I worked all the mad out of me. I wanted to go back to the house, but she'd told me to stay away. I came here to the Down Home and had a few drinks with the gang. Then Sonny and I took a coupla cases of long necks to my place and drank 'til we fell asleep."

"Sonny who?"

"Sonny Barrow. That's his pickup over there. You can ask him when we go inside. But, better let me tell'm you're okay. Sonny's kinda quick tempered, if you know what I mean."

I knew what he meant. I grew up in Cisco. "One last question before we go in. When did you find out about the fire?"

"The next afternoon. Sonny and I slept late and woke up with hangovers. I heard it on the radio. The man said the Adams house burned to the ground and the police found two bodies in the ashes." Again, his head dropped but he fought the tears. "I knew, somehow I knew she was dead. Sonny and I drove to the house, then to the county cop station. They said the firemen had found the bodies so we drove over there."

Bubba had been mumbling but now he looked up and stared at me. "That's when I found out Mr. Adams had hired hisself a private cop. I talked to that punk fireman and he told me all about finding the bodies and the Dallas cop who was here to make them look bad. I figured if I waited, you'd be around." He grinned, a look of triumph on his face. "I figured if you wuz any good, I'd hire you, too. You did come around, and I hired you. I'm still hoping you're good."

It was time for me to put on my hard look. I glared at Bubba. "Let's get a couple of things straight. Yes, I said I'd work for you, and yes, I told Jake I'd work for him. But understand this—understand it now. I find out either one of you had anything to do with that arson or those murders, I'll do my damnedest to put you under the jail. You got that. Cause if you don't, we're quits right now."

He rocked back in the seat and stared. I doubt very many people talked to him like that and got away with it.

He clenched his fists a few times as I waited, not sure whether to get a solid grip on my Beretta or take it like a man.

Finally, he said, "Okay. But you better treat me and Adams the same, you understand? You better not let his money buy you, or I'll break every bone in your body."

"Deal," I said.

"Deal," he echoed.

\*       \*       \*

When we walked into the Down Home, the chatter stopped as the patrons stared at us. Except for the TVs and the jukebox, it was quiet as a funeral home at three in the morning. The thick cigarette smoke hung like a gray veil dangling from the ceiling. Bubba walked around the room speaking to first one and then another. They answered him, shook hands and exchanged high-fives, but their eyes stayed on me. When Bubba got to the bar, he said in a loud voice, "Give me two long neck Buds, one for me and one for my friend, Ace Edwards."

I was afraid the bartender might have a heart attack. His mouth dropped opened and his face turned red. Either that or he'd suffer serious eyestrain from staring at me.

Bubba said, "Hojo, you know I don't like to repeat myself, and I don't like to wait for my beer. Now, move it!"

About the time I figured somebody might get hurt with a flying beer bottle, Hojo moved with a speed that belied his size—about three hundred pounds. In the flick of an eye, two uncapped long necks sat on the bar.

Bubba picked up the beers and handed one to me. He leaned his back against the bar, hooking one of his boots on the bar rail. "Y'all listen up now," he said loud enough to gain silence in the room. "Ah want y'all ta meet mah friend. This here's Mistah Ace Edwards. He's an expensive private detective from Dallas and I done hahr'd him to find out who killed Sheila and burnt her house. Ah know you gonna hep him all ya kin."

Was it my imagination or had he cranked up his good ol' boy accent a few notches? "Now, ah want y'all ta come on up heah and introduce yourselves. Maybe later, Mistah Edwards will wanna ask you some questions. Be a good idear to answer him. Oh, one other thing. Tell'm the truth."

Now, I've been in many places and I've been introduced to many people, but this may well have been the most effective introduction I ever received.

A tap on the shoulder caused me to turn toward the bar.

"I'm Ben Wallace. Everybody calls me Hojo 'cause I worked in a Howard Johnson's once. I'm mighty please to make your acquaintance."

Another tap took me back to the crowd. "Mr. Edwards, it's a pleasure to meet you. I'm Sonny Barrow, Bubba's my best friend. We get drunk together all the time."

I met Hojo, Sonny, Arizona, Tex, Little Tex, Cactus, Dogface, Steer, Tattoo and Jonathan. Many of the people I met had pictures in Jake's files, his private investigation files.

I was about to ask Jonathan about his name when a disturbance in the crowd caught my attention. When I looked through the heads, I saw Sheila walking toward me. I did a double-take, shook my head and blinked several times but it was still Sheila—the Sheila I'd known in college, the Sheila who married Jake, a Sheila who could melt every heart in a room.

I watched as she moved closer, pausing to speak with first one patron then another, establishing herself with the crowd.

When she was about five feet away, my mind quit doubting itself, and I saw the differences between Sheila and this woman. Although the style and appearance were similar, this one appeared warmer, more compassionate. And as beautiful as Sheila was, this look-alike was more beautiful.

As she neared, I stepped out to greet her, but she said, "Hello, Mr. Edwards, it's a pleasure to make your acquaintance. I've heard wonderful things about you. I'm Terri Hart."

Taking the hand she offered, I found it warm, soft, and comforting. I covered our hands with my free hand, hoping she wouldn't pull away. She didn't. I'm forty-two years old and balding, although I think I do an excellent job of camouflaging the loss. Yet, this woman opened new portals into my soul. I heard myself answering like a fifteen-year-old, tongue-tied youngster. "Why, ah, Miss Hart, it's, ah, it's a pleasure to meet you, too." That's as far as I got. I was lost in her midnight blue eyes.

She withdrew her hand and tossed her shoulder length red hair. "If I can help, please call me anytime. Sheila was everybody's friend."

She looked into my face and her eyes swallowed me. I stammered, "Do you come here much? If you do, I'll make this my headquarters." I gave her one of my best grins. "Maybe when I wrap this case, we can talk privately."

She smiled, then walked away—the crowd parting like water before a sleek yacht—with my gaze glued to her gorgeous derriere. The straight skirt she wore made her as lovely moving away as coming toward me.

As I stood falling in love, a blow to my back jolted me back to the present. I looked around. Standing behind me, getting ready to slap me again, was a pimply-faced young man. Where Terri Hart brought to mind a sleek yacht, he was a garbage scow.

"Hey, Mr. Edwards. I'm shore glad to meet you. I feel like I know you already. Shucks, you been the talk of the town ever since you blew in. Even my sister talks about you. You must be some stud to turn her thermostat up." He giggled and lifted his arm again. I countered by grabbing his hand in a firm handshake.

"That's nice, but who the hell are you?" I looked for Bubba, hoping he'd rescue me.

"Oh, 'scuse me, Mr. Edwards. My momma'd whup my butt if she knowed I forgot my manners like that. I'm Joey Hart, Terri's brother. Most people call me Joey-Boy. I'd shore be honored if you'd call me Joey-Boy like other folks."

I looked him over. "Okay, Joey-uh-boy. You're Terri's brother?" Once again, I proved the obvious never escapes me. "Any more of you Harts around?"

Joey-Boy threw back his head and laughed, more of a snorting. "Nah, you've met us all, or all that hang out here. My dad's a good Baptist and wouldn't come near this place and Mom, well, she does what Dad says."

"I'm glad to know. Too many Harts can give you a coronary." I grinned at my joke, looking him over. Terri's brother? I had doubts. She was tall and statuesque while he was short and squatty. Her complexion was clear and unblemished. His was pockmarked and splotchy. She spoke as if she owned the world. He talked as if he'd stumbled in from the backwoods. She was a sleek fighter plane. He was a lumbering Gooney Bird.

"You're lookin' at me like ev'rybody does who meets Terri first." A frown creased his forehead. "Let me answer all your dam' questions. Yes, I'm Terri's brother. She looks like Mom. I look like Dad. We ain't no kin of Sheila Adams. Terri just looks like her. Terri's thirty and I'm twenty-two. She ain't married. If you wuz to ask her, she might go out with you, that is if her other business don't git in the way. She ain't no virgin but she ain't easy. We ain't got no other brothers or sisters. Anythin' else you wanna know?"

I was embarrassed at how well he'd sized me up. Every one of those questions had cut a swath through my head. "Ah, thanks. I believe you answered all my questions."

A waitress saved me from further embarrassment as she made her way through the crowd. "Oh Miss," I said, "could you bring me a Killian's, please? Joey, you want something?"

"Shore, if you're buying. Margie, bring me my favorite."

The waitress said, "Your taste is shitty even when somebody else buys." The look on her face said the rest.

51

Joey snorted again. "She don't think much of Louisiana Bayou beer. But man, I'm here to tell you, that's good stuff."

I didn't follow up. I'd never heard of Louisiana Bayou. "Joey, did you know Sheila?"

"Ah shit, Mr. Edwards, ev'rybody knowed Sheila. And, I do prefer Joey-Boy." He lowered his voice and leaned into me. "I don't think you want to call me what most women do—Lovetoy." He snorted a couple of more times.

I stepped back. I did not want to call him Lovetoy. While I tried to think of something new to say or, better yet, a way to escape, the waitress showed with the beers. There was indeed a beer named Louisiana Bayou. It had a strange smell, like formaldehyde. I've heard formaldehyde will speed up the aging.

"How long have you known Sheila?" Since I was stuck with him, I figured I'd learn all I could.

"'Bout two years. Not long after she dumped that dipstick she was married to. Bubba introduced me to her. She was some woman. There ain't many like her."

The look on his face bothered me, a look that might have been pride in ownership. I hoped I misread it. Surely, Sheila hadn't slipped that far.

"Mr. Edwards, I want you to know, I'm gonna help you all I can. You need somethin', you just tell ol' Joey-Boy. You wanna talk to somebody, you tell me, and I'll deliver him, day or night. I might not look like much, but I plow a wide furrow out here."

"Thank you. I'll remember. Start by telling me about Sheila."

He took off talking and I wasn't sure I'd get out of there by midnight. When he finally slowed down, three things were clear. First, he didn't know much, only gossip. Second, he had a serious crush on Sheila. He'd finished several Louisiana Bayou's by then, so the third thing I learned was he couldn't handle his beer.

Then, as if she had floated in above the crowd, Terri was at my side. "Excuse me, Mr. Edwards. I'd better take Joey home. It looks like he reached his limit early this evening. You must have been paying."

"After you drop him off, will you be coming back this way?"

"Well, usually I go home after Mom and I put Joey to bed. One part of me says it'd be nice to come back and have a beer with you, but my more conservative side says that wouldn't be a smart thing to do. Think I'll go with the second and get some sleep. School comes early tomorrow." She smiled and turned to Joey.

I was tongue-tied again, but Joey spoke up in a drunken slur. "See, jus' play it cool. She's hot af'er your bod."

I gave Terri an understanding look as she led Joey away. In return, she rewarded me with another smile. "See you again."

As I watched her leave with Joey, I felt twenty years younger than when I'd walked in. I turned to the bar and looked in the mirror. It took a moment before I recognized the grinning fool who stared at me.

Bubba managed to ruin my mood by tapping me on the shoulder. "Hey, you're on my dime. Let's go. That's as close to love as you're gonna get tonight."

I looked at him, then in the direction Terri disappeared. Obligation won out over yearning. I sighed, set my bottle down with a thump and followed Bubba.

As we walked out of the Down Home, an older man intercepted us at the door. "Bubba, can I talk to you a minute?"

"Not now, I gotta roll," Bubba said.

I took a good look at the man who had tried to stop Bubba. He didn't look like a local, didn't look like he belonged in the Down Home. "Who was that?" I asked.

"Some old guy says he gonna write a book about Cisco. His name's Randy or Sandy or something like that."

I glanced back at him and saw he continued to watch us.

"Look," Bubba said, "I got somewhere I gotta be but Sonny's goin' with you. Just follow his lead." He walked away.

## CHAPTER SEVEN

There are times when I wish I was six-six and filthy rich. Then, I'd do things my way. But, since I'm neither, I left the bar with Sonny. We drove to Lake Cisco in my car, and parked in a spot where I'd have preferred to be with a woman like Terri Hart. It was a beautiful evening with the moon reflecting off the lake, causing me to think more of Terri than the arson.

"You know, Ace, you outta learn to relax. Here, have a beer."

I looked at Sonny as he reached into the back seat and grabbed a six-pack. I wondered how he slipped it in without my seeing it.

He uncapped a long neck and handed it to me. I make it a rule not to insult a client, or his best friend, so I didn't refuse. He took a long swig from his bottle, then looked around. "Lots of people come out here at night. Most of them are young lovers—teenagers—but sometimes older couples come. This was one of Sheila and Bubba's favorite places. He said it was here he first made love to her. Said he was too big for the back seat so they went over there, under that oak tree." He

55

chuckled. "Ain't that funny? Try picturing Bubba trying to make it in a back seat."

The picture of Bubba and Sheila getting it on in a back seat, under an oak tree, or any other place did nothing for me. "It's a great story and a beautiful place," I said, "but you can tell me that story anytime. I'd rather be here with a beautiful woman."

"Yeah, me too. Coupla more things you oughtta know. Bubba loves Sheila, more than you'll ever understand. She shit all over him, but he still loves her. He'd do anything for her, and I do mean, anything. If you've got him on your list, cross him off. He was with me the night the house burned, and even if he hadn't been, I'd still know he didn't do it. He flat loves her too much to ever hurt her."

"Okay, you alibied Bubba. Tell me about Terri Hart."

"I figgered you'd ask about her. You looked like a starving puppy eyeing a T-bone steak." Sonny gave me a silly grin. "You don't want to get mixed up with Terri Hart. You might be a smart city cop but she's too much for you, and her family's mean as snakes."

"If you're trying to tell me something, spell it out in plain English."

"There's lots of rumors 'cause most of the time she acts so uppity. Won't go out with us normal guys. Some say she swings both ways. Me, I don't believe it." Sonny slid down in the seat and took a sip from his beer. "Wanna hear more?"

"Keep talking."

"One rumor has it she had a girlfriend 'til Joey run her out of town. Her name was Laura Johnson and all I know is she and Terri were together all the time. Then

Laura left—disappeared, sudden like. Some people said she took a teaching job in Oklahoma City, but nobody's ever heard from her. Mighty curious."

Sonny leaned back and finished his beer. He placed his empty in the carton before taking another. "When you finish your bottle, don't throw it out. All this trash ruins the envir'nment."

I mentally scored two points for him as a friend of the earth. "That's nice, but I'd rather know about Terri."

Sonny stared hard at me. "Her last steady boyfriend here in Cisco was a guy named Joe Lewis. That wuz a few years ago. He was another teacher at the school, but they broke up when he left town. Some said she had the hots for Sheila. That'd explain why she does all she can to look like her."

None of his story fit what I wanted to believe. "Okay, you've given me the rumors. Now, give me facts."

"Facts? Like I said, I don't know much about her. She's a teacher here in Cisco, teaches junior high. Been doing it since she graduated from college. Everybody seems to like her, but nobody knows much about her private life."

"That's better. How about boyfriends, significant others, husbands, ex-husbands?"

Sonny grinned. "Nope, not married—never been married. As far as I know, she's got nobody special right now. But she disappears a lot on weekends. Some say she's got a rich boyfriend in Fort Worth or Abilene. If so, she ain't ever brought him to the Down Home. I still say you oughtta stay away from her."

"Thanks for the advice." I decided to change gears. "Why the hell am I out here on lover's lane with you?"

57

Sonny looked at me, a questioning look on his face. "Didn't Bubba tell you? No, guess he didn't take the time. While you was making eyes at Terri, Bubba went to take a piss. When he finished, there was a note laying on the sink. Here it is."

He handed me a damp piece of paper. I gingerly took it, holding it between two fingertips, hoping it was damp from water only. Didn't smell funny. I held it up to the light and read, *You want to know who killed Sheila, be at her favorite place at Lake Cisco at midnight.*

I looked at my Timex, eleven thirty-five.

"This was on the sink?"

"Bad echo out here at night," Sonny commented with a chuckle. "Bubba had to run so he asked me to bring you out to solve the case. He's pissed 'cause he figgers you'll wrap it up. He wanted to be in on the kill."

He shut up and I didn't have anything more to ask. We watched the minutes tick by. Five minutes later, I was antsy. I'm not much for sitting in a car waiting for someone to show up. "I don't like this. I'm going to wait over there." I indicated the oak tree where Bubba and Sheila had, well, you know.

I saw Sonny nod in the moonlight as I opened the door and crawled out. I walked into the shadows and peeked to be sure I could see the car. Then I leaned against the tree.

At two minutes before midnight, all hell broke loose. The staccato sounds of an automatic weapon ripped the night. I hit the ground, grabbing for my Beretta. Not there—in my jacket in the car. All I could do was hug the tree, wanting to crawl under it. I forgot what Sheila and Bubba might have done where I was burying my face. I don't know how many shots there were but it was either a big magazine or two of them. The shooting stopped, its echoes reverberating around the lake. I stayed in place.

I heard screaming. Looking from my hiding place, I saw lights. Car doors opened as male voices called to one another. Behind them, I heard the panicky cries of young women. I wanted to join the panic but instead, I rose and walked to my car.

The driver's door hung open, the hinges shot away. In the moonlight, I could see the car was a mess. Whoever had been on the business end of the weapon controlled it well. The driver's side window was gone, and the door showed tight shot groups.

"Sonny," I whispered.

No answer.

"Sonny, are you okay?" I peeked through the window and saw the answer to my question. He slumped against the passenger door, blood everywhere. His head, or what was left of it, was a pulpy mess. Reddish gray matter was everywhere.

I turned away and threw up. A couple of teenagers peeked into the car. They joined me in puking.

## CHAPTER EIGHT

The next night I sat in my recliner mumbling to the boys. Striker curled in my lap, asleep. Sweeper lay on the arm of the chair watching me. I'd like to think he listened.

"Humph, your brother doesn't seem much interested in my welfare. After the shooting stopped, the cops showed up, and I do mean cops—plural. I spent the rest of the night with them. First, two of them talked to me in the back of their cruiser. They proved they passed the interrogation phase of their classes at the Police Academy.

"'What were you and Sonny doing at the lake?

"'Where were you when Sonny was killed?

"'What kind of weapon did you hear?

"'Who killed Sonny?

"'Was he shooting at you?

"'Who are your enemies?

"'Why'd you come to Eastland County?

"'Do you have a permit for this weapon?'

"And so forth, and so forth."

Sweeper yawned.

"Then they hauled me to the Sheriff's office. At first, I was glad to be there. I figured I'd meet some senior guys who'd be more on the ball. Guess what? Yep, same dumb questions.

"'What were you and Sonny doing at the lake?

"'Where were you when Sonny was killed?

"'What kind of weapon did you hear?

"'Who killed Sonny?'

"Et cetera, et cetera."

Sweeper yawned again.

This time I took offense. "Sorry, am I keeping you up past your bedtime?" I think the sarcasm was lost on him.

He switched his tail a couple of times and curled it around his body, instantly asleep.

"Well, guess that answers that. Remind me never to write my memoirs. But consider this, you ungrateful wretch. You'd get awful hungry without me." I stared at Sweeper, then at Striker. Must be great to be able to sleep as soon as you close your eyes. I swear Striker snored.

I leaned back in my recliner, letting my mind float, hoping right brain might kick in with answers. Nothing. I guess I slept because time passed. I know because Striker's claws sinking into my thigh awakened me. It was almost midnight.

"Ouch," I said, sleep disappearing. "What the hell's wrong with you?" Then I heard a low growl coming from Striker's throat. "What is it, boy? What do you hear."

At that moment, Sweeper came awake and stood on his tiptoes on the arm of the chair. Every hair on his

61

body stood on end, and I heard his nails punch through the leather.

As if on a signal, they leapt to the floor and raced to the window. I watched, straining to hear anything out of the ordinary. They reared onto their hind legs and peeked through the glass. One peek was enough. They wheeled and sprinted under the couch. I hit the floor thinking, Did somebody follow me home?

A thunk sounded against the front door, then silence. I lay there, expecting the worst, pictures of Sonny floating through my head. What was it? A pipe bomb? A crazed assassin trying to draw me out? A firebomb? Images of charred bodies flooded my mind.

After a moment of indecision, I moved, grabbed my Beretta and rushed out the back door. I was glad the Eastland Deputies had given the weapon back to me. They kept my jacket. On second thought, they could have the jacket. Sonny's brain tissue saturated it.

I tore around the house vowing no one would take my cats or me without a fight. I moved as quietly as I could, but I was more intent on speed. At the front corner, I peeked around, willing my eyes to adjust to the darkness. I saw nothing, so I waited. I figured if there was an assassin out there, he'd have to move eventually. I froze. Five minutes, ten minutes—no movement. My muscles cramped. I vowed I'd hit the fitness center more often. I crept to the front of the house, surveying in all directions—like they taught me in the academy. Nothing, not a whisper. I pocketed my pistol and walked to the front door intending to return to my nap, or better yet, go to bed.

When I reached for the doorknob, my toe bumped something. I knelt and found a brick. Picking it up, I felt paper secured by a rubber band. "Somebody's been seeing too many B movies," I mumbled.

I unlocked the front door and went in where there was light for reading. The paper was a note, printed in block letters. Like Bubba's note, only drier. I read, *Sorry, I missed you last night. Maybe we can do it again. I'll try not to be so sloppy next time. Been to any good fires lately?*

I don't mind telling you goose pimples crawled my body. I locked the door, feeling like it offered no more protection than my skin.

Striker and Sweeper came from under the couch and paced back and forth, staring at me.

"Meow," Striker said.

"Meow," echoed Sweeper.

Now, that was something I could handle. Their message was they were hungry. My first impulse was to give them hell for thinking of food at a time like this, but then I realized the danger must have passed or they wouldn't be so blasé. I reckoned they didn't want to waste any of their nine lives any more than I wanted to use up my one. We went to the kitchen, and I filled the food dishes.

I got ready for bed and quickly fell asleep. I was bushed from the excitement of last night and the grueling day I'd had. I was awake thirty minutes later. The rest of the night, I slept badly with my Beretta, two cats, dreams of Sonny, Sheila's house before the fire, and two burning questions—Who killed Sonny and who threw the note at my front door? Oh yeah, my dreams also asked why the hell I'd gotten involved?

There were no more thumps at the door to interrupt my restlessness, but Jake came through with his usual sense of timing—his signature three a.m. phone call.

"Hey, Arty, I hear you've got the killers on the run."

I mumbled, "Don't call me Arty."

"Relax, will you? I'm calling to help. From what I hear, you lost your car, and you had to hitch a ride to Dallas. You should have called me. Wanted you to know there'll be a new Chrysler convertible in your driveway tomorrow morning. Use it like it's yours. I hatched a deal with the dealer in Ranger and—"

"Jake, I'm tired. Two nights ago, somebody killed Sonny in my car. Last night, someone left a warning note at my front door. Don't get me wrong, I appreciate your generosity but, right now, a new convertible is low in my priorities."

"Great, Arty. Does that mean I can count on you for more than two weeks? This is working out better than I'd hoped. I'm sure you'll find the assholes who torched my house."

I stifled a yawn. "Right now, I'm more interested in staying alive than I am in *Sheila's* house. Hope you don't mind."

"No problem. I want you alive, too. Otherwise you can't find the arsonist."

I gave up. "Okay, Jake. I'll stay alive so I can handle your case. Now, let me get some sleep." I hung up the phone, then unplugged it from the wall.

While that was going on, Sweeper and Striker snored, curled together. My impulse was to shake the covers vigorously.

The rest of the night I drifted in and out of sleep, dreaming while I was asleep and worrying while I was awake. Both had the same theme—someone wanted to hurt my body.

I woke in the morning, as tired as when I went to bed. You can guess what woke me. Yep, the sound of a car in my driveway. I got up and looked. It was there—a bright red Chrysler convertible. It looked like a big bull's-eye.

As I stood in the shower, alternating the water between hot and cold, I reached a conclusion. I'm not sure when, but it was there. It was simple. The only way I could stay alive was to find the guy or guys who killed Sheila and Sonny. I suspected Jake would be thrilled.

Before I hit the road, I had homework to do. I cranked up my computer and went online. I took the list of names Jake gave me and ran them through the Division of Motor Vehicles, and the state criminal files. I still had enough contacts in the Dallas Police Department to stay abreast of how to gain information electronically. I got lots of hits, if you call driving drunk, driving without a license, creating a public nuisance, and brawling, hits. Nothing that told me who the killer was, though.

I added the names of people I'd met in the Down Home. As I ran Terri Hart's name, I hoped it would come up clean, and it did. But her brother's record was an eye-popper. It looked like he'd committed about every misdemeanor there is, and a couple of minor felonies. His worst arrests were for beating on his girlfriends, something he apparently did frequently. The judge gave him two years probation the last time, and a court order to stay away. That was a year ago.

Randy Rawls

I made a few phone calls to snitches I knew but to no avail. Cisco was too far off their home track.

My last call was to Ms. Jacobs, a cat-loving lady who lived down the street. I explained I had to go out of town, and asked her to check on the boys if I wasn't back in three or four days. She assured me it would be a pleasure to spend time with two such delightful animals. I wondered whose cats she was talking about.

I reminded her of Striker's proclivity for hiding. She laughed as she told me she had her ways of flushing him out—her special kitty-treats. I'd forgotten about those. The boys loved them.

I called the boys for a family meeting. What I mean is I filled their food dishes, gave them fresh water, and rattled the hard food box. I only know two ways to get their attention immediately. The first is what I did. The second is to sit down in my recliner and open the newspaper. The latter is more effective. As soon as I start to read, one or both of them scampers onto the paper and settles down for a long winter's nap.

"Boys, I'm heading out again. Not sure how long I'll be gone, but I'll leave you plenty of food and water. Ms. Jacobs will check with you. Be good to her, she's the one with the great kitty-treats. Oh yeah, try to take it easy on the litter pans, will you?"

Their response was the cracking of their hard food and the smacking of their lips. Sometimes I wonder who's the master and who're the pets in this house.

"You guys watch the place. There's somebody who dislikes me. If he comes around, make sure you chase him off."

Crack, crack, smack, smack.

*Jake's Burn*

I went into the bedroom to pack. When I unzipped my bag, both boys came running. As soon as I folded back the flap, they jumped in and started wrestling. I lifted them out and turned to my sock drawer. When I turned back, they were in the bag again. We went through the drill several times before I was packed. When I lifted them out the last time and zipped the flap, they both gave me indignant looks before they stomped from the room. Somehow, I didn't think their indignation had anything to do with my leaving, only that I was taking a favorite playground.

The new car was a beauty. I appreciated Jake's consideration, but I'd never let him know. He'd enjoy gloating too much. Nothing like the smell of a new car to bring out your manliness though.

I pulled out of the driveway, drove down Frankfurt to I-35E and headed south to Loop 12. I felt good. It was only seven, and I was sure I could be in Cisco by nine-thirty or ten. Disaster struck like it does every morning. There was a fender-bender somewhere in front of me, and traffic backed up. I made Cisco at eleven.

I swung by the firehouse, hoping to catch the fire chief, Sam Raleigh. Al, the EMT, was there again and told me Sam wouldn't be back until six. He had graveyard this week, six p.m. to six a.m. I asked Al if they had anything new on the arson.

"You best talk to Sam 'bout that. He's still not too fired up about you."

"Yeah, I got that impression."

Al's face said I wasn't number one on his Christmas Card list either.

I had time to kill so I turned on the charm. "Look, Al, I wish you guys would cut me some slack. All I want

67

is to find out who torched the house, collect my fee and get the hell back to Dallas. I'm a city-boy now, and want to get out of here as soon as I can."

Al didn't say anything, but the frown disappeared.

"I know Sam will be happy when I'm gone. The quickest way to get me out of here is share with me. You must know who the bodies were."

Al fidgeted, and I knew I'd scored. "Com'on, Al. We're on the same team."

"Well, Sam didn't say I couldn't tell you. It might be all right."

"Of course it is. Hell, it's public information. I'll bet the paper will have it in the next edition, and you know the Fort Worth paper's gonna jump all over it."

"Okay, but you gotta help me if Sam gets mad."

"You got it, buddy."

"They're pretty sure one of them was Sheila, just like we guessed, but you'll never guess the other one."

My impulse was to tell him I don't do guessing games but instead, I said, "You're way ahead of me. I don't have a clue. What's his name?"

Al reached into his desk drawer and took out a small notebook. "That's a her, as in her name—they think it was a woman. They got the ID from the serial number of that burned out hulk behind the house. It belonged to Madeline Millener. She's a hotshot lawyer from Fort Worth."

I pictured the car remains we'd seen. One parked out front, one where I supposed the garage was and one setting on the melted driveway behind the house. Apparently, Sheila's guest had driven to the house and parked in the rear. Did it signal a familiarity, or that the visitor was not allowed to use the front?

Millener? It rang a bell. I'd heard it before, but where? "That's interesting. Got anything else?"

"Nope, that's it. You saw the reason. The coroner and the state boys are still working the remains."

"Thanks, Al. You've been helpful." I walked out of the station. I didn't want to push my luck.

\*     \*     \*

I climbed into the car, trying to find the tidbit of information I knew about Millener. It wouldn't come. I've learned my best bet is to leave things alone until right brain decides to help.

Instead, I wondered what to do until I could talk to Sam Raleigh. I considered finding Bubba but didn't have a clue where to look. Finally, I decided to do something I hadn't done enough recently—visit my parents. I purchased a bouquet for Mom.

I'm no connoisseur of cemeteries—prefer to stay out of them—but Oakwood Cemetery in Cisco is one of the best—dignified without being solemn, quaint without being weird, and most important of all, the resting-place of my parents.

I parked on Second Street. The old high school gym and the football field where I practiced and played was on the other side of the street—home of the Cisco Lobos.

Memories flooded back as I walked through the gate. The cemetery is laid out in rectangles with *streets* named after trees, flowers, and other types of vegetation. I moved toward the intersection of Rose and Gardenia. In front of me, keeping a wary eye on me and moving away if I got too close, were six black goats. Apparently, they were the groundskeepers. They appeared to do an excellent job.

Names on the headstones went back to when Cisco was Red Gap, before the railroads crossed. That was the real beginning of Cisco. I remembered having it drummed into my head in fourth-grade history class. The Texas and Pacific Railroad arrived first in 1880 but the Houston and Texas Central later crossed its right-of-way. The settlement of Red Gap was about a mile from the crossing point. Everyone picked up and moved, bringing Red Gap with them. In 1884, the town of Cisco was officially recognized and a new post office granted. Then as now, money drove events. The town was named for John A. Cisco, a New York financier connected to the Houston and Texas Central Railroad.

I found my parents' graves in the Edwards family plot, side by side, as they'd wished. I admit I was misty-eyed standing there remembering all the good about them. I guess some might say they were simple country folk who raised one son while losing two daughters at young ages. I know better. I know they were two loving parents who gave their stubborn son everything they could while insisting he learn and accept responsibility for himself. Most of all, they gave the most precious gifts of all, love and trust.

I placed the flowers on Mom's grave and, as I stood between their final resting-places, told them about the case. I told them about Jake calling me, about Sheila and Bubba, and Sonny killed in my car. I told them I suspected Sonny was an accidental victim, the bullets intended for me. I confessed I hid under an oak tree while the bullets flew and Sonny died. I didn't mention it was the same tree Bubba and Sheila used for carnal purposes. I didn't think Mom would appreciate the story. Dad might have gotten a chuckle out of it, but I couldn't tell him without Mom hearing.

As I stood there talking to my dead parents, right brain kicked in and gave me my first insight into the case. I excused myself. "Sorry, but I gotta talk to Sam Raleigh."

## CHAPTER NINE

I rushed to the fire station.

Al was in the office. "Told you Sam won't be here 'til six. Whatcha doing back early? I'm not gonna tell you anything else."

"Look, I know it's only two, but I need to talk to Sam now. Where does he live? I'll go by his house."

At first, I was afraid I'd offered Al too tough a dilemma. He stared at me for a moment, then scratched at the top of the desk. As I watched him sort through the alternatives, I wondered if he and Bubba were related. He wasn't as big as Bubba and didn't look like him, but they acted like mental cousins.

After what seemed an eternity, but was only about a minute, he said, "Okay, I'll give you his address. But you better not do nothing that'll get me in trouble." He wrote Sam's address on a yellow sticky and handed it to me.

I headed out of the station fast and was almost to the car when I heard a horn blowing. I looked around to see Bubba pull into a parking space.

"Heard you wuz back in town. Why'n hell didn't you check in with me?"

I stared at him, wondering if he'd said what my ears said he did. I walked over to his Suburban and stopped by the driver's side. "What did you say? I've been having trouble with my hearing recently."

"I said, why'n hell—"

That was as far as he got. I reached through the open window, and grabbed his left ear, twisting as hard as I could.

"Yow," he yelled. "What the hell're you doing?" He tried to open the door but I slammed it shut and twisted more.

"Turn me loose right now, you som'bitch, or I'll kill your sorry ass!" He yelled louder now, and I realized the firemen had come out.

"I'll turn you loose as soon as we get a few things straight." Actually, I wondered how I could end this without losing my head. "I don't check in with you or anybody. I do my own thing and you do yours. Do you understand what I'm saying?" I twisted again.

"Yeah, I unnerstan'. Now, you best turn me loose so we can talk."

I released him and stepped back. He put his hand over his ear. "Ace, that was slick. I always admire a man who keeps a trick up his sleeve. You're right, I shouldn't have expected you to check in. Just 'cause I'm payin' you don't mean you gotta report to me all the time."

"I'm glad we got that straight." I let out a relieved sigh as he stepped to the ground. Behind me, I could hear the firemen whispering and snickering. I stuck out my hand to shake. "Now that we understand one another, we can be friends again."

Bubba looked at me, still holding his left hand over his ear. He reached toward me with his right, and when I

73

looked toward his hand, he hit me with a wicked left cross. I spun backwards into the crowd of firemen. Somebody caught me, held me up, and gave me a gentle shove toward Bubba.

My eyes glazed and my jaw hurt like hell. I spit blood and hoped none of my teeth went with it. I rubbed my jaw then looked and saw Bubba coming at me. I managed to say, "Pretty good shot, Bubba, but you'd better quit while you're ahead."

He laughed and kept coming, stomping straight at me like a vengeful bear. When he was almost within swinging distance, I saw him winding up with a right that would send me to Christmas if it connected. I kicked him below his right kneecap. He grunted and took another step so I kicked him below the left one. He folded toward the ground but to ensure he didn't hop back up, I kicked him in the groin. He collapsed like a giant oak tree in a hurricane.

"Now, like I said, Bubba, I don't check in with anybody and I sure ain't checking in with you. As of right now, you're fired." I turned to walk off then spun back at him. "I'll send you a bill for two days work—that's four hundred bucks you owe me."

I was close to my car when I heard him wheezing my name. I looked back where he was regaining his feet. "Don't leave. We needa talk. Let me catch my breath."

I figured the worst he could do was tear me limb from limb. I waited.

"You're one tough little bastard, and sneaky as hell," he wheezed. "I never been suckered like that before." He walked toward me, bent at the waist.

"What do you want? I got leads to follow. I don't have time to stand around passing the time of day with you." I was on a roll and decided to keep it going. But, to play it safe, I had the car door open between Bubba and me. It partially protected me so I could make a quick getaway.

"Okay, Ace, okay." He held his hands up in the universal sign of truce. "I'm sorry. I was out of line. I just wanted to ask you about Sonny, and let you know the funeral's tomorrow. Sorry about your car. Looks like you got another one, though."

"Yeah, but enough small talk. You got something, spit it out. Otherwise we can talk some other time." I started getting into the car, thinking it'd be best if I left before he recovered.

"You go ahead. I'll be at the Down Home tonight. Stop in and I'll buy you a beer while we talk—if you want to talk." He was a lot more humble than when he arrived.

I pulled out of the parking lot, half expecting Bubba to follow. He watched me drive away.

I drove straight to Sam Raleigh's, violating the speed limit as I went. The knot in my chest told me it was important I talk to him. I knocked on his door and an attractive woman in her early twenties opened it, holding a baby in her arms.

"Excuse me, I'm sorry to bother you. I'm Ace Edwards. Is Sam here? I'd like to talk to him."

She said over her shoulder, "Honey, some guy named Edwards here to see you." She walked away, leaving me on the wrong side of the door.

I stood there for a couple of minutes. About the time I decided to knock again, Sam appeared. "Damn, I hoped it was somebody named Tom Edwards or Bob Edwards. I don't know anybody by those names, but it'd be better than seeing you at my door. What the hell do you want that can't wait until I'm on duty?"

"Look, Sam, I'm sorry to bother you but we need to talk. I've got questions that need answers, and I'm sure you can supply some of them."

He stared a moment, then called over his shoulder, "Honey, I'll be on the porch if you need me. Don't hesitate to interrupt."

He opened the door, came out, and pointed to a padded rocker. "Have a seat. Let's get this over with. Remember though, I may not answer any of your questions."

"I understand. I wish you'd accept that I'm not trying to upstage you." I sat in the chair he'd indicated. "I only want to know why Sheila and Sonny were killed. Fairly basic stuff."

Sam sat in a chair identical to mine. He leaned toward me. "All right. Ask your questions."

"What time did the fire start?"

"As best we can figure, it was about one o'clock in the morning."

"What rooms were the bodies in?"

"Hell, you know that. You were there. One was where the study used to be."

"On the first floor, right?"

"Now where in hell do you think it would be? Of course, the study was on the first floor."

I hesitated a moment, not sure where I was going with my next question but knowing I had to ask it. "Where was the other body found?"

"Damn, Edwards. What are you driving at? You were there."

"Please be patient with me." I leaned forward in the chair. "I have a very cloudy picture I'm trying to clear up." I gave him my best Perry Mason look. "Where was the second body?"

"In the hallway on the first floor, or what had been the hallway. Does that answer your question?"

"Not quite. Do you think she died there? What I mean is, could she have been on the second or third floor?"

I waited, gently rocking the chair. I might have held my breath. Somehow, I knew the answer to that question was important to the case. Only thing was, I didn't know why.

Meanwhile, Sam looked at me so strangely I was afraid I'd grown a second head, or a third eye had popped out of my forehead. "What are you getting at, Edwards? If I knew where you were headed, maybe I could help you."

"Answer my question, then I'll lay out my ideas for you."

"Okay, it's possible. I'm trying to picture anything that could prove the second body was on the first floor but I'm not getting anything. In fact, now that you raise it, I can't be dead sure either body started out on the first floor, although I feel pretty confident about the one in the study. Do you know something?"

At least he'd quit snarling at me. I plunged on. "Do you have plans for the house? I have this cockeyed idea that the second body lay in about the middle of the house where the stairs were. I know it's stupid because I was never in that house, but I get an image of stairs where we saw her body. Jake showed me the construction plans and I swear, the curved staircase went up right where her body lay."

Sam leaned back and rocked for a moment. "You're either the nuttiest cop I've ever known or you're psychic. We'll find out which. I have a copy of the house plans and our reports at the office. We can check'm. Now, you've used up all your time. I gotta wife and baby I don't spend enough time with. I'm gonna feed my baby before I go to work. If you have any more questions, I'll be at the station at six." He got up and walked into the house, leaving me staring at where he'd sat.

## CHAPTER TEN

I left Sam's house, confused and wondering if I were onto something, or if my imagination had run away with me. There had to be more, something I had missed.

I looked at my watch and saw three o'clock, too early for the Down Home and three hours before I could see Sam at the fire station. I drove into the country.

Without thinking about it, I pulled off at the overlook below Jake's house. Surprised at where I was, I got out, walked over to a big rock, and leaned on it. The view was as I remembered—fields, pastures, groves of trees, and hills that appeared to grow from the valleys for no apparent reason. I could see no changes from the way it looked all those years ago when I'd stood here as a teenager.

My body unwound, my mind relaxed. I massaged my jaw where Bubba hit me, knowing I couldn't have taken another shot without folding. My brain zoomed around like a hummingbird, flitting from one point to another without settling on anything. There was something there. I knew it, but what? What was I missing?

I started through it again. The house caught fire at about one a.m. One person was in the study, and the other was either in the hallway, on the stairs, or on an upper floor. Maybe I misread Jake's plans. What room was above the hallway on the second floor, on the third floor? Was I seeing fire ants where there were only doodle bugs? To hell with it, I decided, I'm going for a six pack.

I crawled into the car with no answers but somehow feeling better. Suddenly, one other question popped into my head. Where was Jake when the fire started? I realized he never told me.

I drove into the valley, headed for Cisco, then decided to swing by the sheriff's office. I pulled into a visitor's space. Getting out of the car, I noticed the difference between my Chrysler and the older beat-up civilian cars parked around me. They probably belonged to the underpaid deputies. That was another reason I'd quit the force. Risking my life for peanuts didn't impress me. Of course, I was still working for peanuts, but seldom had to risk my life. A vast improvement.

I walked into the station and found myself face to face with that most feared of all public servants, the desk sergeant. "Can I help you?" he said.

"I'm Ace Edwards. Like to chat with the sheriff about the fire at the Adams place."

"Edwards, yeah, I know the name. You were with Sonny when he bought it. Sonny and I went to school together. I wanna know who did him and why. You got any of them answers?"

Oh boy, here I went again. Another guy who wanted a piece of me. "No, I'm sorry but I don't. I also want to know who killed him. If I had the bastard, I'd ask him if he was gunning for Sonny or for me. You guys got any leads yet?"

"None that I'd tell you about. Don't like meddlin' big city private dicks."

I wondered if my breath had turned him off. I'd had onions for lunch. Next trip, I'd remember breath mints. "Is the sheriff here? I'd love to talk to him." I was determined to charm him.

"Hold on, I'll check if he'll see you."

I sat on a straight-backed, wooden bench, then picked up a *Time* magazine. The cover asked, *Can Clinton defeat Bush?* I didn't bother to check the date as I carefully placed it back where I'd found it. I feared I might scar a collector's edition.

There was nothing more current to read, so I studied the area. Dingy walls. I tried to guess what the original color had been—gray, tan, off-white, pale yellow, light blue. Could have been any of them. After analyzing the color, I concentrated on the stains—dried blood brown, puke yellow-green, a distinctive faded yellow, and a few other hues I decided to pass on. The ceiling was next in my analysis, but fortunately, before I was halfway through counting flyspecks, the desk sergeant called, "Hey, Edwards. Com'ere."

I walked to his counter. "Well, do I get to see the secret passages or not?" My urge to charm had slipped.

He glowered at me. "The sheriff will see you. Walk to your right, down that hall. A deputy'll meet you and take you to the sheriff. Oh yeah, your right's that way." He pointed down the hallway as a grin split his face.

I decided to let him win one. I walked in the direction he pointed, hoping he knew my right from my left. A deputy stepped out and asked, "You Edwards?"

My normal sarcasm reared its head, but before I let my mouth get my butt into more trouble, I answered, "Yes sir. I'm here to see the sheriff."

"Come with me. I'll take you to his office."

We wandered a maze of corridors, obviously laid out to keep me from escaping if I tried to make a fast break. I felt uneasy as I pictured myself trapped like Charlie in the old Kingston Trio song about the Boston subway. The deputy nodded toward an open door. "In there."

I complied and found myself in a nice office with an attractive secretary, telephones, freshly-painted walls, a fax machine and a modern looking computer. Quite a switch from the front of the building.

"Through that door, Mr. Edwards. Sheriff Yardley is waiting for you," the secretary said,

I gave her my sexiest smile and walked into the office. The man sitting behind the desk was about sixty years old, but looked like he worked-out every day. His hair was gray—mostly he was bald. His tan department-issue cowboy hat hung on a wall hook. It was sweat stained and dirty, giving it character. The star pinned to its front had SHERIFF in block letters pressed into it.

"I'm Ace Edwards," I said with my best phony smile. "I appreciate you making time to see me."

"Have a seat, Edwards. I wondered when you were coming by. Heard you were here the other night. Sorry I missed you."

He almost sounded like he meant it. Maybe he and the desk sergeant had attended the same acting class. He went on. "I remember when you ran the ball in high school. I was a deputy then, and worked traffic control at the games. Always thought the coach should have given you more carries. You were much better than that big palooka he used all the time."

Now that approach threw me for a loop, but I liked it. I managed to stammer, "Ah, thanks. That was a long time ago."

Sheriff Yardley leaned forward, his eyes boring into me. "Tell me everything you know about the Adams fire and Sonny Barrow's death. I don't like arson and murders in my county, and I don't like meddlers who come in and think they can walk all over us."

Maybe there was a subtle change in his attitude. I looked into his eyes and was sure of it. "Sheriff, I'm on your side. If it looks like I'm meddling, I'm sorry. All I want is to find the bad guys who burned the house, and killed Sheila and the other woman."

"You mean that lawyer?" he answered in a sarcastic snarl. "If that's what you want, start talking."

Lawyer. That was it. Madeline Millener was Maddie Millener, the lawyer who'd represented Sheila in the divorce.

"I really don't have anything to tell you. I'm not even sure who the killer was after. I'm pretty sure it wasn't Sonny, though. It had to be me or Bubba. Sonny was there by accident and it all happened so fast, no one would have known. The note was passed to Bubba—and it was my car."

"Makes sense. But not new. I already grazed that pasture. Give me something new. What about Jake Adams? He had reasons to want Sheila and Bubba dead. From what I'm hearing, he don't have no alibi for either time. How 'bout you? Who'd be gunnin' for you?"

He might be a country sheriff, but his logic was big city. "Second part first," I said, not convinced about

Jake. "Down this part of the country, I can't think of anyone specific who has reason to want me dead. Back in Dallas, a few husbands I caught straying from the home hearth don't like me. I can't believe they'd follow me here, though, or try to kill me anywhere. They might want to break a few bones, but, nah, they wouldn't try to kill me."

"So, you think the killer was after Bubba?"

"No, I didn't say that. It could be the arsonist trying to take me out before I stumble onto him."

"Again, not new. I want something new. How 'bout Jake? What'd he tell you?"

I was embarrassed to tell him I'd never asked Jake where he was when Sheila's house burned or when Sonny died, so I countered with, "What about Sheila's lawyer. Who were her enemies? She might be the key to all this. Maybe someone was after her and Sheila happened to get in the way. What was she doing at Sheila's at one in the morning?"

"Good questions. We're looking into it. From what we've learned so far, she was probably an accident, like you say Sonny was. The Fort Worth folks are working it from their end and have come up with nothing. She had lots of people who didn't like her, but no more than any other high profile lawyer."

He glared at me. "Me, I think Sheila was the target. If you don't know anything new, I'm busy."

He picked up a folder and pulled out some papers. His message came through loud and clear.

"Thanks, Sheriff. I'll be in touch."

He didn't look up as I left his office. His secretary still looked good, and gave me a big smile. I gave her one back and entered the maze wishing I'd left a trail of breadcrumbs. As I wound my way through the corridors toward the entrance, I wondered if she was married.

Sergeant Jones glared at me when I rounded home into the lobby. I grinned at him. "Have a nice evening, Sergeant."

## CHAPTER ELEVEN

I had a choice to make. It was five-forty-five. I could head for the fire station and butt heads with Sam, or I could head for the Down Home and hope somebody would talk to me before they got too loaded. Remembering that Bubba might be at the Down Home, I opted for the fire station.

I pulled into the parking lot as Sam got out of his pickup.

He waved. "Hey, Ace. Come on in. I'll buy you a coffee. Then we can look at the plans."

I sat there for a moment wondering if there were two guys named Ace around here. He sounded downright friendly. After the shock wore off, I went into the firehouse. Sam sat in his small office studying some papers.

Before I could speak, he said, "Here's your coffee." He didn't bother to look up as he pointed to a cup that had somehow appeared on his desk filled with a steaming black liquid.

"Dammit, Ace. You might be as good as Adams said. You're right. She was on the stairs, the second floor or the third floor. She couldn't have been killed where we found her remains."

"Stairs go up there?"

"Yeah. Look at this." He turned the plans around. "See, her body was right here. Now, look at this. She couldn't have been on the first floor. The curving staircase covers that area. She had to be on the stairs or one of the upper floors."

He threw the second floor plans on top of the first. "Look. There's a hallway on the second floor directly above where we found her body." A flip of his wrist and we were looking at the third floor. "Ah, shit. There's a hallway on the third floor, too."

He leaned back in his chair and stared at the ceiling, massaging his temples. He mumbled, "That explains the lack of alligatoring. Man, that answers several questions."

"Slow down," I said. "All we know was she may have fallen. She could have been on the stairs."

"Not unless she climbed stairs in the nude."

"Huh," I said. "What do you mean, nude?"

He looked at me and his eyes told me he'd decided to let me join his team. "I held out on you. We sifted all the ashes around her body. We found no evidence of clothing, no jewelry, no metal snaps, no metal or plastic buttons, no metal zippers, no nothing."

While I digested that, he added, "To me, that equals naked, or some kind of lightweight negligee with no bra. Now, do you think she was on the stairs nude, or in a negligee?"

He had me off balance so I did what anyone would do. I changed the subject. "What did you mean by alligatoring?"

87

He ignored my question and started talking, as if unburdening himself. "After you left this afternoon, I sifted through everything I knew while I fed the baby. Two things have bothered me from the first reports. The first was the lack of alligatoring, and the second was any proof of clothing. Your cockeyed idea answered the second one and that fed the first one."

"I'm glad I'm so good," I said. "But what is alligatoring?"

"Alligatoring is an effect we find when the perp uses an accelerant. The first floor was oak flooring laid on a concrete slab. Alligatoring occurs when the wood burns so hot it ends up in a pattern like alligator hide. We found alligatoring or distinctive burn trails everywhere he poured gas. There was none around the second body."

He paused while I played catch up. "What about the other body?"

"Yeah, big time. My best guess is her body was drenched in gasoline. The flooring around her was so toasted you could see her outline. He must have stood and poured a can of gas over her. That's why she burned so bad, and that's why I'm sure she was on the first floor."

The picture of her charred remains sent a chill up my spine but I had to push on. "And the other woman?"

"She was burned the same, but there was no alligatoring around her. That had me buffaloed. Now, I believe it's because she was upstairs. I should have thought of that. Thanks, Ace."

I decided to risk another question. "What about the body in the study—clothing I mean. Was she dressed?"

"Same. No evidence of clothing. Doesn't make sense, does it?"

"One more. Do you know how they died, what killed them?"

He flipped open a folder and took out a sheet of paper. "The coroner says the lady in the study may have died from extreme trauma to the head. Her skull was cracked. He has no guess about the other one. Both bodies were burned too bad for normal procedures. In fact, there's no sure way to know how or when the crack in her skull occurred."

"What did you mean, sure way?"

"Well, the coroner said if she was hit with something hard enough to crack her skull and kill her before she burned, the skull should be cracked in. On the other hand, if the skull cracked from the heat of the fire, it should have cracked out because of the pressure built up inside the cranium. That's the easy part. Sometimes, a cracked in skull will blow out from pressure, especially if the fire is really hot."

"What about the body in the study?"

"Out."

"And the other?"

"Out, also. But, the coroner says he's convinced hers was from the fire. He's not sure about the one in the study."

I thought for a moment. "So, all we can do is guess that neither was wearing any metal or plastic, and one was not on the first floor when she died."

"And, the one in the study was drenched with gasoline."

I shuddered. "Yeah. I hope she was dead when that occurred."

89

We talked on and he promised to re-check the ruins tomorrow. He wanted to verify his sketches, and pin down the exact spot where the second body lay, and from where it might have fallen.

As I walked through the parking lot toward my car, I checked the time. Seven-thirty. It had been a long day. Again, I had two choices. Get a motel room or head for the Down Home. I chose the room. I wanted to speak to Jake.

I drove down Eighth Street toward Interstate 20. A chain had built a motel at the intersection across the street from a popular truck stop. I had no problem getting a room. After moving my luggage in, I again faced a choice—the Down Home or hiding out. I admitted to myself I had been ducking the Down Home and the face-off with Bubba. It had to happen, and I knew I couldn't put it off any longer. But first, a conversation with Jake was in order.

Several unsuccessful phone calls later, I gave up. I'd left messages at his office, his home, and had paged him. Even his cell phone took my message. Hopefully, he'd call back.

\*       \*       \*

I pulled into the parking lot and looked around. Bubba's Suburban wasn't there. That was a relief. Maybe he wasn't here tonight. I got out, wiped the dust off my boots on the back of my jeans and walked in. Like my last visit, the noise was deafening and the smoke thick enough to count lung cancers—figuratively. The country-western music screaming from the jukebox

90

fought with the sounds from two television sets, and the crowd yelling over the noise.

I stopped in the doorway and surveyed the room. I saw what you always find in a country Texas bar— attractive young ladies in dress ranging from office formal to jeans and boots, and young men in jeans, boots, and western hats or gimme caps. No change in the sawdust on the floor. I could tell because the same wet chips were in the same places as when I was last there. Also, some of the chips had a strange color that caused the patrons to step gingerly around the area. Nothing different about the bar—a collection of beer bottles advertising brands sold over the ages, and dusty liquor bottles that looked like they hadn't been touched by this beer crowd in years. What I didn't see was Bubba.

I walked to the bar where Hojo held court with a couple of the locals. "Hey Hojo, give me a Killian's."

Hojo glanced toward me then went back to his conversation. I waited patiently for about ten seconds, then said in my most courteous voice, "Barkeep, I'd like a Killian's *now* if you have the time." Okay, maybe I put extra emphasis on now.

Hojo ignored me. It was times like this I wish my dad had been six-foot-five. When you were the runt of the crowd, people always thought they could either shove you around or ignore you. I've visited that neighborhood too many times.

I walked down the bar and shouldered my way between the two guys with whom Hojo had his interesting conversation going. As I separated them, I said, "Excuse me, gentlemen, but Hojo is hearing challenged so I thought I'd get closer to him." I said it that way so they'd know I was politically correct.

91

Hojo was now in front of me. "Now my good friend, if you can't understand this difficult order, I'll slow it down for you. I—want—a—Killian's—now."

Hojo looked down on me from his superior height, turned his head, and uttered something to one of his friends. I may have cheated history of some deep philosophical statement. I reached across the bar, grabbed Hojo by the throat, squeezed with my fingers and slammed the back of my hand under his chin. From experience, I knew this was a show-stopper. Whatever he was going to say came out, "Ugh, ugh."

While trying to watch his friends, one on each side of me, I said, "In case you've forgotten, that was a Killian's for immediate delivery."

Out of the corner of my eye, I saw one of his friends make a move. Fortunately, it was the one on my left, since my right side was busy. As he drew back his fist, I dipped at the knees and slammed a sharp elbow into his stomach. He bent forward with an audible "Whoof," so I spun and kneed him in the groin. Several hostile husbands taught me to look for an advantage, and grab it first. He crumpled to the floor in such a way I knew there was one less to worry about. There are advantages to being short.

Then came that sound you always hear in a low-life bar fight. What a shame so many beer bottles get shattered. Wonder if that's why they're not refillable like pop bottles used to be.

The guy on my right said, "All right, super cop. Now, you get yours. This is for Sonny."

I turned Hojo loose, grabbed the bar towel, and wrapped it around my left arm as protection. From behind, I heard wheezing from the guy I'd kneed. Hojo was busy massaging his neck and trying to squeeze sounds through. I figured neither was in any condition to help me, although I wasn't sure that would be their first priority. Of course, that also meant they couldn't help the beer bottle guy either.

"Edwards, you're a dead man," he shouted. "You shoulda been dead the other night. Now, I'm gonna finish what some dummy messed up."

He jabbed with the beer bottle and I took it on the towel, praying it wouldn't cut through. At the same time, I chopped down on his forearm with the edge of my open palm. I heard a distinct cracking sound that didn't come from my hand. He yelped and the bottle hit the floor. He grabbed his arm. With my towel-wrapped arm, I slammed him across the face driving him backward. He toppled over a chair and hit the floor, his head cracking on the sawdust-strewn concrete. He no longer presented a challenge.

Behind me, Hojo regained his speech and expressed doubts about my heritage as well as my parents' marital status.

"Excuse me, Hojo. I'm waiting for my beer," I said.

He stopped his tirade and looked at his two friends who were still out of action. He rubbed his throat again and reached into the cooler. I played it cool, refusing to rub the edge of my hand which hurt like hell.

As he placed a Killian's in front of me, a voice yelled, "He's got a gun!"

I turned to see the beer bottle guy pulling a gun out of his boot. I grabbed my Killian's and drew back my arm to throw it.

"You best put that back, Buster, or I'm gonna twist your head so you can keep a close watch on your ass."

93

Randy Rawls

Bubba. His appearance was fortuitous. Of course, on second thought, he could be saving me for himself.

Beer bottle, I assumed his name was Buster, put the pistol away. I took a swig of my rescued beer. If it was my last, I'd enjoy it.

Bubba stepped to my side. "Don't you ever slow down? You gonna whup all of Eastland County while you're here?"

Before I could answer, Bubba turned toward Hojo. "You done disappointed me now. I 'spect you best move away from behind us." He addressed the room. "Shut off that damn juke box. Hojo, kill the sound on them TV's."

Well, here we go, I thought. He's asking for silence so he can tell everyone he's going to reduce me to another off-color spot in the sawdust. I tensed, ready to defend myself as best I could.

As the sounds died, he said, "Now, ain't that better. I got somethin' ta say and y'all best listen. This here little man," he pointed at me, "is my friend. I thought I made that clear the other night. He didn't kill Sonny so don't blame him. Instead, help him find the sonafabitch what did kill Sonny and whoever killed Sheila. Now, you don't do that, I'm gonna be awful mad. And I'm gonna tell you right now there ain't but one muther in this room can whup my ass."

Bubba stopped talking and looked around. I looked too and saw everyone doing the same. The unspoken question was who, who's Bubba talking about?

After letting the suspense build like a good Hitchcock movie, Bubba said, "Now, who could that be? It's this damn midget right here." Again, he pointed at me. "He whupped my ass this afternoon down at the fire station in front of all th' damn firemen. So, if nobody

94

around here except my friend, Ace, can whup my ass, who do you think can take both of us?"

My opinion of Bubba grew by the second. This dude knew how to work a crowd. You could have heard that proverbial pin drop.

He continued. "The answer is nobody. Ain't none of you or no bunch of you good enough to take us. Don't waste your time or teeth or . . ." He looked at the guy I'd kneed, "Yo' fam'ly jewels messing with us."

He laughed and turned to the bar. "Hojo, give me one of them Kill'an things." There were nervous laughs all around the room.

I stood with my back to the bar, figuring Hojo had had enough for the night. I was far more interested in the reaction of the crowd. They busied themselves, but cast glances at Bubba and me. I couldn't tell if they were friendly or not. The guy I'd dropped with my sharp elbow and a well-placed knee made it to his feet and walked away, bent at the waist. I hoped he didn't have a date tonight.

As I surveyed the room, I saw Terri Hart working her way toward the bar. If my luck held, she'd come close enough for me to talk to her. It did, and she did. In fact, she walked straight to me.

"Why, Muster Edwards, I do declare, y'all jist enough to make a poor country girl's heart go all a'flutter. Y'all sho' be one tuff city boy."

"Terri, knock it off, will you? I happen to know you attended the University of Texas, and majored in English. Use it. I've heard enough people play stupid today."

She threw back her head and laughed, a sound like clear spring water tumbling over stones in a streambed, a

95

laugh that sent ripples of pleasure through my chest. Her hair and make-up were different tonight. Except for the hair color and those beautiful eyes, she didn't look at all like Sheila. I didn't mention it, and didn't care. She still looked good.

"Why, Muster Edwards. Are y'all accusin' little ol' me of fakin' an accent?"

"You're a beautiful woman, Terri Hart, but a lousy actress. That accent wouldn't fool anyone, not even the boobs in Hollywood. Besides, with a voice as musical as yours, I prefer to hear its natural tones."

Terri ducked her head and looked up at me through her long eyelashes. "Okay, I'll be good. But don't give away my secret. I have my students to consider."

She looked at the spot where the guy I'd kneed had fallen. "You don't fight fair, do you?"

"Depends on what you call fair. Way I see it, fair is me winning. Unfair is when anybody else wins. I fight fair."

Again, she laughed with her head thrown back and her shoulder length red hair floating. "Sounds cockeyed enough to make sense."

"Have you had dinner?" I asked. "You must know a nice restaurant where a tourist wouldn't look out of place. Go with me and I'll swear off fighting for the rest of the night."

I saw a flicker of hesitation in her eyes before she responded, "Sorry, I'd better not. I'm—"

"Whoa, I'm not asking for your hand in marriage, at least not tonight. All I'm requesting is a simple dinner for two. You know you can trust a home-town boy just returned from the big city." I gave her my best grin.

"No, well, maybe, ah . . ."

"Wonderful, you're wavering. Here's the coup de grâce. You pick the restaurant and we can go in separate cars if you want. That way, you can—"

Her laugh filled my chest again. "Ace Edwards, you're everything I've ever heard about you. Okay, I'll trust myself in your car. But it's dinner only, then quickly to bed—separate beds. You in yours and me in mine."

"Deal," I said, sticking out my hand.

"Deal," she responded and gave my hand a hearty shake. "There's a nice restaurant in Ranger where the clientele isn't as boisterous as this Down Home group. We can go there."

I think she was right about the restaurant although I have no idea what I ate. All I did was feast on the phenomena that was Terri Hart. And, as promised, I delivered her to her car at the Down Home at a reasonable hour, then went to my motel alone.

# CHAPTER TWELVE

My sleepy brain registered the ring but my body fought moving. I pushed to my left and reached for the phone with my right hand while trying to read my watch. "Hello, Ace Edwards here," I mumbled.

"It's seven o'clock. This is your wake-up call." A click followed this announcement.

I swung my legs around, untangling them from the sheet while mumbling unkind things about my lack of judgment in requesting a wake-up call on Sunday morning. Then I remembered why. Terri. I planned to call and ask if she'd spend the day with me.

I asked the previous evening but she refused to make a commitment. I warned her I'd call in the morning and keep calling until she agreed. She laughed and said I should do just that.

Here I was, dragging myself out of bed at seven a.m. so I could call her at eight. I wanted to be shaved and ready to face the day before I spoke with her. I stumbled into the bathroom and cranked on the shower.

An hour later, I was showered, shaved, dressed, and sipping a cup of coffee I'd made in the miniature pot in the room. The second numbers on my watch counted up to double zero, and the hour number clicked to eight. I punched in her phone number.

"Good morning, Terri," I said when she answered. "I hope I didn't wake you, but if I did, it's your fault for not committing to me last night."

Her chuckle filled my ears. "It's okay, I've been up for a couple of hours. I'd begun to think you weren't going to call, that you were out doing whatever PIs do on Sunday."

"Nope, I'm giving the bad guys a day off. And hearing your voice makes me glad."

"Oh, Ace. Do you always wake up with your sense of humor intact, and a compliment for a woman?"

"Only a beautiful woman whose single kiss can turn a toad into a prince. What's your decision?"

Terri chuckled at my attempted witticism. "How do you know? I haven't kissed you yet, well, not really kissed you. If I did, you'd know the difference."

A chill rippled over my body, anticipation at its most dramatic.

She continued, "You might say I've made a decision, but now you have to agree with it."

"I'm game. Let'er rip."

"After your performance in the bar last night, I thought you might want to go to church this morning. From where I stood, it looked like Someone watched over you."

"Church? You go to church?" She caught me without one of my astute comments. There were many things she could have suggested, and I'd have been more than happy to add a few others, but an invitation to church didn't rank high on the list. I hesitated, trying to remember when I was last in church. As far as I could

99

remember, it was when I followed a straying husband one Sunday morning.

That guy's wife had been flabbergasted when I told her where he'd taken his bimbo. She'd said something to the effect he never went with her. Then she switched into a string of obscenities her pastor would not have appreciated. Last I heard, she named the church as a party in her divorce.

"Yes, Ace. I go to church. Not as often as I should, but I go. Does that surprise you? Now, would you like to go with me this morning? It is Sunday, you know." Her tone said she didn't appreciate my question.

I thought fast. "Gosh, Terri. All I have with me are jeans and sport shirts, not appropriate for church. If I'd brought something dressier, it'd be great to go with you." Saying it, I knew my morning would be spent in church if that was my best excuse.

Terri responded without hesitating, "Who do you think you're talking to, a Yankee tourist? This is Cisco. Wear your nice boots with those jeans and you'll fit right in. And your Stetson to complete the outfit."

"Okay, you've got me." I laughed, still stalling. "What church do you attend? My folks had very strict standards." My brain raced but came up with no reason to refuse her.

Before I could dig myself in deeper, she answered, "I go to the First Baptist of Cisco. It's not far from you at Ninth and E. You must remember it. It's the big brick church with the white columns. Please come with me." Her voice took on a more appealing quality. "I'd love to show you off."

The way she said love sealed my fate. I knew she'd won the discussion, and I wanted to go with her.

100

"First Baptist, yes, I remember it well. When you said the name, my ear hurt. Mom used to twist it to keep me awake, or keep me from shooting spitballs, or keep me from whispering, or . . . Well, I wasn't a very good churchgoer when I was young, but Mom and Dad attended the First Baptist and dragged me along."

"Then it's time you went again." Terri faked a contrite voice. "I promise not to twist your ear."

"Wonderful," I heard myself say, which surprised me because I still had pictures of us in different settings. "What time should I meet you and where?"

"I'll come by the motel about ten-fifteen."

"Wonderful, I'll have brunch waiting and we can dine in my room."

"Nice try, but no go," Terri replied. "If I go into your room, you might not let me out, and we'd miss church. The way you've been behaving, I think you need church first."

My hopes soared. "Does that mean we can have lunch in my room after church?"

"No, not then either. You're far too virile and attractive for a po' ol' country girl like me to be in your room on an empty stomach." She paused. "Promise me dinner, who knows? Now, I have to get dressed and you need to shower and shave. Make sure you shave close enough to last all day. I hate beard burn."

"I already shaved," I said but the phone went dead in my hand as I sat there dazed, replaying her last remarks in my mind. I rose from the edge of the bed, poured myself another cup of coffee and sat to watch the seconds tick away.

Terri called from the motel office at ten-fifteen sharp as I pulled on my boots.

"Okay, I'll come right up. Are you sure you don't want to come to my room to pick me up?"

"You have two minutes, then I'm on my way to church, with or without you." She sounded like she meant it.

I scrambled out of the room, grabbing my Stetson on the run, forgetting my Beretta as usual. When I walked into the office, she looked at her watch and tapped her foot. All I could do was stare at her. She was so beautiful she took my breath away. She wore a pale blue, knee-length dress that reached from her throat to her knees. It accented her deep blue eyes and made them appear huge. She was the very essence of a virtuous church-going, Texas lady school-teacher. I think that's when I discovered I was in love with this woman, deeply, irreversibly in love. I was stunned. Since my marital experience, I'd had a few girlfriends but nothing that came close to the feelings that now made me weak.

"Did I make it?" I asked.

"Mr. Edwards," she lectured. "According to my Sunday-only-watch, you made it with only ten seconds to spare. Because you have met the deadline, I will allow you to escort me to church." Her mouth was set in a straight line, her lips pouty, and her eyes smiling.

The desk clerk looked from me to her, then back to me.

I bowed from the waist and said, "Your chariot awaits milady. Shall we go henceforth from this place and find a pastor to bless our pairing? Should we cross a dragon in our journeys, have no fear, for I shall slay it with my mighty penknife and present its head as a trophy." I took her elbow and steered her toward the door.

"Ooh, I love dragon heads," she said, slipping her arm through mine.

The desk clerk followed our every step, a look of confusion on his face.

The church was more modern than I remembered, but the message from the pulpit was the same. The pastor was against sin. I felt like he spoke to me. After all, my life had not been perfect in every way— enjoyable, but not perfect. I was glad I'd forgotten the Beretta. It would have been out of place here. I'd have felt worse if Terri hadn't held my hand, and given it an occasional squeeze.

In the Southern Baptist tradition, after the service the pastor stood at the door shaking hands with the congregation and making small talk as they departed. When I came to him, he said, "It's good to have you back, Ace. I heard you were in town. I hope you'll come back more often."

I looked at his wizened face and realized he was Pastor Dinwiddie who had been the pastor of the church when I was a kid. Before I could say anything, he turned to Terri. "Ah, Terri. It's always nice to have you in the congregation. Your beauty and your voice add so much. Please come back soon."

As we walked away, Pastor Dinwiddie called to me. "Ace, if you visit your parents, please give them my best and thank your mother again for her fried chicken."

We drove away from the church and I said, "I know lunch awaits us, but where? That service made me hungry enough to eat a horse, or some good fried chicken."

"Head toward Eastland. I know a nice place that serves an excellent Sunday brunch. Now, you've been holding out on me. What did the pastor mean by his remark about fried chicken."

I grinned as memories flooded in. "Like I said when you called, Mom and Dad attended the First Baptist of Cisco. Pastor Dinwiddie, who was new to town and much younger then, ate a lot of Sunday dinners at our house, mostly fried chicken. My mother was known throughout the area as the best chicken fryer around."

I stopped, remembering those dinners with Mom, Dad and the pastor. "He was proud of taking over a church with such a history. Do you know that it traces its roots back to Red Gap in the 1870s? He said it started as the Red Gap Baptist Church and moved here after Cisco was founded and Red Gap gradually disappeared. According to him, the church has stood on the same site since 1882."

"That's interesting," Terri said. "Tell me more."

"Okay, but don't interrupt, I'm just warming up." I hesitated, and said, "Hmmmmm," as if searching my mind. "The tornado of 1893 destroyed the church but the congregation got together and rebuilt it. Everything was fine until 1924—I think it was '24—when it burned. By then, the oil boom was petering out and there was no money to rebuild. The pastor held services wherever he could find a place. Being the good Baptists they were, the congregation scraped together the money, and rebuilt the church on the site where it had previously stood."

"Ace, you never cease to amaze me with how much you know about Cisco. I hope my kids are learning their history as well as you learned yours. Would you like to come to school one day and talk to them about the history of the area? You know so much about it, and lived through so much of it."

My face flushed—I felt it. "My ego thanks you for the invitation and hopes to recover from that crack about my age. Is this your day to be kind to an old man?" I was only half-joking. No man likes his age to be the subject when with a beautiful young woman.

"Oh, you know what I mean. That's one of the things I like about you. You're young for your age."

I was quiet for a moment, replaying her words, trying to decide how to feel. I wondered how old she thought I was. Finally, I decided, To hell with it. Knowing I was with a beautiful, desirable young woman who found me interesting soothed my ego.

I drove to Eastland to the restaurant Terri selected where we had lunch and tons of conversation. Afterwards, we whiled away the afternoon doing nothing except enjoying one another.

We went to Lake Cisco and skipped rocks on the water, and to the Cisco City Park and swung on the swings. We checked out the new high school. We rode around the countryside, stopping whenever we saw anything we wanted to investigate closer. Terri asked me to stop and we examined a large prickly pear cactus clump. We remarked how beautiful, but nasty, they can be, and how sharp the quills are. I told her how much it had hurt when I stumbled into one when I was ten years old.

She directed me to an ostrich farm. I watched in fascination. A few years ago, ostrich and emu farming promised to be a new oil boom for Texas. Ranchers and farmers rushed to buy ostrich and emu chicks at costs far above the common sense level. But, as with most get-rich-quick schemes, it bombed. The bottom fell out of the market and the ranchers were stuck with birds that no one wanted. But they were still fun to watch.

Later, I drove to the remains of Jake's house and we sat quietly, each of us lost in thought. A clean-up crew had begun its work but the three chimneys still stood guard over the valley. The bathroom sink was gone, no longer swaying in the breeze. I wondered if it had fallen on its own, or someone had taken it down.

"Can we walk up there?" Terri asked.

"Sure," I replied as I opened the door and got out. I walked around and opened Terri's door. When she looked up at me through the open door as I reached for her hand, I felt like the luckiest man alive.

"Where was Sheila's body? Where was she killed?" Terri's voice quavered as she asked.

We walked to the edge of the foundation arm in arm. I stopped her as she lifted a foot to step onto the concrete. "One body was laying right over there." I pointed toward the spot where we'd found the first body. "Let's stop here. You'll get all dirty if we go any farther."

"How did she die? Have you discovered the cause of death?"

"No and I'm not sure we ever will. She was burned pretty bad." That reminded me I needed to follow up to see if there was anything new on the causes of death of Sheila and the lawyer.

We walked around the remains of the house. "Such a waste," Terri said. "It was the most beautiful house I've ever been in. Jake poured his heart into it, and he did love Sheila." She looked at me. "I'm glad he hired you."

\*     \*     \*

About five o'clock I drove into the motel parking lot. "Can I invite you in for a cold beer? I stocked your favorite."

She reached over and took my hand as she stared into my eyes. "Didn't you promise me dinner? We can start with a beer and order carry-out later. This afternoon has made me *very* thirsty."

She moved her car closer to my room and we walked in together. As soon as I closed the door, I reached for her. It was a short reach because she had already stepped into me, and nestled against my chest. I don't know who kissed whom, but our lips pressed together, and I knew they were born to meet. I had no idea any woman could taste so sweet. Her tongue gently probed, and I returned the favor.

We came up for air and she gently pushed me away.

I tried to pull her close again but she resisted. "What's the matter?" I asked through quick breaths. "What did I do?"

"Nothing, Ace, and . . . and everything. I can't do what I want, what we want. I simply can't—not now. I'd better leave."

Those words slammed me back to earth in a crash landing. "If you wish, but I don't want you to go."

"I'm not looking for a quick roll in the hay. The next man I make love with is going to be special. You may be him but not this quickly. Give me time to work out some of my life. Move slowly with me, Ace, and we'll both be better off."

107

I stepped away from her, and tried to smile. "Whatever you wish. I'll be here when, and if, you want me."

## CHAPTER THIRTEEN

I snoozed in my motel room dreaming of Terri when a pounding on the door shattered my fantasy. "Edwards, you in there? Wake up."

My first instinct was to wonder where the cats were but gradually consciousness seeped in. "Who, who the hell's at my door?"

"It's me, Sammy. Sammy Waltham. I needa talk to you."

I rolled out of bed, stumbled toward the door in the dark, and kicked a chair with my bare foot. I danced around a moment, emitting noises that made me sound mean and upset. When I opened the door, a guy who looked familiar stood there emitting nervousness. "What the hell do you want?" I growled.

"Excuse me, Mr. Edwards. I'm Sammy Waltham. We met at the Down Home. I kin come back later if you want."

"Whaddaya mean come back later?" I said, checking to see if he was alone. "Hell, it's still dark out there. You got me up, now get your ass in here and tell me what you want." I stepped aside and waved him in, hoping I wasn't inviting the killer into my room.

109

Waltham came into the room and looked around, as if looking for something or somebody. "I mean it. I can come back after work if it'd be better. I didn't know you'd still be in bed."

I flipped on the bedside lamp and took a good look at him for the first time. It was the guy whose family-making potential I'd assaulted the other night in the Down Home. He looked a lot bigger than he had then—about a foot taller and forty pounds heavier. I figured I'd better keep tough or he'd realize how small I am. "Okay, you're here. What the hell do you want? I'm not used to having some dude beating on my door at, at—hell, what time is it?"

"It's five-thirty, Mr. Edwards. I'm on my way to work and thought I'd stop by. You want I should come back later?"

"Oh, shut up and sit down. Five-thirty, you go to work at five-thirty?" I felt sorry for him. Nobody should go to work that early. That was a time to be getting in, not commuting.

He sat in the only chair in the room.

"Now, why are you here?"

"I been thinking about what Bubba said, and I wanna apologize."

Now that threw me for a spin. I sat on the edge of the bed. "Apologize? What for?"

"For treating you bad in the Down Home. I know now we wuz wrong, I mean, Hojo, Buster and me. We shouldn'ta treated you that way."

This was too weird. I fouled this guy bad, bad enough to be ejected from a professional hockey game, and here he was apologizing to me. Well, on second thought, I guess a simple elbow and knee lift aren't bad enough to be ejected from a hockey game—five minutes in the box maybe, but not an ejection. "I understand. You feel bad," I said. "But why are you here?"

"Bubba said you wuz our friend, that you wuz trying to help us. I got some information might help you. I wanna tell it to you."

I looked at the clock. It was too early for this crap. "Good, Sammy. That's real good. But it's five-thirty and I'm tired. Tell me what you know and then get the hell outta here."

Sammy jumped, then started talking. When he finished twenty or thirty minutes later, I was wide awake and thanking him for waking me.

As Sammy left, I knew it had to happen today. It was time to have a serious talk with Jake. There were questions he'd better have answers for. But in the meantime, sleep was top priority.

I crawled into bed and slept until nine o'clock. By the time I'd showered and shaved, it was ten, and I felt human again. I knew I should call Jake first but I felt the need to pursue something more important.

I dialed the school. "I'd like to leave a message for Terri Hart, please. Ask her to call Ace Edwards at 555-3478, room one-twenty at her first opportunity." Terri had told me she had a break at ten-thirty.

I flipped on the tube and watched Fox News until the phone rang at ten-thirty. "Hello, Ace Edwards here."

The voice that came through the phone reminded me of one of those commercials I'd seen a few minutes ago. You've seen it. A beautiful woman with a sexy voice is talking as she runs her fingers along the top edge of her open-necked blouse. She's talking about perfume but she's selling sex. "Ace, it's so good to hear from you. Did you sleep well?"

I lied. "Yeah, like a rock. How about you?"

"No, I had a terrible night. I kept re-playing yesterday and how nice it was being with you. Do you want to see me tonight? If that's why you're calling, the answer's yes."

I knew she was the cat, and I was the mouse, but it didn't matter. I hadn't felt like this since I was fourteen and my older neighbor took me into the barn. She gave me the number one experience I'll never forget. Terri was my number two experience, or maybe she came in at 1-A. I was star-struck, infatuated, in love, in lust, whatever name you want to give it. I stammered, "Yes, that would be wonderful. When and where should I pick you up?"

"I'll meet you at the Down Home at eight. Please don't get in any more fights."

Her voice was like warm syrup pouring over a stack of pancakes—smooth and sweet. My heart pounded and my pulse raced. The fourteen-year-old kid inside me said, "Great, I'll be waiting for you. I promise, no fights."

I hung up with a grin that must have stretched from ear to ear. It was so wide I was afraid it might push my hairline back. My next call wouldn't be as pleasant.

I dialed again. After working my way through to Jake, I said, "We need to talk. I'm coming by your office so clear your calendar."

"What the hell are you talking about, Arty? I have a morning full of appointments. No time today. Look, I'll put my secretary back on. She'll find you a slot tomorrow or next week. Good to talk to you."

"Don't hang up, Jake, and don't transfer me to your secretary. Today, Jake, today, we gotta talk."

"Arty, Arty, Arty. What is it? Am I late with your check? I'll get one out today. Now, I have to run. Set something up with my secretary."

Click. He hung up. I hit re-dial and his secretary answered, "Mr. Adams' office."

"Miss, you've only seen me once, and I've only seen you once. From that one meeting, you can't know what a mean, sarcastic, snarling pit bull I can be. Don't hang up on me, or I'll come over and chew your leg off."

"This must be Mr. Edwards. Mr. Adams said you have a terrible growl, but in your heart, you're a teddy bear. We've never met. I wasn't here when you came before but I did hear about your visit. How nice to talk with you. I'm fine, and how are you?"

She was cool, but I refused to be diverted. "Yeah, this is Ace Edwards, that's Ace, not Arty. You tell your boss I'm headed his way, and when I get there in about one hour, we're gonna talk. So, I suggest you clear his calendar. That's Edwards, Arthur Conan Edwards, commonly known as Ace."

"But, Mr. Edwards, you don't have an . . ."

I left her trying to tell me something when I hung up. I sat back with another grin on my face—not as big as the one earlier, but a big one. Sometimes, it felt good to shove the shoe on the other foot, especially when it was another person's foot—especially when it was Jake's foot.

I thought of Terri, I thought of Jake, then I thought of Terri again. She was a more pleasant subject.

Now, what I needed was coffee and a doughnut to fuel my trip to Fort Worth. I headed for the closest Seven-Eleven.

## CHAPTER FOURTEEN

I stopped outside Jake's executive office suite, arranged my face so it carried my tough-guy look, opened the door and stepped in. Jake's executive secretary glanced up as I walked in. I realized she was right, I hadn't seen her before. But, seeing her reminded me that Jake had a great instinct for selecting beauty and brains in the same package. Sheila had been that way. My tough-guy look dissolved and in my most gracious voice, I said, "Hi, I'm Ace Edwards. We spoke earlier. I'm here to see Mr. Adams. I believe he's expecting me."

"Good morning, Mr. Edwards. It's nice to meet you. Mr. Adams is expecting you. Before we go in, I'd like to make an observation, though."

"Okay, roll the dice." I was still in my tough guy mode.

She continued in her soft voice. "I think you're too nice to act like a horse's ass like you did on the phone earlier. I'm sure your mother would never approve of your behavior. If you ever do that to me again, I'll cut your nuts off and roast them over an open fire like

115

chestnuts." She smiled, stood, and walked toward the door to Jake's office. "Now, follow me, please."

My mouth dropped open. From her behavior and appearance, no one would have known she'd cut me up into fondue-size chunks. Fortunately, she turned and walked away as I blushed. Watching her walk brought me back to reality, though, and gave me a whole new appreciation for the fair sex. I followed her.

She opened the door. "Mr. Adams, Mr. Edwards is here."

You'd have thought Jake and I had planned this reunion for months. He jumped out of his chair and after several steps, rounded his massive desk with his hand outstretched. "Arty, come in, come in please." He spun toward his secretary. "Kathy, please bring us coffee and spring water."

He turned back toward me. "Anything else you'd like, Arty. Kathy will be glad to get it for you."

"No, coffee's fine," I mumbled as I turned to watch Kathy walk away, thinking he shouldn't ask questions like that.

"Ain't she something?" Jake whispered. "Having her around makes a man feel ten years younger."

I stopped watching Kathy and looked back at Jake. "Yeah, she's up to your standards." I'd decided while driving in that I'd try to get him off-balance. Maybe he'd give something away. "Why'd you have somebody following Sheila all the time?"

"Arty, are you getting absent-minded in your old age? I told you I hired a private eye to check on her." Jake had settled back in his chair in his relaxed executive mode. So much for my surprise tactics.

"Yeah, I know. But you didn't tell me you had a team on her twenty-four hours a day, every day. You didn't tell me it was a close surveillance so she'd know they were there. You didn't tell me she was terrified. Why, Jake? Were you jealous?"

Jake jolted forward and slammed an open palm on his desk. The desk didn't vibrate. At its size, nothing short of a thousand-pound bomb would have moved it. His face was ugly. "What the hell are you talking about? I've never been jealous of anybody in my life, and you, of all people, ought to know that. Now, knock off the bullshit. You've screwed up my day. What the hell do you want?"

I stepped forward with my eyes locked on his, placed my hands on his desk and leaned toward him. "That's just too freaking bad. I agree. Knock off the bullshit. Where were you between ten and two the night Sheila died?"

Jake settled back in his chair, a look of incredulity on his face. "I've been through all this crap with the cops. Do you doubt me?"

"Yeah, I do. Now, answer my question."

Jake and I went back a lot of years. In high school, we had our ups and downs. A couple of times we came close to blows over a girl. On the football field we yelled at one another, but I'd never seen a look on his face like I saw now. I swear his jaw never moved as he said, "Pick up your check. I don't need you anymore. You're fired, as of this moment. Now, get the hell out of here!"

I had to admire him. His enunciation was perfect. "Firing me won't solve your problem. If I walk out now, my next stop is Sheriff Yardley's office. Do you think he'd find it interesting that you had a PI on Sheila

117

twenty-four hours a day, that you have no alibi for the night she was killed? You can talk to me or you can talk to him. Your choice, buddy. No skin off my ass." I sat, almost disappearing in one of those wingback chairs. I leaned back, hoping what I'd said would soak in—and I could get out of the chair.

The door opened and Kathy entered pushing a cart with a coffee service and spring water. There was also a selection of sweet rolls. "I thought Mr. Edwards might have been too busy this morning for breakfast."

Her smile hid the true meaning of the words as I felt smaller and smaller.

When she left the room, I stood, poured a cup of coffee and took a sweet roll. Why not? It was Jake's dime.

In my most nonchalant manner, I sat back down, sipping and nibbling.

Jake glared at me. I thought I could hear his Rolex ticking. With what they cost, I always assumed they were silent. But then, the closest I'd ever been to one was on Jake's wrist. What did I know?

Tick-tock, tick-tock. The antique grandfather clock along the wall recorded every second. The office was as quiet as a church mouse as I stared at Jake. Church mouse. You ever wondered where that expression comes from. In my experience, all mice are quiet. Otherwise, they are dead. I figure there's a great book title there, patterned after Louis L'Amour's *The Quick and the Dead*. It'd be a western about mice and I'd call it *The Quiet and the Dead*. Obviously, a cat would be the hero.

I wasn't gonna move until Jake did. I found myself wondering if this was one of those battles of wills we hear about. Beats me, but I decided it was time for Jake to make a play.

I stared at him as he stared at me. A classic case of who blinks first. Tick tock, tick tock. Jake blinked. "Okay, Arty, I'll answer your question. Yeah, I had a PI on Sheila. Hell, she and that man-hating lawyer took me for a bundle of cash and my home. I wanted to know how she spent it."

"Nice try, Jake. Very nice. Now, here's the sixty-four dollar lifetime question. Where were you the night Sheila was killed?"

"You're buggin' me, Ace. I don't have to answer to you!"

"Only if you want me to find whoever torched your house. Or maybe I already know. Maybe you torched your own house after you killed Sheila and the lawyer. Maybe the sheriff would love to have that as a theory—if he hasn't settled on it already."

"Okay, I get your drift." Jake relaxed and settled into his chair again. "Look, I don't want to tell you where I was when the house was burned—trust me, it's best you don't know. All you need to know is I'm innocent, and have an ironclad alibi."

I was less than impressed. "Try me. I'll let you know if I agree."

"Don't force me to tell you. Trust me, okay?"

I couldn't figure what he was trying to pull, but I wasn't about to back off. "No, you tell me. If I believe you, I'll stay away from the sheriff."

"Suppose I fire you. Will you quit then?"

"No, Jake. You know me better than that. I want to know what happened. My dad always said there's a bulldog in our family tree. Once an Edwards locks on to

119

something, he doesn't turn loose until he wins. That's me, Jake."

"Yeah, that's what I thought. Ace, it's not that I don't want to tell you, but if I do, you must promise the story will stop with you. Do you understand?"

I noticed he'd quit calling me Arty but decided not to bring it up. Instead, I said, "Tell me, I'll make my own decision on what to do with it. No promises."

"Damn you, Arty!"

So much for his not using my obnoxious nickname.

"Let me try again?" Jake said. "For reasons I don't want to get into, my reputation is on the line here. If the word gets out before I'm ready, I'll be a laughingstock. I need your support, and I need to know I can trust you."

I leaned back and studied my fingernails. My intent was to show Jake how unimpressed I was with his plea. Don't know if it worked, but I noticed my fingernails needed cleaning. In my most detached voice, I said, "It's getting late, Jake. I've got better things to do than sit here listening to your crap. Tell me where you were and who you were with. Otherwise, I'm getting out of this body-swallowing chair and drive straight to the sheriff's office. Your choice now, my friend, I've made mine."

I was glad I wore my lead skivvies. Jake's stare would have burned through anything less. He glared at me for what seemed like an hour and a half, probably the longest thirty seconds I've ever endured.

"I was with a woman, Ace, a lovely, vulnerable woman. We were together from early in the evening until I left her in my bed after the phone call from the Eastland county cop. I hope you're pleased you dragged that out of me."

I stared back, trying to burn through his outer layer. "Bullshit, Jake. Why should I believe you? That's no reason for you to play coy with me. A woman, hell, we'd all like to spend the night with a desirable woman. You gotta do better."

I could see Jake's thought processes as they crisscrossed his face. His Adam's apple jitterbugged up and down his throat. Again, we played our stare game, eyes locked, intense looks on our faces. I almost smiled when I realized we probably looked like my cats when they do their stare-down routine.

"Arty, if we weren't old friends, I'd come over there and kick the shit out of you. You always were too damn big for your britches. I've said all I plan to tell you. If it's not enough, get out of here. We won't need to talk again."

We sat there glaring at one another like two fifth graders, each afraid the other would make a move. I'm an expert at this game. I play it with the cats all the time.

Jake caved. "Trust me, Arty, trust me. I need your help to find who torched my house and killed Sheila. Believe me when I tell you it wasn't me. Like I said, I was with a woman. I can't tell you any more. If you'll think, you'll figure out why."

I studied his face. The last time I'd seen him that serious was when he'd announced he was proposing to Sheila. I had to accept what he said. "Okay, Jake. I'll buy it for now, but hear me and hear me good. If I don't find somebody with a better reason for wasting Sheila, I'll be back, and you and I *will* pick up where we're leaving off." I hit the word will hard.

"Okay, you've made your threats. Now if you don't have anything else, I have work to do."

I squirmed out of the chair and started toward the door, then turned back toward the coffee service, and refilled my cup. "Great coffee, Jake." I'd decided to hell with his work schedule. I might never get another chance to stick it to him.

"I do have more." I dropped back into the body-swallowing chair. "I'm here until I get a few answers to some questions. What do you have on Madeline Millener, the lawyer who represented Sheila? I'm sure you've heard she was the second body in the house."

"Yeah, I heard. No great loss there." Jake's look was sour. "What makes you think I have anything on her?"

"Just a guess, Jake. Just a guess."

He leaned back and appeared to think for a moment. "I don't know much about her. She's from a small firm here in Fort Worth. Give me a minute and I'll dig out what little I have."

"You rang, Mr. Adams."

I turned toward the entrance to his office where his secretary, Kathy, stood in the doorway. I guessed he had a hidden call button connected to her desk.

"Check the records and get me any info we have on the lawyer who represented Sheila at our divorce," Jake told her. "Mr. Edwards will need it. Run a print-out."

"Yes sir, Mr. Adams." She left the room.

As soon as the door closed behind her, I looked at Jake. "I'm impressed. Do you think my little one-man shop can afford someone like her."

Jake relaxed and chuckled. "Hell, on what I'm paying you alone. One problem though. There's only one Kathy. She's good, the best." He stopped and frowned. "But a guy'll come along. She'll fall in love, and I'll lose her to a maternity ward. Happens every time."

I sat straighter. My feet came close to the floor. "Do you mean she's single and available?"

"Not for you. She's got better taste, and if she doesn't, I'll fire her. With my luck she'd fall for you, marry you and then double-cross me by not having babies. Then, I'd have you snooping around my office all the time."

We were friends again as we both laughed at his joke. There was a discreet knock on the door, a hesitation, and it opened. "I have the information you wanted, Mr. Adams. We don't have much."

"Give it to Arty."

I scowled at him as Kathy leaned over and handed me a one-page printout. I wanted to grab it and read, but my eyes wouldn't shift from her cleavage.

She stood and I scanned the report, but before I finished the first paragraph, Jake interrupted.

"Ace, I don't mean to be a prick but I do have work to do. Your sitting there is costing me double—what I'm paying you and what I'm losing by not getting my work done. Do you have anything else for me?"

I laughed. "That's the first time I've ever heard you concerned about money. Are you turning human in your old age?"

"No, I'm just tired of looking at your ugly mug. Now, get out of here and earn your pay," he replied, chuckling.

The chair released me again. "The lawyer, her name was Millener? That can't be real."

"Yes, it was. She was a partner in Millener, Millener and Millener—her mother, her sister and her.

That's a law firm, not a hat shop. The three of them were all partners and the only lawyers."

We parted company much friendlier than we'd been when I arrived. If we had been playing a game, I'd have had to score one for Jake.

In the lobby of Jake's building, I used a pay phone and called one of my contacts in Dallas. I asked him to find out everything he could about a Fort Worth lawyer named Madeline Millener.

## CHAPTER FIFTEEN

I was about halfway to Cisco, trying to make a picture out of the few pieces of the puzzle I had when my pager went off. I checked the number and smiled—Terri's number at school. I shoved the puzzle to the back of my mind and thought of her.

I pulled over and took out my cell phone. People who drive with one hand while holding a phone in the other scare me. I called Terri's school.

"Hello, this is Ace Edwards. . . . No. Ace, A-C-E. . . . Yes, Ace." This was one of those times when I wished my dad had called me Tom, John, Bob or anything in common usage. "I'd like to get in touch with Ms. Hart. Can you tell me when her next break is? . . . Thank you. Please give her a message that I'll try to contact her then." I broke the connection and stared at the highway. I hoped she wasn't calling to break our date.

I think I counted the minutes until twelve-thirty when Terri would be free to take a call. Finally it arrived, and I heard her incredible voice say, "Ace, I'm glad you returned my page. I want so much to talk with you."

My heart skipped enough beats to get thrown out of a musician's union. "I'm glad you paged. What is it? Is something wrong?"

"No, nothing is wrong—I mean, nothing unless you're tied up this afternoon after school."

"Nothing except putting a few felons in jail, but they can wait. No matter how many I incarcerate, a new one pops up to take his place." I hoped she'd hear my attempt at humor, not the anticipation in my voice.

"Good, I'll come by the motel about four-thirty. I'll call you from the office. I want to see you up close, but I don't trust myself in your room again. You know what would happen." Her voice had a huskiness that sent my emotions soaring.

"Anything wrong with that?"

"No, nothing at all. But, we need to save it. Anticipation makes the feat so much sweeter."

All I could muster was a shaky, "I'll be waiting."

She rang off.

I sat, remembering the previous day.

*       *       *

Although I tingled with anticipation about seeing Terri, I still had time to kill and a case to solve. I remembered what Sam said about Sheila and the lawyer being naked. Like Sam, I couldn't think of anything to explain it. Only the killer knew for sure. Rape was the one possibility I came up with. Maybe the county mounties had developed better answers. If so, I needed to convince them to share with me.

I drove to the sheriff's office and parked, noting that older model cars were still parked in the reserved spaces. When I went into the station, Sergeant Jones was once again on duty. "Good morning," I said in my most gracious voice. "It's good to see you again. I'm—"

"I know who you are, Edwards. Hell, everybody in Eastland County knows you. Everybody knows you're sticking your nose into police business. Now, whaddaya want?"

It seemed Sergeant Jones and I would never be close friends. I wondered what he'd do if I invited him to the Down Home for a Killian's. "Thank you, yes, I'm feeling fine. How nice of you to ask. I see by your attitude that you're feeling snarly again. I'd like to see the sheriff. Would you be good enough to ring him?"

I don't know if my sarcasm was lost on him or not, but his response didn't make me warm and fuzzy.

"Edwards, you're gonna overstep your bounds one of these days and I'll love it when they bring your ass in, dead or alive." He rose and started around the desk. "In fact, I might—"

"Ace Edwards. Good to see you again. What brings you by?"

I turned and saw Sheriff Yardley coming toward me. I relaxed from my fighter's stance and Jones settled back behind his high desk. "Sheriff," I said, sticking out my hand in greeting. "I'm glad you're in. I have news I want to pass on to you. Do you have a minute?"

He shook my hand as he looked toward Sergeant Jones. "Sure, come on back." He slapped me on the back shoving me up the hallway.

I turned back toward Sergeant Jones. "Good to see you again, Sergeant. Have a nice day."

After we were in his office and I was settled in a straight back wooden chair with a cup of coffee, the

127

Randy Rawls

sheriff said, "Edwards, you're going to piss Jones off too much one day and he's gonna snap your neck like a pretzel. The reason I stepped in out there is I don't want him in trouble. He's a good cop so stay away from him."

"Sheriff, I assure you, that was the least of my intentions. Do you think he's prejudiced against short, balding people? It seems—"

"Enough of that crap. That's what I mean. Now, you said you wanted to talk, so do it. I have a meeting in thirty minutes and I like to get to the conference room early. Your time is limited. Talk straight and talk fast."

I sat up and put on my serious face. "Okay. Are you aware that both Sheila and the lawyer were naked?"

"Yeah, so what and how did you find out? That's privileged information. It hasn't been released to the public." His face flushed red. "Who told you? I'll have his ass."

Before I could reply with a suitable lie, he blurted, "That dumb-shit fireman, right. The boys said you been spending a lot of time around the firehouse."

He had me and he knew it. "Yeah, it was Sam Raleigh. Or, I should say he confirmed what I guessed. Remember, I was there when the bodies were found, and I noticed there was no evidence of clothing. When I confronted him with my supposition, he agreed." Yeah, I know it was a lie but I owed Sam. He felt like an ally.

"Yeah, right. He's like you, loves to play cops and robbers. I'll deal with him another time. Now, tell me everything you know. And for your own good, don't leave anything out."

"Not much more to tell. Sam and I went over the house plans. Sheila's body was in the study and the lawyer must have fallen from the second or third floor.

128

Or maybe she was on the stairs when she died. Sam said the analysis of the ashes around the bodies showed no evidence of clothing."

Sheriff Yardley leaned back in his chair and hooked his thumbs under his suspenders. "Interesting, your theory about the body placements. When Raleigh told me, I figured he was overreaching." He hesitated. "You buy that? It could throw a whole new light on things? What do you think?"

I relaxed. Maybe, we could work together, and maybe I'd taken Sam down from the meat hook I placed him on. "Right now, I don't have anything definite. What comes to mind is rape and murder. I suppose it's possible someone broke in, made them strip, then raped and killed them."

"Possible, possible. But, if that happened, why weren't the bodies together."

"I don't know," I replied. "Maybe one of them, the lawyer I'd guess, made a break for it. She might have been headed up the stairs when the killer caught up with her, and he killed her on the spot. Maybe he shot her as she climbed the stairway. Any evidence of bullet damage?"

"No, the lab boys didn't find any of the bones had been struck by a bullet. Of course, it could have passed through without hitting a bone and we'd never know. You saw the condition of the bodies."

"Yeah, I did." The picture flared in my mind, making my stomach queasy.

The sheriff leaned forward again. "You're talking like you know there was only one killer. Why? Way I see it, two or more fits better. Maybe there were two, and one had Sheila downstairs while the other took the lawyer upstairs."

"Could be," I said. "I'm not ruling out anything yet. Could have been one, two, or more. Like you said, two makes the separation between the bodies easier to understand." I went back to my earlier question. "Cause of death? What killed them?"

"We don't know except both skulls were cracked, and that was enough to kill them. But it could have happened after they were dead. If rape happened, we'll never know. The coroner says he can't determine the exact cause of death or any flesh damage that might have occurred before death. They were burned too badly. This is one of those where the cause of death officially goes down as unknown."

He spoke so freely, I plowed on. "Any suspects? Anybody who might have a case against either or both of them?"

"Nothing concrete. The lawyer was from Fort Worth and slammed enough ex-husbands to make some guy wish she was dead. The Fort Worth police are working that. We talk at least once a week. They haven't developed anything yet."

"Yeah, I get the same input. How about out here? I know she worked here. Anybody in Eastland County that would want her dead?"

"Other than Jake Adams, you mean?" He looked at me and added, "What about your friend, Jake?"

I responded without thinking. "He's clean. He has an airtight alibi for the night of the fire." Even as I said it I realized I wasn't covering for him, I believed it. Jake was off the hook with me.

"Humph. You believe his story about being with a woman—a woman he won't identify? Maybe, maybe not, or did he tell you who she is? That still don't clear him. He could have hired someone to do it. He's got enough money to buy near anything."

I stood and paced. "Yes, I believe his story, and no, he didn't give me a name. You have to understand how much he loved that house. I don't know whether he's capable of killing or having Sheila killed, but I know he'd never burn the house. That's why I believe him."

"Oh, sit down. If you'd run a football the way you're talking now, you'd never have gained a yard. I'll keep checking on your buddy and so will the Fort Worth police. But, back to what you asked me. We haven't come up with anything firm to finger a suspect. Whoever did it knew what he was doing and covered his tracks. Either that, or he's one lucky amateur. If you know anything different, you best tell me or I'll slap obstruction of justice charges on you."

I chuckled. "Nope, you know as much as I do, probably more. How about Sonny? Anything new? Have you verified the target?"

"Sorry, Edwards. We've come up empty on that one, too. My gut feeling is you were the target. We haven't found any reason to believe someone would be gunning for Sonny. As far as Bubba goes, only Jake Adams has a motive to go after him. Adams' name seems to pop up a lot when I think about this case. On the other hand, maybe you brought some nut out here behind you, or maybe Sheila's killer wants to take you out because he believes your reputation."

He stood looking at his watch. "Now, if you don't have anything else, I've got a meeting."

131

"Whoa, before you go, how about protection? Seems to me there's somebody out there gunning for me, and that doesn't feel good."

His grin tipped me off before the words came. "Simple. Leave town. Go back to Dallas and stay out of Eastland County business."

I grasped his not-so-subtle hint. "Thanks, you've given me feelings of safety and confidence. I hope your people soon solve this mess."

"Edwards, I've already told you about being a wise-ass." He stood and walked toward the door then turned back. "Dammit, I knew your father and your grandfather, and I respected them. Hell, I worked as a delivery boy in the drug store when I was a kid. Watch your back. I agree somebody wants you dead. From what I hear, you stomped toes since you left the force in Dallas. You made enemies. Play it safe, go home and spy on husbands. Leave the crime solving to real cops."

He stepped toward the door, then again turned toward me. "Oh, one thing that might or might not tie in. We got a call saying somebody stole three jerry cans filled with gas. Could be the ones used in the fire."

"Who called?"

He threw a name at me, then made another attempt to leave the office as I considered his answer. At the doorway, he turned back toward me. "When you pass Sergeant Jones on your way out, it'd be a good idea to keep your mouth shut."

Mom always said I never knew when to stay quiet. As I left the building, I said, "Have a good day, Sergeant Jones. I hope to see you again soon."

His hostile glare made me feel better.

*     *     *

When I arrived at the motel, I called my contact. "Tom, what'd you get on Millener?"

Tom Roberts was an ex-cop like me, but unlike me, he invested his retirement fund in education. He took enough courses to become a computer nerd and now made a large and steady income solving other people's problems. Not bad for an ex-cop. Of course, being an ex-cop, he kept his ear to the curbstone. If you needed to nail a rumor, Tom Roberts had heard it. Since we'd been together on the force and I'd pulled him out of a few tight spots, he did research for me on the cuff. I assured him I'd pay him when my first oil well came in.

"Looks like you tied into a hellcat this time. She was with a three-lawyer firm in Fort Worth, her mother, her sister and herself. Up front, they're typical ambulance chasers. You've seen their ad on TV, haven't you?"

I thought for a second. "Are they the ones who promise to get you double what any man can, and faster?"

"Yeah, that's them. Their gimmick is they're better than any male ambulance chaser. But your gal. She was the crème de la crème. She chased ambulances, but her love was divorces, those where the ex-husband had a bundle. Her nickname was Maddie—some called her Mad, The Mad Millener, or," he chuckled, "The Mad Hatter."

I laughed, "That fits. She blocked a friend of mine in a divorce."

Tom continued. "Word on the street was when she took a divorce case—and she only represented wives—she was a tigress, and would use any trick to win."

"Example?"

"I have no direct knowledge, of course, but someone heard she wasn't above a hint of blackmail to win a case."

"How?"

"Don't know if you ever saw her, but my sources say she was a good looking woman. She could turn on the charm and get to any man."

I remembered Jake's divorce. Yeah, it fit. She was a looker.

"The story goes she tried to get her cases on the dockets of male judges. She'd get the judge alone in chambers and tell him she might leak to the news media that he harassed her. The media might find out he tried to grope a female lawyer during an office conference. Rumors say she never lost a case after a one-on-one with the judge."

"Sounds like a sweetheart," I said, wondering if that's why Jake got burned. The judge had been putty in her hands. "What about enemies, any that might want to see her dead?"

Tom began to laugh and kept laughing. I tried to be patient, but I had to interrupt. "Tom, do you mind? I must have missed the joke."

He stifled his laughter, "Ace, you're priceless. After what I told you, you ask if she has enemies. How about every man she took to the cleaners, plus a few judges. Any one of them would love to see her planted."

"Yeah, that's logical. But why? Is there anything on the street explaining why she hated men?"

"Nothing more than the usual problems—her dad took off when she was young and left her mom and older sister in a hurt. They never heard of him again, except when he died.

"Her mom swore off men, vowed to never let another one in her bed. She worked two and three jobs and somehow finished law school. When she went into practice, she set the standard of no males allowed. The two daughters made it through law school also and when Maddie graduated, they launched Millener, Millener and Millener.

"Since then, they've been rolling in dough. Women flock to them. Nobody accuses them of catering to the rich, but they're not known to do pro bono work. A few years ago, they threw a big party, women only, when they learned the old man died."

"Interesting trio," I said. "Even for this age, it seems extreme. Ever charged with sexual discrimination? Hasn't any judge stood up to them?"

"Several times."

"What happened?"

"What do you think? They're women. The cases were dismissed before they ever came near a jury."

"Okay, I get it. Anything else?"

"That's it. Are you investigating Maddie's death?"

"Indirectly. My charge is to find the arsonist who did the house where Millener and Sheila Adams were found dead. If I have to backtrack her, I will. If you hear anything, let me know."

"Sure, good luck."

I rang off from Tom with a final remark. "Thanks for your input. All you've done is make my case twice as difficult." I softened it with a chuckle.

135

## CHAPTER SIXTEEN

My motel room was shrinking, no doubt about it, and my watch had stopped. No, I could see the seconds changing—very slowly. I walked to the door and opened it expecting to see the sun sliding down behind the row of rooms across the parking lot. What was it doing holding high in the sky? I looked at my watch again. Four-fifteen. Couldn't be. It was four-ten an hour ago. I picked up the phone and punched zero.

"Front desk."

"This is one-twenty. What's the correct time?"

"Umm, it's four-fifteen."

My watch was right. "Thank you." I hung up and realized the receiver was slick with sweat. Ridiculous. I was acting like a green kid.

The phone rang. I leapt to grab it. "Hello."

"Ace, it's me, Terri."

Bells rang, cherubs flitted around the room, the sweet aroma of roses appeared, and the walls returned to their normal positions. "Terri, you're early." I mentally kicked myself for that opening as I fell onto the bed feeling great. The phone base slid, dangling between the bedside table and the bed.

"Well, a little. I just wanted to see you as early as I could. You're not busy, are you? Not solving an important case or something?" Her chuckle sent ripples through my body.

"No, I'm, uh, I'm not doing anything except waiting for you to lend glamour to my otherwise drab life. Are you in the office?"

"You're still full of it, aren't you. Yes, I'm in the office. Are you—"

"I'll be right there." I rescued the phone and hung up all in one smooth move, then grabbed my jacket as I headed out of the room. After a few strides, none of which touched the parking lot, I opened the door to the motel office.

A beautiful woman stood there, and I knew it must be Terri. I say it that way because I might not have recognized her in a crowd. It wasn't any of the Terri's I'd seen before. This Terri looked studious, intelligent, every bit the teacher of children. Her red hair was pulled into a French twist, and she wore a dark blue pants suit. Navy blue shoes, and a discreet touch of blue eye shadow completed her wardrobe. I considered the four looks of Terri I'd seen. The others were more glamorous, but this was a Terri I could adore more—a Terri who brought out the love I yearned to share.

"Excuse me, I'm looking for Terri Hart." What else could I say? A corny approach was my only hope. "Have you seen her around here?"

"I, I knew I should've gone home and changed, but I got stuck late at school. Do you mind?" She gave me an embarrassed look, and I swirled into the vortex that was her eyes.

137

"Mind? No. You're beautiful." Out of the corner of my eye, I noticed the desk clerk watching us. I couldn't decide whether he was trying to improve his English or debating whether he should call 9-1-1. "Maybe we'd better get out of here."

We walked to my car, and I resisted the impulse to invite her to my room for a glass of water. I was afraid she'd say no, and I was afraid she'd say yes. My emotions were in turmoil like I'd never felt before.

"Where to? Any place special you want to go?" I asked as I drove out of the parking lot.

"No, you pick something. I'll spend my time unwinding. It was another of those days at school."

The cherubs and smell of roses had followed us into the car. I loved the pudgy little guys. "I haven't walked around downtown in a long time. Do you mind?"

"Whatever you'd like to do," she replied as I melted and ran into my shoes.

I drove into Cisco and turned onto the main street—Conrad Hilton Avenue. It used to be Avenue D but someone decided to rename it to honor Mr. Hilton.

I parked and we left the car. As we moved along, I sneaked looks at Terri. I had trouble accepting the feelings that raced inside me like the mechanical rabbit at a greyhound track.

To get myself under control, and maybe stop the flood of water pouring from my palms, I commented on what we passed. "Across the street there. Isn't that about where the bank was that those robbers hit that Christmas when they had the big shootout, and they were caught because a little girl wanted to talk to Santa Claus?"

"Huh?" Terri looked at me like I'd emitted a blasphemy in a monastery. "If one of my school kids phrased a question like that, I'd stand him in the corner until he figured out what he wanted to say. Now, would you like to try again, or should I attempt to interpret?" The chuckle that sang out of her mouth reminded me of birds on a fresh spring day.

"Okay, guilty as charged. Which street corner do you want me on?"

"Maybe we'd better get back to the robbery," she replied, smiling. "They called it the Santa Claus Robbery, didn't they? I remember my granddad telling me about it. He said my great-granddad was one of the townspeople who chased after the robbers, guns blazing."

Her great-grandfather! One of the cherubs tumbled down, dropped by her great-grandfather. My grandfather always claimed he shot out one of the bank robbers' tires. Did the sun go behind a cloud or was it my imagination twisting my fantasy toward reality?

I must have looked as old as I felt because she asked, "Are you okay, Ace? You're pale as a ghost."

"Something I ate wants a second chance at life." What else could I say? "Yeah, it was the Santa Claus Robbery—December 23, 1927 or 28, I forget which. As the story was passed down in my family, four bad guys blew into town in a big car and robbed the First National Bank. They might have gotten away except one of them dressed like Santa Claus. Kids saw him on the street and wanted to make last minute requests."

"Can you imagine?" Terri said. "He must have been stupid. What happened?"

Although I suspected she played to my ego, I continued. "According to Dad, a young girl dragged her mother into the bank to see Santa. This was after the bad

139

guys were well into the robbery. When the mother saw what was happening, she took her little girl's hand and walked straight through the bank out the side door into the alley. The robbers must have been dumbfounded. They didn't stop them. She went to the sheriff's office and told him what was happening. All hell broke loose as the word spread. Everybody came pouring out of their homes and stores, all packing heat."

"Can you imagine?" Terri interrupted. She looked around as if seeing the street for the first time. "It always seemed like such a sleepy little town. I can't picture the townsfolk running around with guns blazing."

"I guess they did, or that's what Dad said. There was a big gun battle but the robbers made it to their car and took off. The townspeople jumped into their cars and gave chase.

"Now, one of the funnier or dumber parts of the story came into play. The bank robbers had stolen the car up north and driven it for several days. When they tore out of the alley beside the bank, the gas gauge sat on empty. Although they got a good jump on the townspeople, they had to stop and steal another car when theirs ran out of gas. Eventually, the white hats caught up and recovered the money, but not before several people were killed, and others wounded. It must have been a wild time back then."

"Is it different today?" she asked, a sad look on her face. "In the last few weeks, two women are dead, and Sonny killed in your car. Who knows what might happen next, or to whom? I hope it's not you." She gave me a look that could have sweetened a lemon grove.

I took her hand. I wanted to do more. "Don't worry about me. I've been ducking a long time, and nobody's gonna get me now. Besides, the Santa Claus caper came to a fitting end when the guy who dressed as Santa was dragged from his cell in Eastland by the loyal townsfolk and lynched. Of course, that was after he killed a guard in an attempted jailbreak. That can't happen to me, I'm one of the guys in the white hats."

She gazed at me, a tear carving a path down her perfect cheek. It left a glistening trail of moisture—no makeup to travel through. Covering her perfect features with makeup would have been like a rock arrangement of Ravel's *Bolero*—a sacrilege.

I knew if I looked at her much longer, I'd do something that would scandalize all of Cisco. I'd take her in my arms and kiss her right in the middle of town in bright daylight. "Maybe we'd better move on before we draw a crowd."

She laughed.

We walked down Conrad Hilton Avenue.

I was glad there were few pedestrians. My heart beat so loudly, I was sure anyone passing would hear it. The cherubs floated merrily around my head, making beautiful music on their lyres.

"Ace, my curiosity is killing me," Terri said squeezing my hand.

"About what?"

"Your name—Ace. Where does it come from? There must be a story there."

I laughed. "A story? Well maybe, but there's nothing mysterious about it. My full name is Arthur Conan Edwards. If you take the first initial of each, you come up with Ace. That's what my dad branded me and that's what I carry today."

Terri chuckled. "Arthur Conan Edwards. Any connection with Arthur Conan Doyle? Or is it a coincidence?"

"My dad was an avid Sherlock Holmes fan. He had every mystery Mr. Holmes ever solved and had read each of them many times. He always said if he had a son, he'd name him Sherlock Holmes Edwards." I stopped and chuckled at the memory. "When Mom was pregnant, Dad told everybody his son's name. Mom hated it. One day in her ninth month as she sat at her desk doodling, she wrote Sherlock Holmes Edwards. When she looked at it, the initials leapt out at her. According to her story, she jumped up and raced to the drugstore." I laughed out loud. "Picture that. My nine-month pregnant mother racing into the drug store shouting, 'John, John, it's SHE, it's SHE.' Dad always said it took him ten minutes to quiet her down enough to figure out what she was talking about. If he named me Sherlock Holmes Edwards, my initials would spell out SHE." I stopped and enjoyed Terri's laugh. "It took Dad less than a second to change my name."

We walked on, both grinning at the story.

"Since I have you in a confessing mood, one more point," Terri said through her chuckles.

"Shoot. I have no secrets from you."

"Arty. Why are you called Arty?"

I flinched at the name. "That's another part of my legacy. It was my mother's pet name for me. Unfortunately, some people heard her use it. I'm stuck with it."

"Arty. I think it's kinda cute," Terri said smiling.

"Don't you dare," I replied with my best glare.

She grinned, squeezed my hand and pointed toward a two story brick building on the corner of Fourth Street. "Look, there's the Mobley Hotel. Let's visit the museum. I haven't been there in years. Maybe there's a homework assignment for my kids."

"That's the hotel Conrad Hilton ran, isn't it?" I wanted to hear her talk for awhile.

"Yes, according to my great-grandfather, he bought it in 1919. Great-Granddad said he came to town to buy into one of the local banks but the owners reneged on the deal. So, he bought the hotel instead."

She had highlighted our age difference again. I remembered hearing the story from my grandfather. But all I said was, "Oh, I remember, this is where Hilton got his start, or something like that. Right?"

She looked at me as if doubting my question. "Yes. He kept the hotel for about six years. I'm sure you know the rest. He went on to build an international chain of hotels and hobnobbed with heads of state and all the other important people of the world."

"Yeah, if I ever solve a really big case, I might be able to afford one of his hotels."

Terri grabbed my hand and picked up the pace. "Come on, let's hit the museum. They used to have some great stuff."

We went into the old hotel and signed in like tourists. I dropped a fiver into the contributions jar. Terri led me up the stairs to the second floor and into the room which houses Cisco's history.

"Ace, look at these." She pointed to newspaper clippings documenting the destruction of downtown Cisco in 1893 by a cyclone. "It must have been terrible.

Look at all the buildings that were destroyed. It doesn't say how many were killed."

She moved down the exhibit. "Here are photographs of families and town dignitaries that go back to the 1800s." She chuckled. "Look at the dresses. Don't they look funny? I can't imagine wearing a dress like that."

"Not much funnier than the suits on the men." I looked at Terri and knew I'd love her no matter what she wore.

We wandered around examining the collection documenting Cisco and Eastland County. It was nothing like big city museums. Here, little was under glass. This was a hands-on place.

We stood before a yellowing photograph of a wedding party. Terri took my hand, and gave it a gentle squeeze. The cherubs strummed their miniature harps with gusto.

As I reached for her, she said, "Let's check out the Conrad Hilton exhibition. I still need an assignment for my kids."

We spent another twenty minutes in the upstairs hallway that documents Conrad Hilton's life. Terri pulled a small pad from her purse and took notes. There were large photographs with short captions, showing him with the most famous people of the century. Terri was quiet as she wrote line after line in her notebook.

I guessed there would be a run on Conrad Hilton biographies at the library after school tomorrow.

Walking away from the hotel, I looked at Terri and then back at the building, feeling like I could have flown off its roof.

She took my hand. "How long has it been since you had a picnic?"

"Longer than my memory. Sounds good, but then anything with you sounds good." I squeezed her hand. "What do you have in mind?"

"Let's pick up some sandwiches."

"I can live with that. I think there's an old blanket in the trunk of the car." If not, I'd have happily bought one—cashmere, if she wanted it.

Following Terri's directions, we assembled a picnic basket that turned out to be more than sandwiches. She added three kinds of chips, pickles, potato salad, fried chicken, coleslaw, beans, cookies, and lemon pie.

You should know by now I'm not the type who wouldn't contribute. I added a cold twelve-pack of Killian's. "Okay, where to?" I asked when everything was packed in the car.

"Do you remember Scranton Academy?"

"Sorta. That's the old school in Scranton, isn't it?"

"Yeah, the place that's been falling apart as long as I remember," she replied. "I've always loved it. When I was a kid, I used to play fort with my friends. Later, after I got my driver's license, I'd search for Joey there. It was his special hiding place."

"I'm game. Is there a good place to spread a blanket?"

"The lawn's flat, and there's a shade tree."

"Are there any fire ants? I don't think it'd be a very good picnic if we had to share it with those nasties." I'd learned through several defeats that I did not want to sit where they could find me and treat me as their main dish. Each time it happened, I itched for days. I'm not

145

normally allergic to insect bites, but fire ants are bad news.

Terri laughed. "Is my ferocious PI afraid of little old ants?"

Before I could reply, she added, "You should be safe. Although it's been a while since I've been there, I'm sure the county folks keep the lawn cleared—tourists, you know?"

While we talked, I had driven out of Cisco, heading up 183 to I-20, then west to State Highway 206. The quickest way I knew was south on 206 then 569 to Scranton. Actually, the town of Scranton, like the Scranton Academy, belonged to history. A gas station, closed for years, and a few houses were all that was left. Once it had been a thriving community. A couple of oil pumpers, recycling themselves into rust, were reminders that oil once brought wealth to the area.

Terri was right. There was a nice tree to spread the blanket under. I shook the blanket several times to rid it of cat hairs. I'd used it to wrap Sweeper and Striker at various times to keep them under control for eye drops or pills or toenail clipping or whatever. I probably ate a few hairs but I didn't say anything. I assumed Terri did the same.

Scranton Academy has always intrigued me, and must have been a beautiful bit of architecture in its heyday at the beginning of the twentieth century. Now, everything was gone except the remains of the stone walls.

"Tell me about being a tough private eye," Terri said. "It must be exciting."

We lay on the blanket after stuffing ourselves with the picnic extravaganza. I couldn't help but chuckle.

"I've been a PI for ten years. I can't begin to remember how many errant husbands I've followed, or how many angry wives I've briefed on those husbands." I turned on my side toward Terri as she squirmed in closer to me.

"The funniest part of this business is the reaction of the wives. They come in hell bent to pin something on the husband so they can rip him off in divorce court. But when I come back with the proof, they most often end up acting like it's my fault. Guess that's what they mean by shoot the messenger. I learned on my second case that wronged wives have a vocabulary matching the most hardened waterfront barfly. She was a sweet little thing from a high-class family, but she could sure cuss. You'd have thought I'd heard it all in locker rooms, but she taught me new words."

Terri laughed. "Maybe you ought to write a book."

We continued chatting, making small talk and a slight dent in the banquet we'd brought. I felt wonderful. Who could be expected to eat when his heart soared with an orchestra of musical cherubs plucking their harps?

I emptied my third Killian's and Terri finished her second. She turned toward me and took my hands. "This has been wonderful, Ace, a time I'll always remember, but now I have to be serious. I've tried to summon courage all afternoon. It's time for us to talk, really talk."

I looked at her and saw that her attitude had changed. She looked serious, very serious. Even her body language was different, exuding a determination I hadn't seen before. Her hands were damp on mine, and her eyes had lost the beautiful glow I'd grown accustomed to. Panic threatened to grab me, but I shook it off. "Okay, what is it—our last day together?"

147

"I hope not. But that'll be up to you." A frown furrowed her beautiful forehead.

We sat for a moment in silence. I'm sure I held my breath, wanting to postpone what now seemed inevitable. Finally, I couldn't take it anymore. "What is it? The look on your face is ripping me apart."

"I'm sorry about how I might look, but I'm serious. My brother, Joey, asked me to talk to you, to warn you. He says he likes you and he's worried you might get hurt."

Now that tossed me a pickle. There were lots of things I'd thought she might want to talk about, things I didn't want to hear, but Joey was not on the list. "Joey? What do you mean?"

"He thinks the guy who killed Sonny was gunning for you. He says you might not be so lucky next time."

"What does he suggest I do?"

"Give it up and get out of town." She took a sip of her Killian's before looking into my eyes. "Of course, I wouldn't like that, but if it'll keep you alive . . ."

I waited but she said no more. Finally, I said, "Thank you for your concern, and Joey's. But I can't run. I told Jake I'd find the arsonist who torched his house, and I told Bubba I'd find Sheila's killer." I took a deep breath before I plowed on in a lighter tone. "I don't go back on my word unless there's a whole lot better reason than just getting dead." I hoped I could joke her out of her mood.

"I know Jake's paying you fifteen hundred a day, and you need the money, but is it worth your life? You can pay your bills some other way. Let it go. Let the police find the killers. Go back to Dallas and chase cheating husbands and wives, find lost kitties, anything less dangerous." She dropped her head, and I thought I saw a tear creep down her cheek. "Just come back to see me sometime."

"Husbands are no problem, but wives are wildcats when you expose them." I still hoped to get a chuckle out of her. "The worst beating I ever took was from a wife who caught me running surveillance on her and her boyfriend. She came after me—"

"Quit it, Ace. I'm serious. Joey knows the people around here—much better than you do. If he says somebody's trying to kill you, you can believe it."

That did it. If she wanted to play serious, I knew the game. "If Joey knows who's after me, he also knows who killed Sonny and Sheila. Tell him to let me know, and I'll wrap this mess up before anyone else gets hurt. Otherwise, tell him not to waste my time."

She stood, an indignant look on her face. "Take me home. If you're intent on getting yourself killed, I'm wasting my time. There's no future for us." She took a step, then turned back. "No, take me to my car. I forgot, I left it at your motel, and that's all I want at your motel."

I had little choice but to follow. I swooped up the picnic stuff in the blanket. She stood beside the car, waiting for me to unlock the door.

I tried to talk to her, but she proved the old adage about redheads—their tempers match the color of their hair. The only responses she made were grunts and frowns. Cherubs lay around me hurting and, I feared, mortally wounded.

## CHAPTER SEVENTEEN

As the taillights on Terri's car disappeared into the darkness, I looked at my watch. It was only eight-thirty but my world had tumbled down. Somehow, in a short four hours, I'd moved from king to serf, from pharaoh to peasant. I sniffed the air, hoping to recover the aroma of roses—nothing but wild onions. I looked for the cherubs who flitted around my head all afternoon—AWOL or KIA, Killed in Action. Or they'd deserted in the face of adversity.

I parked in front of my room and walked disconsolately to the door. As I inserted the key, an alarm went off in my head. I stepped back and looked around. Something was wrong. I sensed it. It's one of those traits I inherited from my father. Unfortunately, it normally kicks in late. I backed to the wall of the motel, reached for my Beretta, and surveyed all directions. Nothing out of the ordinary, nothing I could see. And nothing where my Beretta should have been. It was always somewhere else when I needed it.

Carefully, and as quietly as possible, I unlocked the door. I leaned against the outside wall and pushed the door open, waiting. I wasn't sure what I waited for, but it felt right.

I started counting to myself, "One Mississippi, two Mississippis, three Mississippis, up to thirty Mississippis. Nothing, not a sound. While I counted, I had one eye closed. I lay down on my belly and peeked around the corner of the doorframe. I knew I was silhouetting myself, but only at doorsill level. All I saw was dark. I switched eyes, using the one I'd kept closed while counting. It worked. My night vision was good enough to see furniture shapes in the room. I lay there, roaming the room with my seeing eye. Everything looked normal. After another moment, I opened my second eye and its night vision had caught up with the first. I rose and stepped into the room.

I spun to my right and felt the breeze of something rush by my head. Someone grabbed my arm and pulled me to the left as a hard blow landed in my midsection. I doubled over, gasping for breath, wondering what had happened, who was here.

A second blow to the stomach dropped me to my knees. I struggled to recover, looking for my assailant as a chop to the back of my neck drove me to the floor. I reached out, grabbed a leg, and yanked as hard as I could. A thud against the wall was my reward. My assailant was down.

I tried to rise but found my legs unwilling to cooperate. I made it to my knees, gasping for breath. My eyes refused to focus. I heard noise on my left—the sounds of someone getting to his feet. Inspired by fear of what would happen if he made it before me, I struggled upward. I reached out trying to grab something. Air filled my hands.

I heard a harsh laugh and a "You sonafabitch," as another blow to my gut doubled me over again. Then the inevitable happened, a knee to my groin. I pitched forward, putting the lights out as the end of the bed frame jumped up and smacked me in the head—end of game. Nasty Guy 1, Ace 0.

I woke, hurting all over. Pain. An intense ache started in my groin and ran up both sides of me out the top of my head. My first recollection was of the pain, but fear quickly replaced it—a cold sweat fear knowing I had walked into an ambush. Was my assailant waiting to finish me? I forced myself to freeze, breathing as shallowly as possible. Slowly, I turned my head, looking for feet, a reflection, a light, anything that might show where the thug waited. Every time I moved, the pain slammed into me.

Nothing. I couldn't see a thing. I quit trying to see the room and listened. If an ant had crawled across the carpet, I'd have heard him. I know my hearing has never been so acute. Someone in a room across the quadrangle flushed, and I cursed because it seemed so loud I was afraid it might cover a noise in my room. Nothing, absolutely nothing, not a sound from my immediate vicinity.

The door. I remembered I had stepped through the open door. I twisted my throbbing head looking in that direction. I could not see outside. Maybe the bad guy had left, and closed the door behind him. It was so dark in the room, I might have thought I was dead except for the pain. I didn't figure being dead involved pain, maybe a burning sensation, but not the kind of pain I felt.

I reached up and felt my forehead, but quickly withdrew my hand. There was a lump and my touch hurt. It didn't seem to be bleeding, or at least my hand didn't feel wet. I felt my neck and it hurt, but it was also dry. My groin throbbed in that way only a man can understand, but the pain in my mid-section had dissipated. I took several deep breaths, wishing I were anywhere else.

Someone had attacked as I entered the room. Another of the choice moves I'd made in this case. I wondered if I should find another line of work. My body said he'd hit me with everything he could think of, and a few tricks I would've used if I could. Whatever, it was effective. I wondered how much worse it would have been if my instincts hadn't protected me from his first shot.

I relaxed, looked around, and realized I lay on the floor with my head under the edge of the bed. A huge dust bunny tickled my nose every time I breathed. If I'd felt better, I might have called the office about the housekeeping—major dust bunnies under there. I put my hands down to push up, barely missing another bump to the head.

There was something under my left hand. A shot of fear coursed though my body as my adrenaline flow surged. I froze again, wondering what I felt and how lethal it was. I cupped the object and held it before my face. Whoever had been waiting for me hadn't been considerate enough to leave the lights on so I could see what it was. It felt like a book of matches, and I slipped it into my jacket pocket.

I lay another moment, then summoned my courage. There was no point in waiting any longer. I had to find out if it was safe to move. I concentrated on rising to my feet, a difficult chore in itself as my head spun ever faster with each movement.

When I approached upright, I twisted and sat on the edge of the bed while the spin of my world slowed. Although the room was dark, I could feel it revolving around me. The pain in my head gradually eased until it was only slightly worse than a root canal—without anesthesia.

After a few more minutes, I switched on the bedside lamp. It was the brightest light I've ever endured, and my eyes struggled to cope. Five minutes passed before I had the strength and courage to walk to the mirror to examine the damage. A large red lump on my forehead was the only damage I saw, evidence that a bed frame can be a wicked weapon. I vowed never again to attack one with my head. My neck had calmed to a dull ache and looked none the worse for whatever I'd been hit with. A cold wash cloth felt great on my head, then on my neck.

Although I preferred to stand and feel sorry for myself, I knew I had to move. I examined the room. Everything looked normal except the piece of paper laying on the bed. I picked it up although bending over was not my strong suit. It was in the kind of block print I was getting used to. *Get out of town. We don't want you here. Next time, we won't get the wrong man. And we won't be as gentle. This is your last warning.*

My eyes zeroed in on the word *we*. Did that mean I'd angered more than one killer? As my head throbbed, I wondered what they would have done if they weren't gentle. As usual, I didn't have a clue. I sniffed the paper, realizing paper sniffing was getting to be a bad habit. The whole scene was getting weirder, and I wished the bad guy would enlarge his vocabulary, or show himself, or both. I supposed I owed Joey an apology. There was someone out there who did not understand what a wonderful person I am. I'd have to remember to tell Terri.

I limped around the room without touching anything, but there was nothing else to find. After satisfying myself I hadn't missed anything obvious, I walked to the vanity and checked myself again to make sure I wasn't bleeding. Nope, still nothing but a nasty lump turning dark. I put another cold compress on it figuring I'd have a beauty of shiner by morning.

I closely observed the toggle on the zipper of my shaving kit. Yep, it had been moved. I checked for the hair I always leave under the toggle. It was gone.

I learned the hard way during an early case that it was smart to leave booby traps so I could tell if anyone visited my room. In that case, I lost notes and photographs that it took me two weeks to assemble. It was only a straying husband but, without proof, I collected no fee from the upset wife. She had wanted hard evidence. The worst part was I had no idea who stole the material or when it happened. All I knew for sure was the notes and photographs weren't there when I was ready to deliver them. She had not been thrilled with my explanation, and let me know in infinite detail.

After that, I began to leave the toggle on the zipper of my shaving kit in the same position each time, pointing toward the right front of the bag. In addition, I always left a hair under the toggle. I supposed it wouldn't be long before I'd have to find a trick other than the hair—I didn't have many hairs to spare any more.

After satisfying myself that someone had gone through my shaving kit, I checked everywhere. All I found were two more of my booby traps disturbed. I had to assume everything had been searched. Whoever was here was good. Except for the booby traps and the lump on my head, there was no evidence anyone had been in the room. Fortunately, I didn't have anything in the room that would give away my case. But unfortunately, the reason I didn't was because I still hadn't made the case.

Even my Beretta was where I'd left it, hanging in its shoulder holster in the closet. I slipped into the rig and checked to make sure the Beretta was still loaded and would slide out easily. I felt confident, one more door locked on an empty barn. I vowed we'd never be separated again.

I walked to the door and opened it, expecting the worst. There was nothing there. I stepped through the doorway, slid along the outside wall and carefully looked around, afraid my friend might be waiting for me. Fear ran rampant through my body. Nothing. The parking lot was quiet, no one moved. There were only a few cars—a bad night for business—and no one was near any of them.

As my fear subsided, I turned back to the door and took out my penlight. I examined the lock on the door and all around the bolt. My visitor had either had a key or he knew how to slip a lock without leaving a trace. After examining the doorframe a bit more, I realized it wasn't a cracker box but it wasn't a vault door either. A decent burglar could pop the lock. Guess that's why they have chains on the inside of motel doors.

I went inside to the only chair and remembered the object I'd picked up and stuck in my pocket. It was a book of matches from the Down Home Bar. The cover carried the motto, *The Down Home is just like down home.* Cute. I flipped the cover up and saw a series of numbers written on the inside—a telephone number, but whose? I checked the matchbook carefully for other information but found nothing except, *Smokers are welcome at the Down Home.* I could vouch for the integrity of that bit of advertising.

I picked up the phone receiver and dialed the number. One of those awful recordings kicked in. You know the one—a mechanical imitation of a female talking through her nose, "I'm sorry. The number you have dialed is no longer in service."

I thought for a moment. How long had the matchbook been under the edge of the bed? I supposed it could have been there when I checked in. Judging from the dust bunnies I'd felt, it could have been there for years. After all, I hadn't checked the room for suspicious items. Then again, maybe my intruder had dropped it.

I took the phone again and dialed the operator. When she answered, I said, "Miss, I'm trying to reach 555-7654 but I get a recording that says it's disconnected. Can you help me?"

"Just a moment, sir. I'll check." Telephone operators are one of the few groups left in our society where you can depend on courtesy. A moment later, she was back on the line, "I'm sorry, sir. That number is not in service. May I help you with anything else?"

I decided a shot in the dark wouldn't hurt. "Can you tell me who last had the number?"

157

"I'm sorry, sir, we're not allowed to give out that information."

Oh well, nothing ventured, nothing gained. I thanked her and hung up with a smile. My next call was to Tom Roberts. "Can you track the number 555-7654 for me? I need to know who had it last. It's out of service now, in Cisco's area code."

"No challenge, Ace. Give me thirty seconds. You can time me, starting now."

Twenty seconds later, he was back on the line. "Sheila Adams. It went out of service—"

"I can guess when. Thanks, Tom. I owe you another one."

Now that was interesting—a book of matches from the Down Home with Sheila's number under my bed. If my intruder dropped it, it pointed toward his involvement with Sheila. It also lessened the possibility that Sheila's lawyer was the target. On the other hand, with Sheila's reputation, she may have used this room with the guy who dropped the matches. I looked at the bed and got a strange feeling in my stomach.

I thought about it, and decided to go with the theory the intruder dropped the matchbook. That ruled out Maddie Millener as the primary target in the arson-murder case. Worse, it ruled in that the intruder was keeping a close watch on me. While I hadn't tried to hide, it bothered me that I was under surveillance. It was time to make his job more difficult.

I re-read the note. There was no longer any doubt about who'd been the target at Lake Cisco. I shuddered as a cold chill ran up my spine. What was that cliché? *Like someone walking on your grave.* I hoped it would remain a cliché.

158

I turned off the lights and walked to the motel office. The clerk let me know with her look that my request was wacky but she gave me a different room—after a fresh imprint of my credit card.

I returned to my room and moved my stuff to 101, right beside the office. It had to be the safest room in the motel. The clerk could see the entrance door from her desk.

I shifted the Chrysler to the parking slot in front of room 150 on the other side of the parking lot. I'd decided not to advertise which room I occupied.

I went to my new room and, without turning on the lights, sat in the chair. If my visitor were out there, I didn't wish to present a target. The shoulder holster was uncomfortable so I laid the Beretta on the table beside me, within close reach. I leaned my head back, willing myself to sort through what I knew, trying to find a single thread that ran through everything.

What I had wasn't much. Two naked women killed, and a house burned down around them. One woman a lawyer and the other an ex-wife who played the field. A guy killed in my car. A brick with a note thrown against my door. My motel room searched and a book of matches left behind with Sheila's phone number. Somebody attacking me when I entered my room. If I assumed Sonny was an accidental victim, three out of four pointed toward my unpopularity with someone. But who?

I toyed with those four facts like a dog worrying a bone, but nothing came out—nothing except the nagging feeling I knew more than I realized.

## CHAPTER EIGHTEEN

The night passed. I know, because I was awake most of it—or it seemed that way. I spent the night cycling among being scared, jumping at every noise, dreaming of Terri, adding up the meager evidence I'd collected, wishing I had a boring book on police procedure to read myself to sleep, and catnapping.

Catnapping. Never have understood why they call it catnapping. Whenever Striker and Sweeper are catnapping, they're snoring. I'm sure I didn't make it to snoring during the first two-thirds of that night.

At some point, my mind relaxed enough to allow me to sleep. My best guess is it was between five and five-thirty. I say that because I'm sure I hadn't slept more than an hour when I was awakened by the beep, beep, beep of my pager. I rolled over, picked it up, and looked at the number. As the numbers sank into my sleep-deadened brain, my eyes snapped open. The phone number was mine—my number in North Dallas.

I grabbed the phone and dialed. On the second ring, a female voice answered, "Hello, Mr. Edwards's house."

I recognized the voice as Ms. Jacobs, my cat-sitter. "Ms. Jacobs, this is Ace. Did you page me?"

She began a torrent of conversation that I was unable to interrupt, although I tried. As she poured out her story, I attempted to assimilate the meat of it. It came out in this order. She was terribly sorry to bother me because she was sure I was in the midst of solving an important case. The front door was open when the police got there. She'd gone home and made fresh kitty treats with more of the secret ingredient. The police had looked all over but didn't find anyone, and she had come over as soon as Mr. Harbinger called. Striker might have run away through the open front door. Mr. Harbinger said he saw someone sneaking around. Sweeper was fine and loved her high powered kitty treats. She couldn't find Striker. Mr. Harbinger called her at three o'clock in the morning.

I thanked her, and told her I was headed for Dallas right then. I dressed as fast as I could and made sure I put on my shoulder holster with Beretta included. I cursed as I raced across the quadrangle to get to my car—too far from my room, then laid rubber as I tore out of the parking lot.

As I drove, I tried to find order in Ms. Jacobs story. As best I could put it together, Mr. Harbinger, my nosy neighbor who lives across the street, saw something that caused him to call the police. He then called Ms. Jacobs. He's a bachelor, she's a widow, and I've always wondered about those two. He called her, or shook her to wake her. I chuckled at that scene. She rushed to my house, arriving about the same time as the police and found the front door open. Striker could not be found. Sweeper was happy with all the extra attention. That's all I put together from our conversation.

161

I was glad Texas speed limits are high and flexible as I sped toward Dallas. I was also relieved there weren't many big pickups and SUV's on the road. Between Fort Worth and Dallas, the inevitable happened—a serious accident brought traffic to a near halt. An SUV had run through a small sedan. I reached home at nine o'clock. There were no police but Ms. Jacobs was out front, waiting for me. After interrogating me about the lump on my head and my black eye, she verified that I understood her story.

I entered the house, trying not to disturb anything. Sweeper sat at the top of the steps, licking his chops. He'd probably been in Ms. Jacobs' kitty treats. He came rushing to me, and when I picked him up, his motor went into high decibel purring. That lasted about a minute before he decided he'd rewarded me enough and jumped down. He went to my recliner and gave himself a thorough bath.

I called for Striker and looked in all the standard hiding places. Nothing—no Striker. I was getting worried. "Sweeper, how can you sit there gnawing at your toes when your brother is missing? Find him, you old sot."

Sweeper looked at me, yawned, and went back to biting at his right front foot. Now I knew why humans were superior to cats. We had the ability to care about our friends. Cats did not.

Ms. Jacobs and I searched the house, yard and neighborhood, but didn't find Striker. I sent Ms. Jacobs home. She was driving me nuts with her constant comments on what might have happened to Striker—cars, dogs, catnappers, mean neighborhood kids, poisoned kitty treats left out by diabolical neighbors, and other more gruesome endings.

After she left, I called the local police to get the official side of the story. They told me essentially the same as Ms. Jacobs. They'd gotten a call, had investigated, found nothing, and left the house in her care. As I thanked the senior officer on the scene and was about to hang up, he said, "Oh, one thing, Mr. Edwards. You shouldn't leave a can of gas like that. It's dangerous, you know?"

"What can of gas?"

"The one between the hedge and the front of your house. There's a five gallon gas can setting there full of gas. I suggest you put it somewhere away from your habitat."

A can of gas? Yes, I pictured something I'd seen when I looked for Striker. Why hadn't it registered? I must have been more worried than I'd ever realized.

I hung up and rushed out front. There it was—a five gallon can of gas sitting as the policeman had described it. There was one problem. It wasn't mine, and I hadn't put it there.

I called the police again, explained I'd never seen the can before, and they came back to my place. I noted that it looked similar to the ones I'd seen at Sheila's house. A fingerprint crew checked for prints but found none. They took it away, promising to try to trace it to the owner. I had little hope they'd succeed.

I thought of Ms. Jacobs. I wasn't sure I'd ever get her to take care of the boys, excuse me, Sweeper again. I was glad she wasn't there for the discovery of the can and my conversation with the police.

The loss of Striker seeped in as the excitement of the morning dissipated. I felt pretty low when I noticed The Dallas Morning News laying at the top of the stairs. Ms. Jacobs must have brought it in. One last idea came to mind. I picked up the newspaper and walked to my recliner. Sweeper was still there working at his right front paw. I picked him up and placed him on the floor as I sat in my chair. He jumped up on the arm of the chair as I noisily opened the paper. I flipped open the sports section, which, as usual, had a headline about the Cowboys.

I popped the paper twice and tried to do it the third time. I couldn't because an orange and white bundle of fur landed in the middle of it. "Sweeper, get out of here, I'm trying to see if Striker will—" I stared at the back of the cat that was contentedly curled in the middle of my paper. No white splotch—Striker.

"Where have you been, young man? Ms. Jacobs is worried sick about you," I scolded as I picked him up and turned his face to mine. There were dust stringers hanging from his whiskers. Were they a clue?

Striker looked at me, yawned, twisted himself free, jumped down and headed toward Ms. Jacobs' kitty treats. What could I say, "Hey you, don't eat those until you explain your absence!" Nah, he'd ignore me.

I called Ms. Jacobs and told her Striker was safe. She was thrilled and started chattering. It took me a few tactful minutes but I got her off the phone. I returned to the puzzle of who had broken into my house, who had left a can full of gas out front, and what had stopped him or her from doing whatever he or she had intended—probably torching my place. As was becoming routine, there were no solid answers. This case was causing seepage in my container of confidence.

I walked to my chair. Sweeper was still on the arm, gnawing at his foot. I picked him up and placed him in my lap. He licked me once and went back to his foot. I realized he had been at that paw most of the time I'd been home. I held him and pressed on it.

"Yow," he yelled as he squirmed to get free. I held him and spread his toes again. One of his claws was raggedly broken with blood around the base. When I touched it, Sweeper hissed, something he'd never done before. Well, maybe at the vet, but never at me.

I stroked and talked to him until he settled down.

Striker walked in to see what was happening and sat back on his haunches cleaning his face, obviously sated on Ms. Jacobs' kitty treats. He looked at me. "Meow."

I returned his look as I continued to stroke Sweeper. "I don't know what you're trying to tell me, but I'm not happy with the way you hid from Ms. Jacobs. By the way, where is this secret place of yours? None of us could find you."

"Meow," he replied, and ran down the steps into the foyer. So much for conversation with my adopted son.

I turned my attention back to Sweeper. "Okay, guy. Let me take at look at your nail. You might need medical attention. What the heck did you do to it?"

"Yow."

I spread his claws again to get a better look. Something was caught at the base of the nail. It was red and wrapped tightly. I worked it loose as Sweeper squirmed and fussed at me.

Striker ran up the stairs from the foyer to see what was happening, but must have found it boring. He went back down.

I looked at what I had taken from Sweeper's claw. It was a tiny piece of material, more than a thread but less than a swatch. I stared at it, trying to imagine what it was and how it got there. Finally, I wrote it off to whatever he'd been sharpening his claws on when he broke the nail.

As soon as I removed the tiny piece of material, Sweeper calmed down and curled in my lap.

"You seem to be okay. Good, that saves us a trip to the vet." When I said vet, Sweeper gave me a look that needed no interpretation. He must have been satisfied though, because he fell asleep. His gentle snoring assured me he was okay.

I laid my head back and closed my eyes, again letting my mind float, hoping it might land somewhere useful. It felt great after getting so little sleep the previous night. I sat there with my mind as relaxed as it had been in days, perhaps weeks, when my subconscious was invaded by the pitter-patter of little feet, specifically the racing back and forth of those little feet.

As consciousness returned, I realized it was Striker I heard. What the heck was he doing? I lifted Sweeper, who didn't change his breathing pattern, and stood, placing him in my chair. He resumed his snoring.

"Okay, Striker, what are you up to?" I walked to the top of the steps and looked into the foyer. Striker was practicing his soccer skills as he swiped at something with his paw, demonstrating a perfect sidekick. He then raced in front of the object and trapped it before using a low drive to slam it toward the corner of the foyer, a perfect two-touch.

I watched him, a grin spreading over my face. I felt like yelling, "Goooooooooooaaaaaaaaaallllllllll," like the guy who's gotten famous for his goal calls. Instead, I said, "We could have used you when I was in college. You have better skills than most of the players on my team."

Striker ignored me and continued passing, trapping and shooting until my curiosity got the best of me. What was he playing with? I walked down the steps and earned his animosity as I grabbed his toy.

I held it up and looked at it. It was a small diameter, thin golden loop that pulled open. What the heck was it? The only thing I could identify it with was a gold earring. But how did it get in my foyer? Earrings are not an accouterment I find appealing.

As I looked at it, right brain kicked in and, after calling me every degree of idiot, reminded me of the game Sweeper and I play when I break into my house. Could Sweeper have attacked the intruder like he does me during our make believe break-ins?

I sat on the bottom step to think about this new revelation. Sweeper showed up by my side, rubbing against my leg. I stroked his fur. His purring made me feel better.

He reached out with his right front paw and hooked a claw through the loop, tugging on it. "No, leave it alone. Did you rip it off someone?"

"Meow."

"Is that a yes or a no?"

Striker sniffed the floor of the foyer and Sweeper joined him. I studied the gold loop trying to make up my mind if it was an earring.

"Meow."

"Meow."

They both stared at me. As soon as they had my attention, they sniffed the floor. Then both stopped and swiped at different spots on the floor while looking at me.

What the heck were they doing? I looked at them. They looked at me. They said, "Meow." I looked.

"Okay, guys. Are you trying to tell me something?" I knelt and looked at the floor closely where they stood. There were little reddish-brown specks and an occasional larger red-brown spot. I rubbed one and it moved with my finger. I wet my fingertip and rubbed another. It smeared. I sat back, not daring to believe what my instincts told me. Blood, it looked like blood.

I again called the local police. This time I asked for Detective Harasky, a friend I'd worked with before. "Bert. I need your help." I told him about the break-in and my cats' behavior. I finished by telling him I might have blood droplets in my foyer, and a tiny piece of what might be blood-soaked material I'd taken from Sweeper's broken claw.

Under other circumstances, his laughter and snide remarks would have gotten a rise out of me. This time I waited, saying nothing.

"You're serious, aren't you?"

"Yes, Bert. I'm serious. It may sound weird but it's true. Can you get an evidence team over here before my cats wipe out what I think is a blood clue?"

"Okay, we're on the way."

Bert's team swooped in and when they'd finished collecting lab samples, I had the cleanest foyer in town. Sweeper and Striker walked around sniffing the floor, apparently inspecting the job.

I hoped the police would solve the case before my house burned, or I was taken out. Or worse yet, my cats were injured.

When Bert Harasky's team left, I slumped into my chair. Sweeper assumed his normal position on the arm and Striker curled in my lap. I checked my watch, three o'clock. It seemed a lifetime since last night when Terri had, in effect, told me to kiss off. I napped.

As my eyes struggled open, I realized the sun streamed into them. There are disadvantages to a living room facing west. I discovered that I was alone. Striker and Sweeper had deserted me while I napped, probably finishing Ms. Jacobs' kitty treats or fouling their litter boxes. I looked at my watch. Four o'clock. I'd slept an hour. I felt better, or lied to myself that I did.

I dragged myself out of my chair and wandered into the kitchen, straight to the refrigerator where I was faced with a choice between the Killian's I wanted or a bottle of flavored water I knew was better for me. The water won—this time. I stripped the plastic covering off the cap, took a long swig and leaned against the stove, trying to decide what to do next. Maybe I should call Terri. No, she'd made herself clear last night.

I needed to call the motel and reserve my room for a few more days. The answers I sought were in Cisco, not Dallas. But, there might be a major crime in Dallas if I didn't find the perpetrator in Cisco soon. And I might be the victim.

169

I reached for the cordless phone I kept in the kitchen and saw the blinking light on my answering machine. I punched the play button.

"You have one message. Message one. Three a.m. I will play one message."

Don't you love those mechanical chip voices? The chip quit and the recording started, "Arty. Arty? Pick up the phone. Are you trying to ignore me? . . . Dammit, Arty, are you there? . . . Oh, crap. Okay, you must not be home. I lost your pager number. We need to talk. Call me as soon as you can. We need to get together now, not later."

Well, that was interesting, and ironic. On a night when I couldn't sleep, Jake had lost my number. Talking to him last night would have helped pass those long hours I'd lain awake. The interesting part was he wanted to talk to me in person. I wondered if he'd come up with something new on the lawyer.

My first impulse was to call immediately, but then I had a better idea. I chuckled to myself as I thought about it.

First though, I had to make plans for the boys. I couldn't leave them home again—not with some nut running around with gasoline. Plus, he proved my front door was no deterrent. I grinned when I thought about his entry. He must have been one surprised villain when Sweeper landed on his head. I wondered if he knew he'd left his earring behind, if that's what it was. So many if's, and so little time.

I called a nearby kennel with nice facilities for cats, and opened early. I'd used it before and liked the people there, although they were strange. If they found out I called it a kennel, they'd probably blacklist me. They called it the Cat Hotel and operations duplicated a people hotel. No manager, a concierge. They didn't have attendants, they had bellhops who took the carriers when you arrived, room attendants who changed the litter, and a dining room with a maitre d' where the guests took their meals. You get the drift.

The boys didn't share my opinion, but I didn't give them a vote this time. The kennel, whoops, hotel, folks gave me a reservation for six the next morning. In keeping with their approach, they took my credit card number and rewarded me with a confirmation number. I guess I was supposed to be impressed.

When I hung up and turned around, two angry orange and white cats faced me. First, the hair on their necks stood straight up, then they spun and flipped their tails as they stalked off. They were in no mood to listen to my arguments. How the heck did they know what I'd done?

I spent the rest of the evening making peace with them. I retrieved their carriers from the garage and prepared things for the morning.

At ten o'clock, I grinned as I set my alarm for two-fifty-five a.m. I'd made up my mind. Revenge would be sweet. As soon as my head hit the pillow, I was asleep.

At two-fifty, I awakened, lifted Striker off my chest and lay him beside his brother. I tiptoed across to the alarm and disengaged it before walking into the kitchen where the coffee finished brewing. I poured a cup and sat, watching the big hand on the clock finish its climb toward the twelve. At precisely three o'clock, I dialed.

After the third ring, a sleepy voice said, "Who the hell is this?"

"Hi, Jake. It's me, Ace. Received your message. Got a few minutes?"

"Huh, who? Ace? Arty? You son-of-a-bitch. Are you nuts? What time is it? Call me at the office." Jake's tone let me know I'd scored big on the get-even scale.

"Hey, don't hang up, Jake. I'm ready to talk. It's peak conversation time—three in the morning." I stifled my laughter. "What's on your mind?"

Jake was quiet but I heard a muffled voice in the background. It sounded like a sleepy woman asking who was on the phone, telling him to turn off the light and come back to bed.

I wondered who the gorgeous woman was. Kathy came to mind. I hoped not—too good for Jake.

Jake said in a more normal voice, "Ace, I can't talk now. Come by the office at eight if you can. I've kept the whole morning open. Now, I'm going back to—"

"Touché and good-night." I hung up, threw back my head and let the laughter roll as loud as it wanted. When I looked toward the doorway, I saw two sleepy cats staring at me as if I were nuts. No way I could explain to them how good it felt to awaken Jake, how good it felt to score once using his rules. As I walked back to the bedroom, I again wondered who belonged to the female voice. Was she his alibi for the night Sheila died?

I dropped the boys off at six and headed toward Fort Worth. Traffic was reasonably light. For the first time in this case, there was no fender-bender blocking me. It was still early, so a Denny's near Jake's office lured me in for breakfast.

Before entering the restaurant, I gave in and called Terri at home. Her answering machine wanted my message, so I told it I'd like to talk to Terri, and requested she page me during the day. I hoped she checked her messages during the day. I supposed she'd left for school.

My waitress was a sweet Texas lady who took care of me as if I were eating in her home. It seemed every time I took a sip of coffee, she refilled the cup and asked if everything was all right. It was—two eggs over easy, a small T-bone steak, with pancakes and grits on the side. A breakfast for champions.

After I ate, read the paper and drank about a gallon of coffee, my watch said it was eight-thirty. Knowing I could now face the day with a full stomach and detailed knowledge of what was happening with the Cowboys, I figured I'd kept Jake waiting long enough. I couldn't push the envelope too far—he still paid my bills.

When I opened my wallet to pay the bill, a small wedge of paper fell from of the bill compartment—the earring Striker found in the foyer. I had put it in my wallet for safekeeping, then forgot to give it to the police.

I walked into Jake's outer office and she was there—Kathy. My memory may have been good on her name but it was faulty about her beauty. She looked better than I remembered.

She stood as I entered the suite. "Mr. Edwards. How good to see you again? Mr. Adams has been waiting for you. Coffee with one Sweet'n Low, isn't it? Your eye looks terrible. Did it hurt much?" She walked toward Jake's office.

She won that round. She made me feel important by remembering me, politely chastised me for being late, then picked me up by remembering how I liked my coffee. I meekly followed her toward Jake's office knowing I had met my match.

She must have signaled Jake because his door opened and he waved me in. "Arty, glad you came. Come on in and let's talk—great looking eye." He turned toward Kathy.

She said, "Yessir, Mr. Adams. I have his coffee order. I'll bring some sweet rolls."

"Thank you, Kathy," Jake said as she walked away.

We moved into his office and he motioned me toward a corner where he had added a conversation niche—couch, coffee table and two more wingback chairs. Even with the extra furniture, the office was not crowded. He took the couch and waved me into one of those human sacrifice chairs. As we sat, the door opened and Kathy entered with the china coffee serving followed by a young man with a silver tray piled high with a selection of sweet rolls.

I should have told them I'd already had breakfast, but I wanted to watch this play out. I wondered why Jake was putting on a show. When Kathy leaned over to pour a cup of coffee, I quit wondering about Jake and remembered her attractions—both of them with a gorgeous cleavage.

As soon as she and the young man left, Jake said, "Thanks for coming by Ace. I hope you'll give me an update on how the investigation is going. Have you come up with anything concrete yet? From what I hear, the sheriff is still baffled."

He sounded nervous.

I gave him a detailed briefing up to and including the break-in at my house, and what I thought might be blood droplets in my foyer. I showed him the good loop.

He picked it up and examined it as I had the day before. "You think this is an earring?"

"I'm no jeweler, but it looks like one to me. What do you think?"

"Let's not guess," he replied. "We'll get an expert in here."

He must have a foot switch, because with the words hanging in the air, the door opened.

"You called, Mr. Adams?" Kathy stood in the doorway.

"Yes. Please look at this," Jake said to her, "and give us your opinion."

She walked over, accepted the gold loop from Jake, and rotated it as she examined it. "What do you want to know?"

"What do you think it is?" I asked.

She looked at me as if my question was absurd. "It's an inexpensive earring, probably gold plated. The kind a lot of places sell when they advertise free ear piercing. You can find them any place that sells cheap jewelry—more stainless steel than gold. You know, you see them on the street all the time. Jewelry on a woman, or a toy for a boy."

I was gratified that my guess had been right but mortified at the lecture she gave me. I had overlooked the obvious in my enthusiasm to identify the gold loop.

"Thank you, Kathy. That's what Mr. Edwards thought, but we wanted to know for sure. You've been very helpful in his investigation."

I couldn't believe it. Jake, trying to save face for me.

Kathy left the room, and Jake turned back to me. "Hope that helped. You think your cat ripped this out of the intruder's ear?" He sounded incredulous. "And you said, there was blood on the floor. Isn't that a bit farfetched?"

"Yeah, as strange as it may sound, that's what I believe."

"Hmmm. One of these days, I want to meet your cats. Not a bad idea, a watch cat. Less upkeep than a dog." Jake grinned. "You might have stumbled onto something here, Arty, for when you retire. Training Watch Cats to keep homes and businesses safe from burglars. Your motto could me, *No mice, no bugs, no burglars*. Yep, if you decide to sell stock, I'll buy in."

He stopped and refilled our coffee cups.

I should have told him I was about to float.

"Do you have any real leads, though? Have you shortened your list of suspects?"

I didn't tell him I hadn't compiled a list. It was still most of the people I knew and everyone I didn't know. I mumbled something about not crossing anyone off until I had more evidence.

He began to reminisce about our college days, about the four of us—him, Sheila, me and my ex—and all the fun we had. As I half-listened, I toyed with the gold earring. I wondered whether it was male or female. Kathy hadn't said. Jewelry for a woman or a toy for a boy? No way to tell. Both men and women wore the same ear loops these days.

The word toy bounced around in my empty cranial spaces, echoing off the walls. Toy, joy, toy, roy, toy, soy, foy, toy, coy, boy, toy, boy. Hmm, toy boy. That had a familiar sound to it.

"Invited you here," I heard.

"Huh, what'd you say? Guess I was thinking about the case." I looked at Jake who eyed me suspiciously.

"I said, it's about time I told you why I invited you here."

"You mean it's not because I'm such a great listener?" I grinned.

Jake scowled. He shifted on the couch and rested his forearms on his knees with his fingers entwined. "Okay, I've been putting it off, talking about times when we were much closer. This is too big though. I can't stall any longer."

Weird introduction, I thought.

"Remember when you asked me where I was the night Sheila died? Remember I told you I was with a woman and then refused to tell you who she was?"

"Yeah, I remember." He had grabbed my attention with his opening. "Are you ready to tell me now?"

"I'll tell you, but I want you to understand why I was obtuse." He hesitated and ran his fingers through his hair, a nervous habit he'd had since high school. "We've been friends a long time and I didn't want you laughing at me."

"Laughing at you?" I knew the echo in the room was bad but I plowed on. "Why would I laugh?"

He stared at me while rotating his pinky ring on his right hand. The diamond in it looked big enough to finance my retirement. He appeared to be in deep thought.

"I wasn't sure how you'd react if I told you I spent my nights with a Sheila look-alike. I was afraid you'd think I still had a thing for Sheila and either laugh at me or suspect me of killing her, think I was jealous.

Jealousy would have given you an excellent motive, wouldn't it?"

I stared at him. "I swear you can talk the wings off a hummingbird. Explain yourself." As I asked, a picture of Terri the night we'd met flashed into my mind.

"You know her. She's from Cisco. You've met Terri Hart, haven't you? She's my mystery woman. She's the woman I was with the night Sheila died. In fact, she's the one who was with me last night when you called. We're engaged . . ."

The rest of what he said was lost in the gray fog that swirled in and settled over my head, impeding my vision and clouding my mind. I dropped into a trance as if he had waved a medallion in my face and hypnotized me. I don't remember but I must have left his office. I have no memory of escaping that man-eating chair, saying good-bye, leaving, or anything else until I was in the car, headed toward Cisco. When the fog lifted, I hoped I'd been courteous to Kathy.

## CHAPTER NINETEEN

The sign said, *Ranger, Ten Miles.* An uncontrollable urge to stop for an early lunch hit me, and I knew where. I pulled off I-20 at the first Ranger exit, and made my way to the restaurant where Terri and I dined a lifetime ago.

I entered and looked about. The booth we'd sat in was vacant.

The hostess walked over, "One? Smoking or non-smoking?"

I pointed toward the booth. "I'm alone. Non-smoking, please. How about over there?"

She turned in the direction I indicated. "I'm sorry, that section's not open yet. We're seating on this side now."

My mouth spouted words. "Miss, it's important I sit in that booth." My mouth continued without my brain having a clue what it might say. "You see, my late wife and I passed through here six weeks ago and stopped for lunch. We sat in that very booth, the one right over there. That was before, before . . ." I gave her my saddest look, and mumbled, "Before my wife was killed in an

179

auto accident. So, you see, when I was out this way today, I had to stop here and sit in that same booth."

The hostess gave me a sad look. "Of course, sir. I'll open the section for you. I'm glad you weren't hurt too badly." Mouth - one, brain - zero. Some days I survive much better if I don't think.

Apparently, she thought my black eye came from the accident. I said nothing although the look on her face made me feel like a heel.

"And take your time. I'll keep the tables around you empty if I can. I'll be your personal waitress. Follow me." She led me to the booth where Terri and I had sat.

I hope the whopping lie I told to get that booth will show you how shook I was. My dreams of Terri and me had burned worse than Sheila's house. In my new world, there were no chimneys, not even a sink left. I looked for the cherubs who charmed me a couple of days ago—still AWOL.

I remembered Terri and I having an excellent meal with cold Killian's in a restaurant exuding ambiance. I couldn't remember what I'd ordered but I was sure it was superb. Today, I ordered chili, a burger and beer. My first beer was warm, the second was warmer, and the third was hot. The décor and ambiance were early bus station. But I had plenty of privacy. True to her word, the hostess sat no one near me. Occasionally, I saw her look my way, sympathy on her face.

I ate half my chili—no spark—and all the tortilla chips and salsa. The chips and salsa tasted better than the chili, and managed to improve the taste of the warm beer. The burger suffered one small bite—tough and tasteless. They didn't have Killian's, and I hate warm beer of any kind.

When I paid the hostess who had been my waitress, she gave me a sympathetic look and said, "Life must go on, sir. I hope you find happiness again." My guilty conscience forced me to leave a large tip. Later, I realized what a funk I had been in—it was a twenty.

The lunch must have helped because my mind drifted back to the case as I drove toward Cisco. I figured I'd swing by the motel first and let them know I'd keep the room for a few more days. Then I'd find some way to kill time until I could hit the Down Home at an acceptable hour. It was still my best bet for finding answers to my many questions. Even if there were no answers, there was a cold Killian's.

I stopped in the reception area and re-introduced myself to the young man working there. "Oh, I remember you," he said. "You're the one that beautiful woman came to visit. Hope she didn't give you that eye." He gave me a leer that would have made Simon Legree proud. All he needed was a handlebar mustache to twirl.

As I turned to leave, he said, "You have messages." He handed me a couple of yellow stickies that I stuck in my pocket. He looked disappointed I didn't read them immediately.

I dropped my bag in the room and decided not to unpack. A fast getaway might be required. I flipped on the TV to Fox News to catch the latest Washington scandals, and stretched out on the bed. The talking head detailed the latest politician who was under suspicion. I listened for a moment, then tuned out. There were so many scandals, they were recycling. The latest was about someone committing perjury—déjà vu.

181

The case rose into my conscious mind. For what seemed like the millionth time, I started through what I knew for sure and what I could speculate about. Both lists were short. Then, without any help from me, my mind took a hard right, and landed on Terri. It started reviewing every word she'd ever said to me. The Sunday we'd spent together took first place. It felt good until I got to the point where she'd dumped me. I realized how she'd known Jake paid me fifteen hundred a day. I'd wondered about that. He probably bragged to her he was carrying me because we were old friends, or something like that. It also explained a few other comments that now drifted into my mind that I'd ignored when she'd said them—like how she knew about the nickname Arty.

I now knew she hadn't dumped me. She'd finished her assignment. What I had no answer for was why Jake assigned her to watch me. What did he hope to gain? Did he tell her to turn on the charm? I thought I knew Jake but this was a side of him, a low-down, duplicitous side I never suspected. And of course, I wondered if it had all been an act, or had I affected her. My ego demanded the latter.

At some point, the droning of the talking heads on TV and my frustration at my lack of leads lulled me to sleep. As I napped, a dream ran its video through my subconscious. It was Terri the last time we were together. It started as I met her in the lobby of the motel. I could see our lips moving but there was no sound, the mute button on my dream had been pushed. The entire episode unfolded again, as it had the first time.

As we sat together after the picnic, her volume came on, "My brother, Joey, wanted me to talk to you. He's worried about you."

I replied, but my mute button was still depressed. I could only hear her side of the conversation. "He thinks the guy who killed Sonny was gunning for you. He says you might not be so lucky next time."

Me again, no sound.

"Give it up and get out of town." Her voice was back on stage. "Let the police find the killers."

. . .

"Go back to Dallas and chase cheating husbands and cheating wives, find lost kitties or something less dangerous."

. . .

"Joey knows the people around here—much better than you do. If he says somebody's after you, you can believe it."

The dream faded away.

I woke, wet with sweat although the room was cool. I struggled to sit up and decided I needed a shower and a shave. I looked at my hands and they shook. Forget the shave. In my condition, I might slit my throat—and I use an electric razor. I stepped into the shower and cranked the water up as hot as I could stand it. I hoped I could burn Terri out of my mind, and out of my heart. A clear head would help me sort out whatever hid in my subconscious. The water stung and my mind churned, trying to find something—something I knew was there. If only it would come forward. After about fifteen minutes, I stepped out, pink as a boiled lobster.

I decided to head for the Down Home for a few beers. A long talk with Joey was in order. I was still curious about his concern for me, especially since I now knew it wasn't because his sister cared for me. The dream must have some meaning, something right brain was trying to tell me.

Back in the living area, I dressed. As I pulled on my jeans, my mind drifted to what I speculated was Sweeper's attack on the intruder in my home. I grinned, knowing the game we'd played for the past year had paid off. Maybe Jake was right. I ought to give up this PI business and train watch cats.

I picked up the earring I thought had been ripped off by Sweeper. Jewelry for a woman or a toy for a boy—boy, toy, toy, boy. There was that connection again that sounded familiar.

I finished dressing, slipped on my lambskin coat, and fumbled in the pocket for my keys. I pulled out two pieces of crumpled paper—the telephone messages the motel clerk had handed me.

I read the first. The call had come at ten-thirty this morning. It was from Terri. *Call me. I need to talk to you.*

I laughed. I bet she needed to talk to me. Jake must have told her he was going to share their secret. I opened the second note. Four o'clock, shortly before I got back, again from Terri. *Call me, please. It's important we talk.*

The second one intrigued me. By then, Jake would have talked to her, and told her he'd confessed their engagement. Why would she call again? I decided to see if the motel clerk could tell me anymore than what he'd written.

I walked into the motel office. There was a young woman behind the counter. "Excuse me. Is the man here who worked this afternoon?"

"No, sir. He works days and leaves at six o'clock. Can I help you?"

"Maybe. I'm in room 101. He took some messages for me today. I wondered if he left anything more?"

She looked around the desk. "No. He didn't say anything, and I don't see anything here. I'm sorry . . . Wait, you said room 101. There's another message for you. It came in about thirty minutes ago. I rang your room but you didn't answer."

"I must have been in the shower. Who called?"

She handed me the message. "It was a woman. She made me promise to call your room every thirty minutes until I gave you the message. I was getting ready to try again when you walked in." She gave me a cute little smirk.

I took the message and looked at it. Terri again. What the hell was she up to? "Thanks, miss. I appreciate your help." I walked from the office to my room, wondering what was going on. Her message read, *I'll be at the Down Home tonight. Please, I need to see you.*

## CHAPTER TWENTY

I checked the room and debated whether I should carry the Beretta. After arguing with myself for several minutes, I decided to leave it behind. The Down Home should be friendly territory tonight. Besides, I didn't want Terri to worry I might go after Jake, even if he deserved it.

I stepped out of the room and headed for the Chrysler. As I hit the button on the remote to unlock the door, a shot rang out. I dropped to the ground and groped for my Beretta. Dammit, for what seemed like the hundredth time, it was where I wasn't. On my knees and elbows, I crawled to the rear of the car, cursing what I was doing to the toes of my boots—again. I rolled over and peeked around the rear tire. A pickup truck spun out of the motel parking lot. As it passed under the light at the exit, I saw it was dark with a white racing stripe on the passenger side. It squealed its way onto Liggett Street toward I-20, cutting off a sedan in the process.

I stood, wondering if I had heard a shot or if I were more paranoid than normal. Maybe it was only a backfire. I decided to humor my paranoia. I went back into the room and grabbed the Beretta and its shoulder holster. I kissed the handgrip and swore we'd never be separated again.

On the way to the car, I checked the parking lot, letting the Beretta dangle from my right hand. I might not be sure it was a shot I'd heard, but I wasn't taking any more chances. From now on, if someone shot at me, he'd better be ready to duck. I approached my car, looking around again. Nothing. No one and nothing moved. "Okay," I said to myself, "if it was the pickup truck, it's gone. If it was your imagination, you're safe. Get in the car and see if Terri's at the Down Home."

I climbed into the car and lay the Beretta on the passenger seat where I could grab it. After starting the car, I exited the parking lot and accelerated onto Liggett. There was a strange breeze in the convertible. When I looked up, I saw the moon through a small round hole in the roof. I knew my paranoia was based on a strong foundation.

\*       \*       \*

I pulled into the parking lot of the Down Home and drove around, looking for Bubba's Suburban and a dark colored pickup truck with a white racing stripe down the passenger side. I didn't find Bubba's wheels but there were at least a dozen pickup trucks meeting my criteria. I wasn't surprised. After all this was Texas where the pickup is a *Texas Cadillac*.

After circling a second time, I summoned my courage and pulled into an empty parking space. I slipped the Beretta into the shoulder holster, and practiced my quick-draw. I knew I wasn't the fastest but, maybe I wasn't the slowest either. I congratulated myself for saddle-soaping the leather when I was in Dallas. It was soft and slick.

Finally, I couldn't stall anymore. I moved toward the entrance, trying to see in all directions at once. Every shadow seemed to hide a shooter, someone who was out to get me. I realized I was in a crouch. To an onlooker, I must have looked like an idiot, but at least a live idiot—well, so far.

Pushing open the door caused me to reel backwards as it did each time I entered the Down Home. The smoke poured out as if released from a genie's bottle, however, the smoke from a ten-thousand-year-old genie's bottle would have smelled better. Eu de Cigarette Smoke would never catch on as my favorite perfume—unless Terri wore it, then Eu de Skunk would smell great. I pushed again, holding my breath until I was inside. Unfortunately, that didn't solve my breathing problem. When I finally gave in and sucked in air, I realized that was not the last of my problems. The noise was assaulting.

I stepped to the right of the door, hoping my eyes would quit watering and adjust to the dim lights and the smoke. They did once I wiped the tears away. I looked around the room hoping to see Terri, and hoping to find Bubba in a protective mood. What I saw were murky shapes through the veil of smoke. As I stood peering into the murky atmosphere, I felt a tap on my shoulder.

"Hey, good-looking. Are you taken, or can any girl stake a claim?"

I looked around. My heart skipped an entire drum roll. Terri stood there with an inviting smile. Tonight, she seemed more beautiful than ever. I wanted to bury my fingers in her red hair and lose myself in those gorgeous eyes. I wanted . . . Whoa. I had to remind myself she was engaged to Jake, not me.

"Hello, Terri. I got your messages. What do you need to talk to me about?" I'd decided to play it cool on the outside, not trusing my emotions on the inside.

Terri dropped her eyes and stared up at me through those long, long lashes. My knees grew weak. She wasn't playing fair. I wished she wouldn't look at me like that.

"Don't be angry, Ace. I want to explain. Can we go outside where it's quieter?"

I stared at her, determined to be tough. Bull, I was putty in her hands and we both knew it. "First let me get a couple of beers. I have a feeling I'll need a case before you finish your talk."

Hojo was quick and gracious when I walked to the bar and asked for two Killian's Irish Reds and one long neck Bud. He served them without comment, but rubbed his throat as he sat them on the bar. I guessed he had a long memory and hadn't forgotten the other night. I hate it when people hold a grudge. Of course I never do.

I handed Terri the Bud and shouted above the noise, "Okay, I'm ready with my liquid courage. Let's hear your story."

We walked outside and around to the side of the building. I leaned against the wall in my most nonchalant pose.

"I . . . uh . . . I need to tell you about Jake and me, about why I agreed to marry him. He said he talked to you this morning and when he told you, you were thrilled. You wished us everlasting happiness. You said you were glad he and I had gotten together. It hurt that I meant so little to you, but I still want to tell you."

I blinked. Did I do that? I couldn't remember what I'd said to Jake but somehow I believed he might have exaggerated. All I could squeeze out was, "Ah, yes. That's how I feel. I hope you're very happy. You both deserve one another." The last sentence was the only part that matched what I thought.

"I don't know how you can have such a don't-give-a-shit attitude about this. I've been a mess all day. Please understand that I care about both of you—you and Jake."

"Oh, great," I replied. "That makes a lot of sense. Okay, so why did you lead me to believe there might be a future for us?"

She dropped her head and hesitated as she crossed her arms across her chest. When she spoke, her tone was soft and unsure. "I was, no, I am attracted to you." She lifted her head, looked me straight in the eye, and went on in a stronger voice. "You're attractive and very lovable, although right now you're being a horse's ass." She hesitated again. "This is so difficult. I can't find the right words."

"Try."

"All right, but don't interrupt." She inhaled. "Jake and I met not long after he and Sheila separated. At first, I think he was attracted to me because I can look like her. For about the first six months, he insisted I dress like her and fix my hair like her. He bought me the same kind of outfits, she wore. There were even times when he treated me like he must have treated her, like a woman he'd been with for many years. I was thrilled that a rich man who could have anything found me interesting."

"That's impressive," I said sarcastically.

"That's not fair, and I asked you not to interrupt. Why shouldn't I have gone with him? Why shouldn't I enjoy the things he gave me? I grew up poor and worked my way through college. Even now, I barely make ends meet on my teacher's pay. Jake was my way into a world I only dreamed of. I may not be as strong as you, but don't be so damned sanctimonious."

"Okay, okay, I'm sorry." I held up my hands. "Please continue."

"I'm not sure when it happened, but I realized I didn't want to be his Sheila. I wanted to be his Terri. I discovered that I cared about him a great deal. I needed something deeper, more permanent, but he never gave me any indication I was more than an ornament for him to show off. Whenever I mentioned commitment, he changed the subject. I'd about reached the point where I thought I had no future with Jake when you showed up. As I got to know you, I became more and more attracted to you. I felt like you might be the man I was looking for, a man I could love and a man who would love me back."

She stopped for a moment and took a deep breath as an orchestra of pianists tickled their ivories up and down my spine.

"It's been the most terrible and the most wonderful time of my life these last few weeks. Although my feelings for you were growing, my feelings for Jake weren't changing. I can't tell you how many nights I lay awake trying to sort through my messed up feelings—each time with no luck. I shed more tears over you than any other man I've ever known. I was falling in love with you but not falling out of love with Jake. What a mess?"

191

She drew another deep breath. "Maybe that's what inspired Jake to propose. Maybe he sensed a change in me. I don't know what caused it, but it took me by surprise." Terri flashed her beautiful eyes at me again.

"So far, it's a great story," I said. "Make a great soap opera. Do you have anybody in mind to play my part? What tilts the scales to Jake's side—his money?"

Her eyes flashed, and she fired back. "No, not his money. You, you and your stubborn dedication to your job did it. My college roommate married a cop. They had five great years together before he was killed on the street one night at midnight. I watched her struggle to keep her life together while raising two children. I watched her wear the same outfits year after year because she can't afford new ones. I watched her life revolve around work and her kids—no time for living. I watched her grow older with no laughter in her life. Today, she looks ten years older than she is."

She continued with the same intensity in her voice. "I asked you to drop this case. I warned you that you were the target, not Sonny. I tried to tell you how I felt, but all you did was treat me like a child. You tried to placate me by being cute. That's when I knew there was no future for us. I'm not going to be a cop's widow, even a private cop. I'm not going to live my friend's life."

"I'm sorry, so very sorry," I interrupted. "If only I'd known—I had no idea you were so serious and why." I stopped, and reflected for a moment. She'd hit me right where I live, but I could only respond, "You made the right decision, though. My dad taught me that a man's word is his bond. I gave my word to Jake and Bubba, and I intend to live by it. When this case is over, there might be room for compromise, but not now—not on this case."

"Damn you, Ace Edwards. You're so stubborn, it's insulting." Her fists were clenched and her lips were a thin line. "Jake is safe and secure. I'll never have to wonder if he's lying in the street bleeding to death. I'll never have to patch his wounds after an angry husband beats him to a pulp. I'll never have to hand him a cold compress to hold over a black eye—like the one you're wearing now."

Ouch, that was a definite gotcha. I had hoped the light was dim enough to hide my eye.

She continued, ripping my heart as she went. "And, most of all, I'll never have to bury him because he was killed living up to his word. I did feel something special, and maybe it could have grown, but you killed it. Understand me when I say I love Jake, and I'm going to make him the best wife any man ever had."

"Fine, that's settled. Now if you'll excuse me, I've got some serious drinking to do." I headed toward the door.

"Ace, please don't go."

Her tone had changed, all the fight was gone. Instead it contained a plea, one I couldn't ignore.

"There, there's another reason I wanted to see you tonight. I, we need your help."

"You need my help? What makes you think I want to help you? Is this how you treat all your lovers after you find someone better?" I was still hurting and the desire to hurt her dominated me.

"Please. Be fair. Accept what I said, because it's the truth. This is more than you and me and Jake. It's Joey, too. I'm worried about him. He hasn't been himself recently. He drinks too much and is sad all the time. Mom and I don't know what's bothering him. I thought, well, I hoped you might help us."

I sighed, the will to fight draining away. "You're something, Terri Hart. You break my heart because I won't stop being a detective, then ask me to help your brother because I am a detective. At least it's not your fiancé. But before we let this go any farther, I gotta ask questions. If you and Jake were so tight, why did you go out with me, let me think there might be a future for us? Did Jake put you up to it, did Jake—"

I didn't get to finish the question that had haunted me all day because my face was spun sideways by a vicious slap.

Since I wasn't anchored to the parking lot, I ended up against the wall. Her hit wasn't like Bubba's fist, but it was hard enough. She didn't look like she packed a wallop but the stinging of my cheek proved looks can be deceiving. Guess that's what comes from clapping blackboard erasers in school, or is it white boards today?

"Oh, I'm sorry, Ace. Are you okay?"

She even looked like she meant it. "Yeah, the lights only blinked. They didn't go all the way out." I rubbed my cheek. I could feel the heat radiating from it. She'd slapped me on the same side as my black eye. I hoped it wouldn't make the eye worse. I was tired of comments about it.

"I'm sorry I hit you, but why did you ask that insulting question?"

"Because I need answers. Why did Jake have you watching me, have you play up to me, have you—well, you know? All he had to do was ask, and I would have told him whatever he wanted to know."

194

Terri gave me one of those looks usually reserved for repelling would-be assailants in dark alleys. "What the hell are you talking about?"

"I'm talking about you—your spying for Jake—"

"I know what you said. I just don't know what you're talking about. Jake never asked me to do anything with you. Nothing. Nada. What I did with you, I did because I wanted to. Whatever gave you such a cockeyed idea? And, what gives you the right to question me like this? For your information, Jake was upset because I spent time with you."

"Crap, Terri. You expect me to—"

She was winding up again so I decided discretion was the better part of valor, and hurt a whole lot less. I threw my hands up in surrender. "Okay, okay, I'm backing off. Maybe we'd better get back to the conversation we were having before we stumbled into this treacherous land where beautiful damsels clobber white knights." I grinned, or tried to.

"Okay," she responded.

Was that the ghost of a smile I saw?

"What about Joey? What should we do?" Her tone was pleading. She seemed more disturbed about Joey than she was about my broken heart.

I swallowed my pride. "I suppose I could talk to him." I remembered my dream. "In fact, I hoped to talk to him. Is he here tonight?"

"Oh, that would be great. He has so much respect for you." She smiled, actually smiled.

His great respect for me was news. I only talked to him once.

Terri continued, "He's not here, though. He couldn't come out tonight. He fell into a prickly pear

195

cactus and scratched his face. Mom says he's swollen and looks terrible. He says he's not showing his face in public until he looks normal again."

"Prickly pear?" I flinched. "That must have hurt. Those things are miserable. How did it happen?"

"Mom said he tripped."

I was about to commiserate with him when bells rang. "Wait a minute. He has a scratched face? What about his ear? Is it scratched and torn?"

"Yes, or Mom says it is. How did you know? His left ear. You know. The one he wore the earring in. It's a mess. He must have gotten stuck directly in the ear lobe. It's swollen worse than his face. Mom wanted him to go to the doctor, but he refused."

I'll bet he did. Toy boy. It finally clicked. The night I met him. I was close, but not quite on target. It wasn't toy boy, it was love toy—it was Joey-boy, the love toy. Joey, Terri's brother. What a mess. If what I thought was true, this quagmire had turned into quicksand, and I was belly-button deep in it.

I knew I had to stay cool and not arouse Terri's suspicion. "Where is Joey tonight? I'd like to talk to him." My insides churned.

"Home, I think. Mom said he was staying in. I don't think it would be a good idea to go there tonight, though. He's not in any condition to see anyone. Maybe tomorrow night."

"When did you last see him, I mean, face to face?" I was digging and I didn't know which way I wanted it to turn out. "Did you see him today?"

"No. Let me think. A couple of days ago. He came by the school and said he had to go into Dallas on business."

*Jake's Burn*

Bingo, I've got bingo, I wanted to shout. It had to be Joey. Joey, who'd been stalking me. Joey, who'd killed Sonny. Joey who'd killed Sheila. Joey . . . Whoa, I knew I had to slow down before I made a fool of myself. Did that make sense? Where was the motive? Why would he have done all those things? In fact, as far as I'd found out, he'd had no association with Sheila.

"Terri, think back. What day did he go to Dallas, and do you know where he was a coupla hours ago?"

"Home. I mean, I think he's home. I don't know for sure. Dallas. It must have been Wednesday. Why? Are these things important?"

I couldn't tell her what I thought. "Ah, I thought I saw him when I came through Cisco. He drives a dark pickup with a white racing stripe, doesn't he?" I was guessing but I thought it was a logical guess.

"Yeah, but it couldn't have been him. I talked to Mom after school and she said he was asleep. He was running a fever so she gave him a fever reducer and a sleeping pill. Mom believes sleep cures everything. He should be out the rest of the night."

"So, he couldn't have been in Cisco about an hour ago then?" If she was right, I was back to square one, but off the hook with Terri.

"Not according to what Mom said earlier. If it's that important, I can call and see if he's home. What's up? You're acting strange. It's more than seeing a truck like his in Cisco, isn't it? You—"

Her voice changed in midstream. "No! Ace! No! If you think Joey's somehow involved in what's been happening around here, you're wrong. He wouldn't, no, he couldn't hurt anyone. That's what you're thinking, aren't you? You think you can pin it all on Joey. You

197

sonnafabitch, you're trying to get even with me, and with Jake. I wish I'd never told you. How could you?"

She continued to argue his case, while I remembered his assaults on women. So much for not being able to hurt anyone.

I gripped her by the shoulders. "Terri, slow down, please. I haven't accused him of anything. But there are things that look bad." I gave her a small shake. "Listen to me for a moment."

I finally got her attention. She stopped her tirade, but trembled in my grasp. I told her about my motel room being searched, the break-in at my house, the earring I'd found and the droplets of blood, the tiny piece of material I'd found on Sweeper's broken claw, and finally, the shot that someone took at me earlier in the evening. I skipped the assault in my motel room. That would have played into her arguments about my chosen profession.

I completed my story by saying, "If you find it hard to believe, I can show you the hole in the convertible top, and the brick at my place that had the note wrapped around it. The police have the gas can."

Terri grasped my arms. "No, no matter what you say, I know it wasn't Joey." Her gaze locked on me, begging me to believe her. "It was Joey who warned you that someone was after you. It was Joey who had me tell you Sonny wasn't the target, you were. It was Joey . . ." Her voice trailed away as she quit talking.

Her face took on a shock and a sadness worse than I've ever seen before. She reminded me of one of those paintings of little girls with the big sad eyes. She was heart wrenching.

"No, Ace. Please don't make me believe my brother tried to kill you—that he killed Sonny. Please, I can't handle that, I'll never believe it." She fell silent with her head bowed, her quiet sniffling the only sign that she cried.

I reached and pulled her into my arms. "I don't want it to be true, I really don't," I whispered into her hair. What else could I say? "But, I've got to follow this to its end. Right now, everything points to Joey. I'm sorry, Terri, but I can't, no, I won't back off. Down deep, I'm still a cop and I have an obligation to put killers away. The difference between Sheriff Yardley and me is I have fewer restrictions. I can go anywhere, investigate anything. Also, I make more money than he does."

Terri pulled back from me. "Can't you be serious for more than thirty seconds?"

I slid my hands down her arms, grasping her hands, not to comfort her, but to protect myself. What I was about to say might get me another smack in the chops. "You want serious, here it is. Help me, and we'll be helping the people of Cisco. If Joey's innocent, we can prove it much faster by working together. If he's guilty . . ." I let my unsaid words hang in the air.

Terri's eyes reflected her pain, sending a ripple of compassion through my heart. She mumbled, "Joey asked about your investigation, about what you found out. He asked me to find what, I mean, if you have any suspects. Could that mean—"

"Hey, Ace. Is that you?" A voice interrupted her.

"Damn," I said under my breath.

Bubba walked up. "Thought that looked like you. Not too many midgets in this area with bright red

Chrysler convertibles. Hi, Terri. Is it true what I hear about you and Jake Adams?"

Terri tore her gaze from me and looked at Bubba with a sad smile. The charming Terri was almost back. "Hi, Bubba. It's nice to see you, too. What have you heard about Jake and me?"

"Hell, I heard you two was getting' hitched." He stopped and looked at me, then Terri. "Uh, nothing, nothing important." He looked embarrassed. "Come on in. I'll buy you guys a beer. Heck, I'm starting to like those Kill'en things."

We had little choice but to follow Bubba into the Down Home. While I would have sworn it couldn't happen, the smoke seemed thicker and stinkier, the noise louder, and Terri sadder, but still beautiful.

The rest of the evening passed uneventfully. For me, there had already been two highlights—the first, being with Terri and the second, my conclusion that Joey was somehow mixed up in the mess. What I didn't have an opinion on was whether he'd acted alone or in a conspiracy.

I decided not to tell Bubba about my suspicions. First, I didn't want Joey to be guilty because of Terri, and second, I was afraid Bubba might go off the deep end and go after him. He could crush Joey with one hand.

Terri hung onto my arm as if she were engaged to me instead of Jake. I didn't mind even if it was for the wrong reasons. Although she was Jake's fiancee, she was still the most exciting woman I'd ever known. Besides, I figured Jake owed me for winning her away before I knew he was in the race. Terri and I stood at the bar and chatted, and Bubba worked the crowd. As I watched him, I realized why Sheila had found him interesting enough to dump Jake. People liked him. When he approached a group, the grins and smiles turned on him. They were bright enough to penetrate the blue-gray haze of smoke that cast an illusion of privacy over each group. Each man had a handshake for him and every woman a hug. Again, I realized how badly I'd misjudged Bubba. He played his role to perfection depending on what he wanted a person to think. For me, he'd played the big muscle-bound lummox and I'd bought it—hook, line, and sinker.

Terri headed for the ladies room and I stood alone for a few minutes sipping my Killian's. Sammy Waltham came over to visit. After we'd shook hands and exchanged insults, he asked, "Have you learned anymore about who shot Sonny?"

"Nothing firm, but it's getting better." I heard Terri's sharp intake of breath as she returned to my side.

"When you catch up with him, let me know, and I'll warn him not to pick a fight with you." Sammy obviously hadn't noticed Terri's distress. "My wife's still mad at you. She said you shouldn'ta hurt the part she gets the most pleasure from." We both laughed. He slapped me on the shoulder and walked off to join another group, faking a limp for the first few steps.

At midnight, Terri announced she had to leave, something about being fresh for her students in the morning. As we walked to her car, I took her hand, "I wish I'd met you before Jake. Maybe I'd have had a chance. Things might have turned out differently. But since it didn't happen, I do wish you happiness. You'll always have a very special place in my heart."

"Thank you. For obvious reasons, I'm not going to think about what-ifs. I'm a one-man woman, and Jake is that man. I gotta admit though that being around you makes it more difficult to live up to what my mama taught me. I already envy the woman who finally gets you." She tried to kiss me lightly on the cheek.

I couldn't allow her to walk out of my life with a sisterly kiss. I pulled her to me, and gave her the kiss I'd wanted to give her since I'd first heard her voice back there in the smoke.

She stepped back, her face flushed, her voice husky. "Good night, Ace. I have to leave."

"That shade of red looked great on her," I mumbled, watching her drive away with my heart breaking, and my mind cursing Jake. I was sure I'd never love another like I loved Terri.

As her taillights turned into little red dots, reality jumped up and kicked me in the gut. Joey, what was I going to do about Joey, and how would I ever square it with Terri and Jake?

## CHAPTER TWENTY-ONE

Morning arrived after another night of near sleeplessness. I'd be glad when this case was over, and Jake and Terri were married. Maybe I could curl up with my cats and get a good night's sleep.

At eight o'clock, I called the Cat Hotel and spoke with the Concierge. She assured me the boys were fine and having a wonderful time visiting with the other guests. She complimented me on their manners in the dining room, and said the maitre d' and the headwaiter were thrilled with them. Their meticulous hygiene habits also drew her praise. Yeah, she used the word meticulous. It's not in my normal vocabulary.

Her comments made me wonder if she knew which two cats I was calling about. Her comments didn't fit the two alley cats I'd rescued from the SPCA. But, I found the whole conversation to be surreal—we were talking about cats in a kennel, not two rich humans in a hoity-toity hotel. Kind of makes you wonder where society is heading, doesn't it? I felt better when I hung up. The boys were okay.

I showered and dressed, killing time. My eye looked better. Apparently, Terri's slap hadn't caused any new damage. At nine-thirty I called the school and left a message for Terri.

While I waited for her to call back, I walked across the road to the restaurant for breakfast. The buffet was the fastest so I loaded up on scrambled eggs, sausage links, grits, toast and coffee—lots of coffee.

I made it back to the room to find the phone ringing. Terri was returning my call during her ten-thirty break.

I started the conversation by saying, "Last night was wonderful, but I realize it was our last. We need to talk more about Joey, though—maybe after school today."

"Sorry, Ace, I can't," she responded. "I'm heading for Fort Worth to meet Jake for dinner and an engagement ring. I'll probably stay over."

"Oh," was all I could manage. I looked around the room for the cherubs. The bums were still absent.

"Please Ace, don't make this any harder for me. You've got my head spinning, but we both have to remember I'm engaged to Jake. I'm going to marry him."

Talk about a kick in the chest to help you digest your breakfast. She'd given me a mule-kick that might keep my heart on hold forever. I swore off women.

My silence must have bothered her because she continued, "I wish things were different, but I've made a commitment, and like you, I can't back away."

All I could think of to say was, "Have a nice evening." Again, I proved I had the perfect response for any situation.

I hung up feeling like I'd lost everything important. It was a good thing I hadn't brought a case of Killian's.

I'd have been into it and wouldn't have quit until I'd reached the bottom. I never expected to be lucky in love, and had been afraid to try again after Janice. The pain that coursed through my chest convinced me I'd been right. Love is for those sentimental saps with the courage to accept rejection. I didn't qualify.

After I'd sat for twenty minutes feeding my feelings of inadequacy, I made a conscious attempt to pull myself together. I had to get back to the case. First, I needed someone to talk to, someone who could fill me in on the rumors that circulated around the Down Home. I thought of tracking Hojo down, but remembered he still guarded his throat every time I came near. Besides, he'd want to meet at the bar, and I wanted neutral ground. Bubba? No, he was still too close to Sheila to give me any rational help. I wondered about Sammy Waltham. He'd said he wanted to help and had been friendly last night. Maybe I could get in touch with him.

I found his name in the phone book, dialed his number, and, to my surprise, he answered. He told me he took the day off for honey-do's around the house. I told him if he'd meet me, I'd treat him to lunch. He agreed.

I had about an hour to kill. I decided to visit Mom and Dad again.

The cemetery was the same as on my previous visit—quiet and stately, paying proper homage to those who had passed on. The same six black goats, or their twins, grazed, keeping the grass and weeds down. I stopped and admired them as they searched out every weed and blade of grass that had managed to sprout since their last visit. I asked them where they went when the guys with the lawnmowers came in. They chewed and refused to answer.

205

I walked back to the Edwards plot, cordoned off from encroachment with concrete rails. "I'm back again. Bet you're surprised. Most I've visited in a long time. I came to tell you about a woman I met—met, loved, and lost. You would have liked her. She's the most wonderful woman I've ever known and I love her more than I've ever loved any woman, except you, Mom." I stood there for the better part of forty-five minutes telling them about Terri and how I felt about her. And how I lost her to Jake before I had a chance to win her. I didn't tell them about the lust I felt for her, how we almost ended up in bed in my motel. Not only were they old-fashioned, but they thought teachers were above reproach, and I didn't want them to think badly of Terri. When I finished my story, I felt better, better than I'd felt since Jake had busted me with the news about Terri and him.

As I walked away, I remembered when I was young, my folks told me I'd feel better if I shared my troubles with a friend. They'd also said they'd always be there if I wanted to talk. I knew now they'd been right, and I was thankful. The talk had helped.

Right brain took that opportunity to kick in and remind me of what Sheriff Yardley had told me about the jerry cans. It was Joey's dad who had called to report three cans full of gas stolen. It fit.

At twelve-ten, I walked into the restaurant and looked around for Sammy. He sat in a booth along the wall. I slid in across from him.

"What's up, Ace? You got news?"

"Maybe. Sammy, you know the folks around here, and I'm sure you hear all the rumors."

"Hey, Sammy, long time no see."

I looked toward the voice and saw the waitress walking toward our table with pencil in hand.

"Do you want the buffet, order from the menu, or can I get something *just* for you?" She gave Sammy a special look as she said it.

Sammy ducked his head and answered, "I'll take the buffet and coffee."

"You still drinking decaf or have you grown up enough to take it *hot and strong*?"

Sammy's head stayed down. "Decaf, please."

There was an undertone that Sammy didn't choose to face.

I knew I didn't want to go there. "I'd like to see a menu, please."

The waitress tore her gaze off Sammy and acknowledged me. "Okay. Want something to drink?"

I ordered a diet cola and, after reviewing the menu, a chicken salad sandwich with chips. Sammy loaded his plate three times. Made me glad he'd selected the buffet. I wasn't sure my expense account could afford to feed him from the menu, even with Jake footing the bill.

We both ordered a slice of lemon meringue pie, my favorite. When he was halfway through his slice, which was twice as big as mine, I brought him back to the reason for our lunch. "Were there any rumors about Joey Hart and Sheila?"

Sammy choked on his pie. "Joey Hart? Not a chance. Most of the women around Cisco won't go near him."

"Why, what's wrong with Joey?"

"I asked my sister the same thing. She said he's a dried-up, pimply, little pipsqueak who abuses women. She said she'd like to buy him for what he's worth and

sell him for what he thinks he's worth. She told me he'd
punched several women who wouldn't put out for him."

I sat, trying not to show my agreement with
everything he said. He had echoed what I found in
Joey's police record.

Sammy continued, "I don't know if it's true, but
I've heard rumors. Also, I don't know any woman who's
been with him recently. What makes you think there
could be rumors about him and Sheila?"

"Just wondering," I replied, cranking up the
sincerity in my voice.

Sammy gave me a look I could only interpret as a
glare. "She already had Bubba, and could have darn near
any man she wanted. You know Bubba. I'd be awful
surprised if she ever gave Joey the time of day. If you
had somebody like Bubba, would you take on a jerk like
Joey?"

"Guess it did sound like a silly question. How about
the lawyer? Did Joey have any connection with her?"

"Not that I know about. About the only thing I ever
heard about her was she hated men. She was a terror
when she represented a woman against a man. Rumor
said she'd do anything to win, not just to win, but to
humiliate the man. I know she was a bitch during the
Adams' divorce. I went to court a coupla times, and she
was something to watch."

"Interesting. Was she married, or have a
boyfriend?"

"No, never married as far as I know. Boyfriend?
No, never heard nothing about her having a male friend
of any kind, romantic or otherwise. But, you gotta
remember, she was from Fort Worth. Hell, them city-
folk and their doings might as well be a thousand miles

from Cisco. Like I said though, she was a man-hater, or that's what I heard."

Sammy took his last bite of pie and sat back in the booth. "That was a mighty fine meal. I shore appreciate you inviting me. Now, if you don't have anymore questions, my wife's home thinking up more chores for me."

He looked over at the waitress. "Hmmm, I might have a chore for her. Nothing like a nooner to settle a big meal."

"One more thing, Sammy. If you were in my shoes and somebody had killed Sheila, her lawyer, and Sonny, and was gunning for you, who would you suspect?"

"That's tough. I'm shore glad I ain't in your shoes. I wouldn't have a clue. But, I betcha you're ready to wrap this up, ain't you?"

"Ah, I'm getting closer." What else could I say? "You've helped me a lot and I appreciate it. Don't work too hard."

After we shook hands in the parking lot, I went back to my motel room and hung the *Do Not Disturb* sign on the door.

I sat at the table with an empty pad of paper and started with my collection of facts and guesses again. I was convinced Joey was the one who broke into my place, the one Sweeper chased away. Terri had as much as verified that. I knew he was abusive to women, documented by his arrest record and what Sammy had said. But that still didn't add up to the murder of Sheila, the lawyer, or Sonny. I had no motives. Hell, I couldn't connect him to any of them, or not in any way that counted.

Despite the lack of motive, I penciled in a sequence of events. It started with Joey showing up at Sheila's house for an unknown reason. Next, he killed either Sheila or the lawyer. It didn't matter which went first. Killing one would have forced him to kill the other since they were together. He set the house on fire to cover his crimes, and it burned to the ground. At that point, he probably believed he'd destroyed all the evidence. Then I showed up in town with Jake telling everyone I was the best. Joey panicked and tried to take me out. Sonny paid the price on that one while I hid under a tree. He searched my motel room trying to find out what I knew. Same thing with his attempt to break into my house. I grinned when I thought how surprised he must have been when Sweeper sailed down the stairs into his face. Along the way, he tried to scare me off with the warnings he passed through Terri.

Logical guesses, but still guesses. I could think of only one person who could verify my mental gymnastics—Joey, himself. I got up from the table. It was about time I picked up a sympathy card for him. After all, falling into a prickly pear cactus, or getting clawed by a cat, was worthy of a card—even if it wasn't sympathy I felt.

## CHAPTER TWENTY-TWO

I strapped on the Beretta and headed out the door. After stopping by the drugstore to pick up a suitable card, not an expensive one, I drove toward the Hart homestead. The front of the card showed a man lying in a hospital bed. The inside of the card said, *They say a stitch in time saves nine—but didn't you overdo it? Get well soon.* I thought it appropriate.

I drove, trying to remember the directions Terri had given me. Their place was near Nimrod off Route 2526. It was a one-story ranch style house with a porch across the front, holding comfortable looking rocking chairs. I could see to the rear of the house and saw cattle grazing in a pasture. I looked and wondered if that was a burro I saw with the cattle. All in all, it was a nice setting and reminded me of Terri.

When I pulled into the driveway, a couple of hound dogs stirred themselves from under a shade tree and ran out to check me, barking loudly. I froze and they gave me a few sniffs. They must have figured I wasn't much of a threat because they turned and went back into the shade. I was glad my cats weren't there. It would have been embarrassing.

211

I knocked on the door and it swung open, revealing an older version of Terri. The blaze had faded in her red hair and her face wore wrinkles, but the remnants of her youthful beauty were there. If I'd seen her in the middle of the Dallas-Fort Worth Airport, I'd have known she had to be Terri's mother.

"Hi, I'm Ace Edwards. I came by to see if Joey's all right."

"Hello, Mr. Edwards." The voice was Terri's but with more maturity. I liked it and wished I'd be around when Terri's voice aged.

She stuck out her hand to shake and I saw the evidence of hard work in it. "Come on in. Both Joey and Terri have spoken of you. You're the cop that's investigating Ms. Adams' death, right?"

"Not cop, ma'am. A private investigator working for Jake Adams."

"Well, whatever. Ms. Adams took him to the cleaners, didn't she?" She grinned, then turned serious. "The deaths of those two women were terrible but I think it was inevitable for Ms. Adams. For the last few years, she's been after almost every man in the area. She even made a play for my Joey, if you can believe that." She paused and chuckled, a deep-throated laugh that brought pain to my chest because it reminded me of Terri. "Don't know why she'd want to go after Joey. He's got a face only a mother could love."

She nodded toward the inside of the house. "Come on in. Joey's stretched out on the couch watching TV. That cactus did a pretty good job on him. He's gotta be the most accident-prone boy ever born. This time, though, he topped his record. He injured himself with that cactus different from any I've seen before. How 'bout coffee? I just started a fresh pot."

I listened to her with a comfortable feeling. It almost made me hope she was right and I was wrong. "Thank you, that would hit the spot." I followed her into the house and saw Joey napping on the couch.

"Joey, wake up. You've got a visitor." She shook his shoulder.

He woke and looked first at his mother, then me. His hand went to his ear, and his eyes got large. "Ace, what are you doing here?"

"Thought I'd check in on you. Terri said you were hurt. Here, I brought you a card." I handed him the card, giving me a chance to get close enough to examine the scratches on his face. Didn't look like cactus pricks to me. I've seen enough evidence of Sweeper's claws on my furniture and my arms, and his face matched my memories.

He swung around, putting his feet on the floor and opened the card. His left ear was bandaged, keeping me from checking his ear lobe. "So, how's the investigation coming?"

"Not bad. In fact, I got a big break. I might be able to wrap it up pretty soon." I stared at him, looking for a reaction.

He cut his eyes toward me, then away. "Uh, care to tell me what you found out?"

"Not much. But I'm pretty sure I know who's been dogging me, and I figure he's the same guy that killed Sheila, her lawyer and Sonny."

"Uh, that's great. Can you tell me?"

"Why don't we walk outside?" I didn't want to get into it in front of his mother. "No need bothering your

213

mom with stuff like this. Not very pretty." I couldn't be sure of her reaction, and I didn't want a she-cat at my back.

"I get the message," his mother interjected as she re-entered the room with my coffee. "I'll go start supper. Can you stay, Mr. Edwards?"

Joey spoke up, "I'm sure he's got some place to go. Don't you, Ace?"

"Thank you, ma'am, but Joey's right. I have to be leaving in a little bit."

"Well, nice to have met you." His mom walked into the kitchen.

"Let's go outside," I said as soon as his mother was out of the room. "I need to talk to you. Terri says you can help me with the case."

He rose from the couch. "Sure, if I can."

We walked outside and sat in the rockers.

"What can I do for you?" he asked.

"First, you can tell me how you got those scratches. I grew up here. You didn't fall into a cactus."

"Oh? I say I did. Can you prove otherwise?" He was relaxed, not taking me seriously.

I pulled the earring from my wallet and held it up where he could see it. "Yeah, I think I can. The police found this earring interesting. After they ran it through special tests, they said somebody left blood on it. They're doing the DNA thing right now. Any guesses about who the tests will identify?"

Okay, it was another of my bald-faced lies. I needed to shake him and it did. He leaned forward in his chair, much more interested than he'd been a moment ago. His cheek jumped as if he had a tic. His eyes cut from left to right, refusing to lock in on anything, especially me.

I continued, "Want to know where I got the earring? Before you answer, I should tell you the police picked up prints at my house and in my motel room. My bet is they're from the same guy—my bet's on you."

Joey's eyes narrowed as he stared at me. "Bullshit. I've never seen that earring before." He hesitated, then added, "Unless it's the one I lost last week. Yeah, I lost mine. I wuz gonna get another but I fell into that cactus."

"Where'd you lose it?"

"Umm, I'm, um, not sure. Must have been, um, the Down Home. Yeah, it wuz in the Down Home."

I laughed. "You're a lousy liar. Don't ever take a lie detector test. Now, want to try again about how you got all scratched up? And I bet your ear lobe is torn. In fact, I bet this earring was ripped out, leaving a nasty tear, and blood on the earring. I bet an orange tomcat ripped this earring right out of your ear."

His face told me I had scored, so I reached farther. "You wouldn't believe what cops'll do to solve a case. They scraped my cat's claws for blood samples. Now, I don't know much about that stuff, but the cop said he got a good scraping. He said my cat had drawn blood, and he was pretty sure they could run DNA on it."

I hesitated, allowing what I'd said to sink in. "Yep, Joey. Looks like they're building a pretty solid case against you. Especially, when they match the prints off the gas can you left in front of my house with the prints they took off the cans they found at the fire. I'd sure hate to be in your shoes."

He clenched and unclenched his fists, as his gaze bored into me. "I got nothing else to say. I done told you all I'm gonna tell you."

I leaned back and rocked for a moment, giving him time to consider his situation. "Hmmm. I'd forgotten how nice it is out here in the country around Cisco." I closed my eyes and took a deep breath. "Your folks got a nice place here. How many cattle do they run?"

"Cattle? What do you care about cows? You're full of crap, Edwards. You got any more tall tales, or should I just kick your ass out of here?"

"Joey, you sure didn't learn your manners from your mother. But since you ask, nothing you've said explains the prints at my house, my motel room, the gas cans, or anything. Incidentally, when we were fighting, you dropped something—something that led me straight to you." I hesitated and looked around as if seeing the front yard for the first time. "That's a good-looking pickup. Is it yours?" I pointed toward a black truck with a white racing stripe.

"Yeah, that's all mine," he said with pride. "What's it to you?"

"Oh, nothing. Kinda looks like one I saw in my parking lot. Well, it wasn't in the parking lot. It was leaving in a hurry after somebody took a shot at me. Do you have a gun, Joey?"

That did it. That was the final tweak that moved him. He sprang to his feet, and whipped a pistol from the back of his waistband.

"Damn you, Edwards. I've had enough of your crap." His voice came out in a near whisper, but the venom dripping from his words left me with no doubt about his feelings. "If my mother wuzn't in the house, I'd blow you away right here. Now, you sit there and don't move. I'm gonna get out of here. If Mom asks, tell her I had to go to town for medicine for my cactus cuts.

Don't try to follow me. If you do, I'll kill you, and laugh at your funeral."

He backed off the porch toward his truck. As he opened the door, he turned back and said, "Remember, don't try to follow me. I won't miss you again like I did that night with Sonny. You ain't got no place to hide now, and nobody to take your place." He climbed in.

I sat for a moment wishing this was a dream. One thing was real, though—the last thing I wanted was bullets flying with Terri's mother inside. As Joey spun out onto the road and around a curve, I moved, ran to my car and dived in. Luckily, I'd driven from Cisco with the top down.

I pondered for a split second. Nothing to do but go after him. It didn't take long to catch up. Pickup trucks are good for a lot of things but road racing against convertibles isn't one of them. I blasted through the curves, the front wheel drive pulling me around. Joey couldn't take the curves as fast, or his truck would roll. I closed within ten yards and held my position. I saw his hand reach out the window and he snapped off a shot. It missed.

"Okay, hotshot. What are you going to do now?" I asked myself. No answer was forthcoming. Apparently, right brain was on vacation. I dropped to thirty to forty yards behind and stayed there. I figured at this distance, hitting me would be a one-in-a-million shot. Since I'd never won the lottery, seemed like good odds to me.

Did you ever notice there are no policemen around when you want one? On the straight-aways, we were reaching eighty to ninety miles an hour, but I heard no sirens from the highway patrol telling us to pull over.

217

We raced around the countryside, finally wheeling into Cisco.

It surprised me when Joey turned into the parking lot of the old Mobley Hotel. I had dropped farther behind him because I'd slowed when we reached the city limits. However, traffic was light and I had no problem keeping him in sight. I pulled into the parking lot, and saw him kick open the door to the old hotel and run inside. I parked and approached the building, the Beretta in my right hand.

The sweat trickled down my forehead as I tried to see into the dark interior. During our race around the countryside, the sun had gone down and night had descended. Clouds had rolled in with the sunset, blotting out the sky.

I wiped the sweat from my right hand, then again gripped the Beretta. With my left, I pushed on the door Joey had kicked open. It swung inward all the way to the wall before reversing its path. All I saw was darkness.

I squatted and duck-walked through the door, cursing myself for the noise. When I was in the reception area, I leaned against the wall, then rose to my full height. I listened with every fiber of my body. Every nerve ending had turned into a listening device.

A noise, the scrape of a shoe. Where had it come from? I fought myself, trying to reconstruct it. Overhead. That's it. It had come from above. The stairs were in front of me.

I climbed the steps, hoping there were no squeaks on the way up. I edged along the wall where the nails would have been driven to anchor the boards. The dark at the top wasn't very inviting, but I had no choice other than to keep climbing. Joey had to be there somewhere. I struggled to remember everything about the layout I'd seen when Terri and I visited.

At the top of the stairs, there was a hallway to my right, and the Conrad Hilton display area in front of me with a large column in the center. The museum room was to the left. There were two other doors, locked when we were there. If they were still locked, and I hadn't heard Joey force them, he could be in any of the other places. Worse yet, he could be standing at the top of the stairs waiting to send me to one of two places I had no desire to visit, a hospital or hell.

I stepped up onto another step, testing it before putting my full weight on it. No squeak. So far, so good. I peered into the darkness above me, trying to decide if there was anything there that could be Joey waiting for me. Nothing. I couldn't see anything except darkness.

I heard something that made me pause with my foot in mid-air. Was it a footstep, and from what direction did it come? My perspective was not trustworthy but it sounded like it came from the right—the hallway. Joey could be standing there ready to shoot me, kick me, push me down the stairs or simply call me dirty names. I could handle the name calling but the other options had no appeal.

Squeak. The noise again—maybe. It was so soft I could have imagined it. I leaned against the wall, guessing I was about three steps from the top. If Joey were waiting for me at the edge of the hallway, he'd have me cold when I stepped onto the landing. I leaned there, breathing shallow. What to do, what to do? This was not an arena where I was at my best. I've hated to wander around in the dark since I was a kid.

219

"Squeak." Yes. I heard it again. It was a real noise. It sounded like someone shifting his weight from one foot to the other, and again it sounded like it came from the top right of the stairs. I knew I had to make a decision and live or die with it. If I were right, I might gain an advantage over Joey—if I were wrong, I might be saying hello to my parents sooner than I expected. Then again, maybe not. I was sure they were in heaven.

Desperation forced me to come up with something, forced me to take a chance that would save me or send me on my way. Moving at the speed of a snail, or slower, I lowered myself onto the stairs, stretching out over the steps, distributing my weight over several while cutting my profile down as low as I could. I considered the old ploy of throwing something into the area above me to make a noise. In the movies, the bad guy always fell for the distraction and gave himself away. But in my case, anything I could throw I would first have to get into my hand. Car keys—too much noise getting them out of my right front pants pocket. Coins—same problem. Anything I could think of to throw would end up drawing Joey's attention to my position. Bad idea, even if it always worked for John Wayne.

I cocked my right leg and gradually, ever so gradually, pushed my way up the step on my belly. The Beretta bumped against the stair and I cringed, waiting for Joey to come sailing down. Nothing, no movement from above. I slipped the Beretta into its holster where it would stay quiet.

I went back to my slow crawl up the stairs. The carpet had a dirty, musty smell to it. I couldn't separate them, but there were several different odors mixed together, none of them very pleasant. I wondered what tourists had had on the bottoms of their shoes as they'd climbed this stairwell over the years. Then I realized I really didn't want to know. The stairs seemed to be carpeted with a synthetic fabric. I figured if I scraped myself to the top this way, I'd build up enough static electricity to shock Joey into submission if I touched him.

Patience has not always been my strong suit. For example, I won't stand in line waiting to get into a restaurant—there are too many good restaurants to wait for one. If I can't find someone to take my money in a department store, I walk. No, I'm not normally patient. Tonight, I was the epitome of Saint Jude. I moved so slowly, there were moments when I wondered if I moved at all.

I reached out with my left hand to grip the step when I saw a soft glow in the darkness in front of me. I froze and the glow froze. I pulled my hand back and the glow came with me. I quit breathing and moving, concentrating. I feared Sam or Al might hear my heart pounding at the fire station five blocks up the street. I stared at it. My heart pounded at a marching rate of one hundred twenty beats per minute, or so it seemed, but the glow held constant. Using the wonderful patience I'd discovered, I reached toward the glow with my right hand. I used several minutes, or maybe it was several hours, to move my right to within a few inches of the glow. I still didn't have a clue what it was. It didn't move, just glowed at me. When I guessed I was within three or four inches, I grabbed with my right hand.

As I look back now, I assume Joey was not looking in my direction. If he had been, I'm sure he would have seen a red light flashing up the stairs—my red face in embarrassment must have radiated outward. I had grabbed my watch.

I sighed and vowed to pay more attention to my watch in the future. Obviously, I didn't know enough about it. After taking it off and shoving it into my jacket pocket, I went back to my stealthy crawl up the stairs. Finally, my left hand felt the landing. I dropped it back and crept up, ensuring my right shoulder stayed against the wall. When my head was close to the landing, I reached around the edge of the wall with my left hand.

I let my fingers do the walking as I inched them along the carpet. When I reached a point close to the wall, I was rewarded as my fingers brushed something. I froze, not knowing what it was. I explored with my fingertips and discovered what felt like a boot. I couldn't be sure because I couldn't touch it with enough pressure to get a good feel. Cloth, material of some kind was my next find.

It had to be Joey. He had to be standing there guarding the stairs, waiting for me to come blundering up. I had to assume he had little respect for my detective smarts. After all, I hadn't passed many tests so far. I tensed, knowing I had one opportunity to gain the upper hand. Before I made my move though, I reached inside my jacket with my right hand and quietly withdrew the Beretta. For one of the few times since I started this case, it was where it should have been.

With the Beretta clenched in my right hand, I again moved my left until I touched what I hoped was Joey's boot. I backed off a few inches and flexed my fingers. Then I lunged with my left hand, and grabbed. I got a handful of boot and jerked as hard as I could. A surprised cry sounded from above me, followed by a thud, a crack, and silence. I figured the thud was Joey's butt hitting the floor, and the crack was the back of his head gaining the same level as his butt. I hoped the silence, the blessed silence, was his quick trip into unconsciousness.

## CHAPTER TWENTY-THREE

I scrambled to my feet and fumbled along the wall until I found the light switch. When the lights came up, I saw Joey stretched out on the floor, moaning and rubbing the back of his head. Remembering the knot on my forehead and the black eye from my motel room, I felt no compassion. His gun had fallen away. I picked it up.

"Touché, Joey. Hurts like hell, doesn't it? You can get up now, and we'll talk."

He looked at me through glazed eyes. "You sonafabitch, I never heard nothin' a'tall. Whut are you, some kind of snake?"

I grinned. "Yeah, I slithered up those steps and got behind you. No challenge at all."

"I can almost believe it." His eyes moved to my Beretta which was pointed at a sweet spot in his midsection. He shifted his attention to his pistol that I held in my left hand. "Looks like you got the fire power. What do we do now?"

"We're going to chat. I've got questions, you've got answers, and we're going to share. Understand?"

"From where I sit, it don't look like I got much choice." He looked around for a moment then back at me, shrugged and said, "Ask your questions."

"Why did you kill Sheila?"

He said, "'Fore I answer that, can't we go in there and sit down?" He nodded toward the museum. "This ain't the most comfortable position I've ever been in."

Since I wasn't comfortable either, I motioned him to his feet. He walked into the room housing the museum and sat in one of the old chairs. I hoped it would hold his weight, since it looked about a hundred years old. I leaned against one of the display cases after slipping his pistol into my jacket pocket.

"Okay, now you're as comfortable as you're going to be until the police finish booking you, so answer my question."

"Hey, let's make a deal. I kin put in a good word for you with Terri. Nobody needs to know but you and me."

"Not a chance. Haven't you heard? Terri's engaged to the ex-husband of the woman you killed."

"Shucks, Ace. That's the second time you said that. What makes you think I did Sheila? Coulda been any number of guys. She loved'm and left'm with regularity. Hell, I bet most of the guys in Cisco and half of Eastland County wuz dropped by her." The grin on Joey's face made me want to smash him although I suspected there was truth in his words.

"It won't work, Joey. Start talking." I searched for an incentive. "If the story's good enough, I might give you a head start before I call Sheriff Yardley—no promises though."

"Shore you will," Joey sneered at me. "All you cops give guys like me a break. Bullshit, as soon as you git your story, you'll be lookin' for a phone." He stopped and appeared to think. After a moment, he continued. "Of course, we'll have to go downstairs and break into the Chamber of Commerce. Those are the only phones in the building."

He leaned back and the chair creaked. I could picture it splintering at any moment.

"Might be tough walking me downstairs. Anything could happen." He had a silly grin on his face.

I walked to the corner of the room where a variety of antiques were stored. There was a rope there. I hoped it wasn't an antique as I pulled it out and held it up. "Yeah, or I might tie you to that chair and leave you here while I go find a pay phone. I was a great Boy Scout. I learned my knots well. One time, I tied my brother to a tree and it took him three days to get free. Yep, earned my badge in knot tying." It was my turn to smile as Joey's grin was replaced by a frown. He didn't know I didn't have a brother.

"Yeah, you're just the type to have been a Boy Scout. Prob'ly helped old ladies 'cross the street whether they wanted to go or not." He laughed, but it was with less confidence than he'd shown earlier.

"Okay, look," he continued. "S'pose I tell you what you want ta know, answer ev'ry question you got. Will you give me a head start?"

"Can't say, Joey-Boy. Haven't heard your story yet. If it's good, maybe we can work it out. But first, you start talking, and answer my questions."

He stared at me, and I could tell he was thinking hard. His eyes shifted all over the area, looking for something—probably a way out. He must not have found it because after a couple of minutes, he said, "All right, asshole, you win. Where do you want me to start?" All the bluster was gone from his words.

"Start with killing Sheila, then Sonny, searching my motel room, my house, throwing a brick at my front door, scaring my cats . . . Hey, shoot the works. Whoops, change that to tell it all." The grin I felt on my face reminded me of the Cheshire Cat in Alice in Wonderland.

Joey stared at me, a look of resignation in his eyes. "Hope you've got a while. It's a long story, and I've got plenty of time. Sheila? Have you noticed how many people ain't mourning her?" He cracked his knuckles. "Most of the people I know said she got what she deserved. Once the word gets out why I killed her, I'll be a hero. Hey, maybe that writer that's been hangin' aroun' the Down Home will write a story about me. Wouldn't that be somethin'?"

I leaned forward and pointed the Beretta at him. "Move on with the story. I can listen to your crap another night." I gave him my most intimidating look.

"Ace, you ain't got no sense of humor. Try to stay with me. I don't want to tell this too many times, and I figger the sheriff'll wanta hear it with a bunch of his lawyers around. I'm one of Sheila's dropees. Yeah, me, little Joey-Boy, the ugly Hart. I ain't pretty like Terri. I ain't big like Bubba. I ain't rich like Jake, and I ain't even as smart as you, but I had her."

Joey stopped and grinned. "I lusted after her from the time I wuz twelve and found out the difference between boys and girls. Whether she was coming or going, she was pure sex. She used to walk toward me

227

with them boobs stuck out, and away from me shaking her hips. I couldn't help but want her." He stopped talking, a look of longing on his face. After a few seconds, he continued, "It wuz one night in the Down Home near closing time. You know what they say, 'They always look better 'bout closing time.' Well, I guess I'm proof of that."

Joey's eyes glazed. "Sheila walked over to me and said, 'You're Joey Hart, aren't you. My ex is making it with your sister. Why don't you come up to my place? You'll go deeper and longer while we do things those two haven't begun to think of. Be ready to go as soon as I hit the ladies' room.' That wuz it. After all the years of lusting after her, she'd said she wanted me. I couldn't think of a thing to say as she walked toward the john."

"When she came back, I wuz ready to go. She didn't have to ask me twice. I followed her to her place where she showed me positions I never knowed existed. If she'da written a book, every man in the country would have bought a copy for his wife or his honey. She could do things—"

"Okay, okay. I get the picture. Try to fast forward through the x-rated parts and get to the murder scene. Was that when you killed her?"

"Killed her? Oh, not a chance—not that night. I would've done anything for her. If she'd asked me to kill, I'd have done it for her, but not to her. I fell for her so hard I laugh at myself when I remember. It's funny. Until her, I thought I wuz a lover, knew all the tricks. I thought I could love'm and leave'm, thought I wuz too much man for one woman—Joey-Boy, the Love Toy. Sheila made me a changed man. I became a one-woman man, and that woman wuz Sheila. It didn't matter how old she wuz—I knew she wuz almost twenty years older than me. I wuz in love, and I wuz sure she felt the same way." He stopped and laughed a bitter, derisive laugh. "Love. Stupid." He paused.

I waited, feeling the pain of what he went through. After a couple of minutes, he continued.

"I waited at the Down Home the next night, 'spectin' her to show up and invite me to her place again. She never came. Same thing for the next three nights. I waited and she didn't show. I must have called her house fifty times and each time, that snotty downstairs maid said she wuzn't there. I left a message each time but she never returned a call. I wuz beside myself. I couldn't understand why. Every time I relived that night, it came out the same. She had to love me like I loved her. Why else had she, had we—well, you know?"

"Yeah, I know," I responded, feeling his pain, but not wanting a colorful description of what they'd done.

"On the sixth night, she showed up at the Down Home with her lawyer, that damn skinny woman. Every time I got near Sheila, she turned away, ignoring me. It hurt so bad. There had to be a mistake, she must have thought I didn't care." He hesitated, then groaned, "What a damned fool I wuz."

He looked at me, pain in his eyes. "When you wuz a kid, did you ever want somethin' so bad, and then somebody give it to ya'. But, before you could enjoy it, they took it away. That's how I felt. I fin'ly got what I'd wanted, but it wuz yanked away. I wanted to reach out, to smash somethin', to get even with the world." His voice softened. "But most, I wanted Sheila."

229

His tone changed again. "After she died, I waited for the sheriff to bang on the door. I wuz sure I'd be suspect number one, but she'd ignored me so completely, no one ever suspected we'd done the bone dance all night. Even now, no one suspects Sheila and me wuz ever together. Shit, I bet nobody'll ever believe it." His head dropped. He looked like an old man.

My patience was running thin. "Get back to the story, Joey. I don't need a step-by-step narrative—cut to the chase."

"Humph, big city cop. I guess you guys don't have time for plain folk like me."

"Wrong again. I'm just in a hurry to hear your story. I'll visit you on death row, and you can give me all the details."

"You sonafabitch!" Joey's eyes reflected what he'd like to do to me, and it wouldn't have been pleasant, but he returned to the story. "She ignored me, she didn't return my calls. I wuz out of it. Mah mind wouldn't think of anything but her. Ten long days and nights had passed. I wuz in the Down Home and had drunk too many Louisiana Bayou's. Eleven o'clock arrived with no Sheila and I decided to go to her house. I sat outside a while watching. The lights wuz on but I didn't see nobody moving around. Sheila's car was out front so I got out and checked it. The hood was cool. Apparently, she hadn't used it for awhile. I walked around the house to see if I could see her through the back windows and saw a strange car parked in the rear driveway, a new Mercedes. I still didn't see nobody so I went back to the front. I listened at the door and it wuz quiet inside."

Joey's eyes took on a hurt puppy look. "You gotta understand, Ace. I wuz desperate and I wuz drunk as a skunk. Nobody answered the doorbell. I tried the latch and the door opened. I went in, walked around, and didn't see nobody. I climbed to the second floor. You know, up that spiral staircase. When I got upstairs, I heard noises from down the hall and walked that way." He hesitated.

"Let's go, Joey. My time is valuable."

"I shore wish you'd show some patience." Joey appeared to gather his thoughts. "I only took a few steps before I knowed it was Sheila's bedroom, the same room we used. As I got close, I recognized Sheila's voice, or maybe I should say, her moans. I heard them all night when we wuz together. The door wuz open so I snuck up to it and peeked in."

His mouth stopped moving and his facial features froze. Emotions rippled across his face as his eyes looked into the distance, seeing things known only to him. He'd kept a straight face but now, it flashed ugly, mad, hurt and several other emotions I couldn't identify, and didn't want to meet.

"There wuz Sheila. She wuz on the bed, naked. Her body all wet with sweat, her beautiful red hair a mess and splayed around her face. She wuz so beautiful, so perfect in every way. I wuz so taken with her beauty that, at first, I didn't notice what she wuz doing, or who she wuz with."

He stopped talking and grinned, like he was milking the punch line of a good joke.

I pretended boredom. "Can you pick it up a little? I've still got time to get lucky tonight, if you don't keep me too long." I looked at my watch. "There must be some Cisco women I can meet."

231

Joey glared before continuing, "Then, she rolled over and the other one rolled up on her, kissing her long and hard. That woke me up. It wuz a dam' woman, and she was naked too. Later I learned it wuz that bitch lawyer. I never seen two women together before, but I knowed what they wuz doing. Hell, the way they wuz wrestling and groping one another, anybody woulda knowed what they wuz doing."

"What?" I couldn't help but interrupt. "The lawyer? You're saying Sheila and the lawyer were in bed together having sex, or whatever passes for sex between women?"

"Yep. Kinda hard to handle, ain't it?" He leaned back and grinned.

I was still reeling from his revelations. "Is that why you killed her, because she was in bed with the lawyer?" From what I'd learned during the investigation, Sheila was a free spirit. Hearing that she was having a lesbian affair didn't surprise me. She was not the young woman I'd known in college. I did wonder how Jake would take it.

"I don't blame you, Ace. I wuz as surprised as you are."

Joey had misread my facial expressions.

"How could a woman like Sheila who enjoyed men be in bed with another woman? Hell, I know for sure she enjoyed me. Ain't no woman can fake all them orgasms. Course, I'm better than guys like you."

Again, he stopped. I refused to comment except to nod for him to continue.

"That ain't why I killed her. I ain't like you old farts, I kin handle them kind of things. Nah, that ain't why she died. Close, but no cigar. Like they say,

'Different strokes for different folks.' Don't bother me none as long as I get mine."

He stopped and looked at me. I gave him my stone-faced stare and he continued. "When I saw the two of them in bed together, I screamed or yelled or . . ." He paused with a befuddled look on his face. "Hell, I don't know. I said something, I don't know what. They both sat up and stared at me. The lawyer pulled the sheet up over her."

He giggled. "Hell, that wuz a waste a her time. Compared to Sheila, she didn't have nothin' worth hiding. I seen better stacked mannequins. Sheila climbed off the bed and picked up her robe, cool as a cucumber. You'd a never knowed she wuz moanin' and groanin' a minute before. She wuz back in total control of herself." A leer took over his face.

Since he'd stopped talking again, I prodded him, "Great, Joey. She put on the robe and acted like she didn't give a shit. Then what?"

"You got it. She slipped on the robe and walked past me into the hallway and down the stairs. She never said a word. I followed. She went in the study and poured herself a scotch and water. Then she asked me what I wuz doing there, what I wanted. She treated me like I wuz the bug man who'd showed up to do his quarterly spraying."

He took on a puzzled look. "It wuz wild, Ace. She won't angry, disturbed or nothin'. She wuz totally cool. I told her I loved her, and I wanted to be with her. She laughed at me—threw back her head and laughed at me. She took another sip of her drink, then threw the rest of it in my face. I guess I snapped. I didn't know 'til later

233

what happened—after I had lots of time to think about it."

He frowned. "I grabbed her and tried to kiss her. She slapped me, laughing all the while. She said the reason she'd brought me home wuz because I wuz such a dork, a pint-sized, no-personality dork. She'd been doing me a favor, like giving a beggar a dollar." He hesitated, a faint grin showing. "She said she'd been raised to believe charity begins at home." He stopped talking again and crossed his arms.

After a moment during which we locked stares, I caved and said, "Let's go, Joey. Let it out. I've known punks like you all my life. You want to tell this story."

The grin disappeared, replaced by a snarl. "Edwards, you're a cold-blooded bastard, but you might be right. Maybe I do want to tell you how I wasted them bitches." Gradually, his face relaxed into something resembling normalcy. "I wuz holding Sheila by the arm, and when she made that comment about charity, I hit her. I must've had a grip on the robe because when I hit her, she stumbled back and fell, and I wuz left holding her robe. As she went down, I remember thinking what a gorgeous body she had. She wuz stacked."

His face changed again, back to his *I'm sorry* look. "Her head hit the edge of the fireplace hearth and I heard a loud crack. I knelt beside her and saw blood coming out of her ears. I checked for a pulse, but couldn't find none."

He stopped and looked at his hands, then spoke without lifting his head. "It wuz an accident, Ace. You gotta believe me, I didn't mean to kill her. Hell, I didn't mean to hit her. If she hadn't laughed at me—"

"I don't need to hear excuses," I said. "Save them for a jury. Get on with the story and pick it up. You're boring me." Part of it was true. I didn't want him to bog down in self-pity.

"You sonnafabitch!" At least Joey hadn't lost his spirit, or his vocabulary. "I sat and stared at Sheila— stared and cried, cried and stared. Yeah me. Rough, tough Joey-Boy. I cried. I might still be sitting there but I heard a noise. That damn lawyer wuz in the door. I'd forgotten about her. She said something, I don't know what, but it pulled me out of my crying jag. My first impulse wuz to explain I didn't mean to hurt Sheila. Then I saw what she wuz wearing—a white robe with a Texas star over her tit, like the one I used when I stayed with Sheila. And like me a few nights ago, she'd been screwing Sheila."

His face changed again. "Damn, Ace, how come women do that? Ain't there enough men out there for them? I mean, why—"

"You don't want to go there, Joey. I know I'm not going there. Get on with your story."

He clenched his fists, then flexed his fingers as he glared at me. "Okay, but someday I'm gonna meet you when you ain't got no gun."

"I don't think so, except when we're in the courtroom."

He glared some more. It was surprising such a young person had mastered a great glare.

"Let's see, where wuz I? Oh, yeah. The lawyer screamed, ran from the room, and headed up the stairs. I followed as fast as I could, and would have caught her except I wore my new boots, same ones I got on tonight. Ain't they nice?"

"Sure, Joey, they're great. Move on."

"You ain't got no sense of humor, have you?"

"Nope. Move on."

Another of his super stares. "The sole of my new boot slipped on the carpet of the steps and I stumbled. By the time I got up and started again, she wuz at the top, turning into the bedroom she and Sheila had been in. When I reached the bedroom door, she had the phone at her ear and wuz dialing. I dived and knocked it from her hand. We wrestled and I tore the robe off her. She fought like a wildcat, a naked wildcat."

Joey stopped and laughed an evil laugh. "You know, right then, she didn't look too bad. If she hadn't been such a bitch, I mighta give her a treat. But she was a fighter. Stark naked, she fought me as hard as she'd fought Jake during the divorce. Only difference was, against Jake she used the law, against me she used everything she had—nails, fists, teeth." He grinned. "Hell, I think she tried to hit me with a tit. I know damn well she spit on me. I proved I'm a better man than Jake Adams, though. I beat her, I choked her. I choked the shit right out of her."

The look on his face made me want to smash him, smash him as he'd done Millener. I didn't know her, but I figured no woman, no human being deserved to die at the hands of a punk like Joey.

"That's the story. Anything else you want?" Joey wore a satisfied sneer on his face.

"You're cool, Joey, real cool, a real sub-human son-of-a-bitch. If I had a son, I'd want him to be just like you. What about the fire, how'd you do that?"

"Huh?" He looked like he was trying to discern my meaning, then gave up. "The fire, yeah. That wuz my best move."

There went that stupid laugh again.

"I'd have gotten away with it if Jake hadn't brought you in. These local yokels would've never caught me."

"Flattery won't get you anywhere," I said. "Get back to the story. Where did you leave the lawyer's body?"

"Right where she fell. We'd fought our way into the hallway on the second floor. That's where I got my hands around her neck and choked her. When she fell, I left her there."

I mentally checked the house plans. What Joey said fit where the body had been found. She'd burned and fallen through from the second floor. That explained the confusion around her remains. "How did the fire start?"

"I went downstairs, and sat with Sheila for a while. I don't know how long. By now, my mind wuz clear, cold sober, and I was trying to find a way out of the mess. I remembered I had several cans of gas in the back of the truck. I brought them in. I started with the lawyer, dousing her good, then the bed they were in. That was the fun part of the night, getting that bitch-lawyer ready to burn. After spreading gas on the second floor, I did the same on the first. I laid a trail from the front door to Sheila."

Joey stopped talking and rubbed his eyes. Could those be tears or was he putting on a show for me?

"I told Sheila good-bye and poured the last of the gas over her. I drenched her pretty good. Then, I gathered all the cans and walked out the front door. Before closing the door, I tossed a match into the trail I laid down. It shore surprised me. That place went up like a Roman candle. There wuz a huge whooshing noise as the flame tracked the gas I'd poured around the place. It scared the hell out of me. I took off running as fast as I could. Somewhere between the house and my truck, I tripped and dropped all the gas cans."

He looked at me. "I heard you guys found'm when you went out in the morning. Think the cops would give'm back? Dad asked if I knew where they wuz." He crossed his arms over his chest again. "That's it. That's the whole story. What's next, hot shot? You got the gun."

"Book matches from the Down Home, I bet. Did you know you'd written Sheila's number inside the cover?"

"Yep, you musta found them. What, did I lose them when we wuz fighting?" He grinned. "I missed them the next day. Wondered 'bout that."

At this point, it was difficult to keep myself under control, I wanted to let him know in an physical manner what I thought of him. But, with a superhuman effort, I continued with my questions. "Sonny. Why'd you kill Sonny?"

"I'da thought a hotshot cop like you would have figgered that out. It wuz a mistake. When you showed up here, I made sure I met you in the Down Home. You thought I wuz drunk. Not on your life. I wuz checking you out, and I didn't like what I saw. You looked too damn sharp for my tastes. Like I said earlier, I don't think the locals would have gotten on to me, but I wuz worried about you. So, I left a note for Bubba figuring you two would head for the lake. I got away from Terri and headed up there, ready to take you out."

"Why Bubba? What did he do to you?"

"To me, nothing. With Sheila, he did all the things I wanted to keep doing to her. He deserved to die. Anyway, somehow you got out of the car without me seeing you. Might've been while I watched a couple of teenagers get it on in a back seat. When I snuck up and cut loose on your car, there wuz only one person there. I didn't know until the next day it wuz Sonny, and not you, or maybe Bubba." He grinned. "I wuz shore disappointed."

"I guess your other attempts at me were the same thing, right?"

"Yeah. That's some animal you've got there. I didn't know what I'd run into when it jumped on me— ripping, scratching and making the craziest damn sounds. I got the hell out of there as fast as I could. I musta been two blocks away before I realized it wuz a damn cat."

"What about the motel, the night you searched my room?"

"Same night that miserable cat of yours got me. I went to your motel first 'cause I knowed you wuz with Terri. When you pulled into the parking space outside the room, the headlights lit up the room and I thought sure you prob'ly saw me ducking behind the bed. Don't know what wuz on your mind but you didn't come bustin' in like they do on TV. I had time to get behind the door while you did your super-cop stuff."

He stopped talking and grinned. "Wish I'da had a video cam. I coulda won first prize on one of them television shows."

I blushed.

239

Randy Rawls

"I wuz beginning to wonder if I hadda come out after you when you came through the door. You musta heard me or somethin' 'cause you put up a pretty good fight. Course I whipped your butt."

He gave me his nasty grin again. "When I got that last lick in, and you crashed into the bedpost, I figgered you wuz dead. I was about to make sure when a car pulled up. It spooked me, and I decided I'd better get the hell out of there."

He looked at me. "You must be a tough sonnafabitch, but your eye looks great. Is that mine?"

I fingered my forehead. "Yeah, it's yours. What about last night? Your mom thinks you were sound asleep at home."

"Mom—what an angel she is. You gotta understand she believes sleep cures ever'thin'. When I wuz a kid and got sick, she'd put me to bed under three or four quilts and give me a toddy to make me sleep. Funny thing wuz, it worked. I'd wake up in a bed of sweat, cured from whatever crud I had. Yesterday, she did the same thing, but instead of a toddy, which I'd rather have, she gave me a sleeping pill. I didn't swallow it."

"How did you get out without her knowing?"

"Simple. Mom settled down in front of the TV and her favorite show. I went out the window as soon as I wuz sure she wuz occupied. After I missed you in the motel parking lot, I went home and crawled back through the window. Mom never knowed I'd been out. You know, you're a lucky sonnafabitch. I don't usually miss what I shoot at, but I missed you twice."

He'd confessed to killing two women in cold blood, incinerating their bodies, and killing Sonny by mistake. Most insulting of all was he'd admitted making two

240

attempts on my life. The way he acted, you'd have thought he was telling me about a Sunday School picnic. I said, "Next, I—"

"Ace, Joey. Are you here?"

## CHAPTER TWENTY-FOUR

Terri! What was she doing here? My concentration wavered and I looked toward the door.

Joey must have been waiting for the opportunity. He was on me like Sweeper, scratching, clawing, and punching like a wild animal. I shoved him back, but as I recaptured my balance, he proved he'd learned the same low-down dirty tricks I used. He tried to knee me in the groin. I saw it coming, and spun. His knee slammed into my thigh causing instant paralysis, then slid into my groin. I dropped, verifying you can see stars indoors.

He grabbed my Beretta and rushed out the door. All I could do was moan.

I heard, "Thanks, sis, you always come through for me."

I was trying unsuccessfully to get to my feet when Terri arrived at my side. "Are you okay? I'm sorry. Did Joey hurt you? Can I help?"

I didn't answer any of her questions, not even the last one, although in any other circumstance, I'd have had a double entendre response. I managed to gain my feet and hobbled to the antique chair where Joey had sat. I dropped into it, thankful that our ancestors had been good craftsmen. Through clenched teeth, I wheezed, "I'll be fine in a couple of minutes, but I'll pass on the orgy tonight."

Terri made me feel much better by cupping my face in her hands and kissing me on the lips. "I love you, you stupid jerk, and I'll make it all better later."

The cherubs sang again but I shushed them. There was a killer out there.

The pain had diminished to something equivalent to an impacted wisdom tooth. "It'll have to wait. I gotta go after Joey. He confessed he killed Sheila, Sonny and Sheila's lawyer. I can't let him get away."

"I'm coming with you," Terri said. "If Joey did what you say, I have to face him, to ask him why."

I wanted to protest, but one look at Terri's face convinced me it'd be a waste of time. I rose to my feet and hobbled to the door. "Let's go then. We gotta get on his trail before he gets out of sight."

Terri helped me down the stairs and out of the building. By the time we arrived at the Chrysler, I was almost walking upright. If only the pain would go away.

I looked around and all I saw was darkness and storm clouds. The wind blew and the lightning and thunder were moving closer. "What a time for the weathermen to be right," I mumbled. "Now we'll never find him. Get in, I'll put up the top."

I opened the door for Terri, then limped around the car, got in the driver's side and started the motor.

"I know where he's headed," she said. "It's where he hid when he was young. Head toward Scranton."

I hit the button to raise the top and thirty seconds later, it was locked in place. I backed up and started out of the parking lot as the storm hit in full fury. It was a typical Texas thunderstorm, a real gully-whomper. Lightning flashed and the rain pounded so hard, I worried about a flash flood. The windshield wipers fought a losing battle.

I drove as fast as I dared, at least ten miles faster than I should because visibility was near zero. My headlights reflected back into my eyes, unable to penetrate the almost solid wall of water that slammed down. Lightning blinded me, keeping my eyes from adjusting to the darkness. The cracks of thunder were deafening. I hunched over the steering wheel, hoping I didn't miss the road. The rain dripping through the hole in the top was my reminder as to why I had to keep going. Things could have been much worse. There was no hail pounding down, and Terri's hand on my thigh equalized everything.

"Where do you think he's headed?" I risked a glance at Terri.

She stared ahead. "Scranton Academy."

"Huh? There's nothing there but the remains of the stone walls. Remember our picnic." I looked toward Terri to see if she was serious, but had to return my full attention to the road when lightning flashed. It was a good thing I did because we were headed into a curve I hadn't seen coming.

"When Joey was a kid, he and his buddies used to bike out there and play in the old ruins. Later, he went there to hide when he couldn't take the harassment from the high school bullies anymore, or when he decided to run away from home. He'll be there."

I concentrated on my driving as my mind pictured what had been Scranton Academy. I remembered it well from our picnic although I spent most of that afternoon looking at Terri.

"Hold on." I twisted the wheel to counteract the slide the car had started into as I stomped the accelerator, praying the wheels would find traction. I'm a firm believer in front wheel drive, and it saved us. The wheels spun, then gripped and pulled us around the sharp curve where State Road 569 turns into 1864. We'd reached Scranton.

"Look," Terri said.

She pointed toward a pickup truck off the road resting against the trees. It was dark with a white racing stripe along its side.

"It's Joey's. I'm sure it's Joey's. Stop, Ace. Please stop." Terri's voice shook.

I slowed to a stop, then backed up. The rain still pounded down, and I couldn't see much, but it did look like his truck.

Terri jumped out.

"Where the hell are you going?"

"To see if Joey's in there," she yelled back over the noise of the storm.

She peered through the window, shading her eyes against the glare of the lightning. After a moment, she came back to the car. "It's empty. He must have gone on to the academy."

"You're nuts, you know," I said. "Why'd you get out in this storm? He could have been waiting for us."

"I had to know if he was in there, if he was . . ." She didn't finish it. "The academy's a ways down there. Watch for the turn-in to the left."

I eased the car forward, looking around, hoping I'd see Joey before he saw us. He had my Beretta and I suspected he wouldn't hesitate to use it.

"Before we go in there," Terri said, "there's something I've got to tell you. Joey's not going anywhere. We don't need to rush. Pull over."

The urgency and seriousness in her voice compelled me to do what she asked. Once stopped, I said, "Okay, but make it quick. I don't want him going to ground where I can't flush him out."

"You've got to know this before you face Joey. I talked to Jake. I had to tell him today, I couldn't wait any longer. That's why I was looking for you when I found you with Joey at the hotel."

Her words struck deep in my psyche, and I reacted without thinking. "Wonderful. You pulled me off a chase for a killer to tell me you talked to your boyfriend? What the hell—"

"Calm down and listen." The urgency in her voice shut me up, told me she was not to be interrupted.

"I told him I couldn't marry him. It wouldn't be fair because I'm in love with another man. That's why I talked to him—to tell him I'm in love with you."

Ever heard the expression, *You could have knocked me over with a feather*. I'm glad she didn't have one or she could have given me a serious thrashing. I pulled her to me, squishing her rain-soaked clothing against me.

"If this is a trick to get me to back off on Joey, it won't work. I'm still going to bring him in." Doubt and hope swirled inside me.

"No trick, Ace. I love you, and we're going to talk Joey into giving himself up."

I quieted her with my lips. A long kiss later, I released her and pulled the car back onto the road.

Love is a miraculous state of being. It can make grouches agreeable—the selfish, unselfish—and the ugly, beautiful. It can make the worst day a beautiful spring morning with flowers blooming and robins circling overhead. That night, it stopped the storm.

With Terri's declaration, there was a last flash of lightning followed by its roll of thunder, and the rain stopped. The moon didn't exactly leap out but I was satisfied. I inched the car along with the headlights off, expecting to catch up with Joey at any moment. He couldn't be too far in front of us.

I concentrated on the road and the vegetation alongside. "When this is over," I said, "we'll go on a long trip, maybe to the Caribbean where we can explore one another."

Her reply wasn't what I hoped for but it would do. "Once Joey's been judged in a court of law, we'll take that trip. Until then, you'll have to accept my love. Joey comes first."

As I considered a way to convince her otherwise, she pointed. "There's the turn-in."

I swung the car in and stopped. The ruins of the academy loomed about fifty yards in front of us, silhouetted against the brightening western sky. All stone, ragged at the top—nothing but broken walls.

"Stay here. Don't get out until I've captured him. I know he's your brother, but right now, he's a fugitive running from justice. Neither of us knows what he'll do."

I climbed out, cursing the courtesy lights as they flashed on, lighting up the area. I dropped to the ground, and rolled, simultaneously slamming the door. I could see the tree we'd picnicked under, silhouetted against the sky so I crawled toward it. I made the tree without incident and squinted at the ruins. Nothing. I couldn't see anything except the walls. I suddenly had a revelation or whatever they call it. I knew he had my Beretta, but did he keep a rifle in his pickup? I tried to picture his truck as I had followed it into Cisco but the image I conjured was the flash of his pistol as he fired at me. I should have asked Terri before I'd bailed out of the Chrysler. He was a Texan. I had to assume he had a rifle.

I lay there soaking up rain water from the grass, trying to think of a way to get Joey to reveal himself, or better yet, to convince him to give up. The last thing I wanted was to kill the brother of the woman I loved, the woman who I now knew returned my love and waited in my car for me to do something to save him.

I knew I couldn't sneak up on Joey if he watched for me, and I was sure he did. I stood and leaned against the tree while trying to think of an approach. I did the only thing I could think of. I yelled. "Joey! Come out, Joey. We need to talk."

Silence.

"Joey, your best hope is to give yourself up. Even if you get away tonight, somebody else'll run you down. Talk to me, Joey."

There was a flash of light and another voice called out. "Joey. Please come out. We want to help you."

Terri. She was out of the car, out in the darkness somewhere. I cursed under my breath. "Hard headed woman. Why doesn't she ever listen?"

I heard a noise to my right and dropped to the ground, rolling in that direction. It was Terri scooting across the ground toward me.

"You sure are noisy," I said. "I'll quiet you down after this is over."

"Let me call him again." Terri called to Joey a second time, but there was still no response. "Poor Joey, he must be terrified."

What could I say to that? I couldn't tell her I hoped he was more terrified than I. I took Joey's pistol out of my jacket pocket where I'd put it when we were in the museum. "Guess I'm going to have to go get him." I stood, trying to blend myself into the shadow of the tree trunk. There was still no movement, or none I could see.

I crouched and stepped from behind the tree, taking small steps. I hoped we didn't get a residual lightning flash. I'd stand out like a nun in the Down Home. I moved toward the ruins.

A shot rang out. I dived and the ground rose and smacked me in the chest and face, leaving me gasping for air. I lay catching my breath and spitting grass. It was a rifle, no doubt about it. I'd been right about his pickup.

While I digested this development, Terri screamed, "No, Joey. No, don't hurt him. I love Ace. We're going to get married."

Her words were music to my ears, and I hoped Joey heard, and wanted me as a brother-in-law. I tried to remember when I'd proposed to her or vice-versa, but gave up. Hey, who cared?

My mouth fumbled at making words but nothing came out. All I could do was gasp for breath and spit grass. I struggled to my feet and started back to Terri, thinking it would be smart for us to get behind the tree.

Joey with a rifle was a whole new game I wasn't keen on playing. That rifle meant he could make whatever rules he chose.

My breathing returned to normal and I moved more quickly. As I got to the tree, Terri stood and wrapped her arms around me.

Although our clothing was wet, I felt her warmth flowing into me. I wanted so badly to forget about Joey, to stand there and hold Terri all night—to hold her for the rest of my life.

"Ace, I was so worried. Please don't—"

Another shot had sounded and Terri grunted, then went slack in my arms. I lowered her to the ground, knowing she'd been hit and hoping the opposite. Leaning over her, I whispered, "Terri, where'd you get it? Where're you hit?"

"Don't blame Joey." Terri's voice was filled with pain. "He didn't mean it. I love you and I love him. You're the two men I hold dearest . . ." Her voice trailed away.

"What Terri, what? Please talk to me. Don't quit on me now. Please talk to me."

Silence. I felt her neck looking for the carotid artery. There was no motion there, no movement other than my trembling fingers. I realized I'd never told her how much I loved her. "Terri, please hear me. I love you. Please don't leave me."

Knowledge far beyond anything I'd learned in school told me I wasted my time. Death had claimed Terri.

I lay her on the wet ground and stood, facing the ruins as tears flowed freely. "You sonafabitch!" I screamed. "You hit Terri! She's dead, Joey! You killed

250

your sister! You killed the woman I love! You're a dead man, Joey!" I ran toward the ruins, squinting, hoping he'd fire again so I could spot his position. I knew I was out of control but I didn't care.

Joey obliged me. The shot whizzed by my ear as I stepped in a hole and stumbled. I fired three quick shots at the muzzle flash, got up and ran. Another shot rang out, but it was far enough off target I didn't hear the bullet. I fired again, remembering the old adage, *You don't hear the bullet that has your name on it*, or something like that.

I neared the base of the ruins as another shot broke the silence. Dirt kicked up at my feet and I tried to return fire toward the flash. I heard the click of the hammer against a spent shell. What a time to run out of ammunition. The son-of-a-bitch hadn't reloaded. One more thing to take up with him when I got my hands around his throat. Hands, yes that would be much better. Guns were too impersonal. I wanted to kill him with my bare hands. I wanted to feel his life slip away.

I heard a long scream, a thud, then silence. I reached the wall and leaned against it, breathing hard, trying to meld myself into it. In front of me I heard a whimpering, a moaning. I suspended my breathing to hear better.

"Ace, I'm hurt, hurt bad." It was Joey's voice, filled with fear and pain, coming from down the wall.

I remembered the thud. "Joey, where are you?" I whispered.

"Over here. The stone is slippery. I fell. I think my back's broke. I can't feel my legs."

"Serves you right, you son-of-a-bitch. You killed Terri. She's dead, Joey, and I'm going to rip your guts out."

I heard him moan again. "No, I couldn't have . . . I didn't . . . I loved her. She was my only friend."

I inched along the wall toward Joey's voice. "Yes, you did, and you're going to pay. Keep talking, you bastard, so I can find you." I stepped closer, trying to ascertain how much farther I'd have to go before I could wrap my hands around his neck and squeeze the life out of him. "You're a dead man, Joey. No judge and jury for you. You're dead." Anger drove me, sadness about Terri and the adrenaline from rage kept me going, made me ignore my empty pistol against Joey's loaded guns.

"No, Ace. I'll save you the trouble. I gotta find Terri. Gotta tell her it wuz an accident. Maybe Sheila'll be there, too."

A shot sounded from near by, and I flattened against the wall wondering if Joey had been suckering me in. As the echo died away inside the stone walls, silence became the dominant feature of the night.

I froze, fearing for my life. The shot had reminded me of my vulnerability. Joey still had my pistol with ammunition and all I had was his pistol. In the dark, I couldn't even see to throw it.

Silence. I waited. More silence. I could hear nothing except my heart pounding loud enough to wake Mom and Dad. "Joey. Joey!" I was in the shadow of the wall and I couldn't see a thing. I inched toward where I'd last heard him, and stumbled over a soft object.

I hit the ground and reached to feel what had tripped me. My searching hands found a body. Joey. He didn't move or make a sound. I ran my hands up his trunk and groped for his carotid artery. I put my hand into a gooey mess. My sense of smell kicked in, and the odor was unbearable. Also, I didn't find a carotid artery. I didn't find a head.

I rose and collected my thoughts, giving my heart time to settle back into something resembling a normal rhythm. I stumbled away and went back to the car where I found a flashlight. I stopped by Terri first and found her still dead, in spite of my yearning. Her body was cooling in the wet air. I opened the trunk, took out the blanket we'd used for our picnic and covered her with it.

When I got back to Joey, I found the same result—he was dead. He'd blown the top of his head off.

I lost it. "You son-of-a-bitch, how dare you do this?" I screamed at him, demanding he get up so I could kill him. I was nuts, out of control. I snapped back to normalcy to find myself with a rock held high over my head, preparing to bash Joey with it.

I sobered, and dropped to the ground with my head in my hands. As far as I was concerned, he cheated justice, and he cheated me. I hadn't wanted him to die from his own hand. I wanted the satisfaction of watching him die after I pulled the trigger. I wanted to dribble him like a soccer ball over the grounds of Scranton Academy.

I walked back to the car, took out my cell phone, and called 9-1-1. Then I sat with Terri to wait. I cradled her and whispered, "I love you. I should have told you, I love you."

When the ambulance arrived, the medical personnel assumed I was injured because of the blood on me and my crying. They insisted on checking my blood pressure, temperature, pulse, and other vital signs. They seemed surprised to find me healthy, and were solicitous as they took Terri's body away.

Sheriff Yardley didn't show as much concern for my well-being. He used terms like *jail, charges, obstruction of justice* and a few other expressions that meant he wasn't happy with me. I didn't care. All I thought of was Terri.

I cried.

He cursed.

## CHAPTER TWENTY-FIVE

Jake and Bubba stood one on each side of me at Terri's funeral. I was between them because I wasn't sure they were ready to be civil to one another, even in grief. Terri and Joey were buried side by side in the Hart family plot. I wished Terri's grave were closer to the Edwards plot. I knew Mom and Dad would love to have her for a neighbor.

Across from us stood Terri's mother and an older version of Joey. I remembered Joey's comment when we'd first met. "She looks like Mom and I look more like Dad." He'd been right. I wanted to do something, say something that would make Ms. Hart feel better, that would let her know I hadn't wanted it to end this way. It wasn't often a mother buried both her children on successive days. I could see the pain etched in her face, making her look twenty years older than when I'd met her a few days ago.

I headed around the grave to express my condolences, but her grimace froze me in my tracks. She wasn't interested in anything I had to say. I couldn't blame her if she held me responsible for their deaths. There was no way I could expect her to understand it

255

was Joey, not me, who was the reason both were dead. She had to be thinking that if I hadn't returned to Cisco, Terri and Joey would still be alive. Maybe she was right. But I couldn't afford to believe that—not if I wanted to remain sane.

I wanted to tell her I felt the loss of Terri as acutely as she did. I wanted to tell her how much I loved her daughter. But, I backed down and returned to Bubba and Jake.

I stood with my head down, feeling sad for myself, cursing my fate at losing Terri.

"Ace, I can't tell you how sorry I am at how this worked out." Jake's voice was soft and sympathetic. "When Terri told me she couldn't marry me because she loved you, I knew who was the richer. All my money packaged with my love couldn't buy what had been handed to you—the most fantastic woman I've ever known."

"Thanks, Jake." I noted that he didn't call me Arty. "I was almost there, wasn't't I? A shot at true happiness. I never really had her, but I miss her more than anyone can ever know." Tears flowed. Embarrassed, I turned toward Joey's grave. He'd been buried the previous day. "At least we know what happened to your house."

"And to Sheila and Sonny," Bubba added. "I lost the woman I love, so I understand what you're feeling." Bubba's voice was soft and filled with sadness. His country-boy accent had disappeared. "I suppose I could use that old cliché that time heals all wounds. But I can tell you from my experience, it leaves a nasty, angry scar. I'll never get over Sheila."

Jake looked at him. "Neither will I, Bubba, neither will I. I tried to hate her, but I could never do it. She was a part of me I'll carry to my grave."

They stared at one another for a moment, and I tensed, fearing the worst while hoping it wouldn't happen.

Bubba changed the subject. "Hojo said he would open the Down Home early today. That's his way of honoring Terri, and he's laying in an extra supply of Killian's in your honor, Ace. He should be there by now. If we don't head out, we might not get in the door. I'm sure the whole Down Home crowd will gather to wish Terri a good trip."

As we turned to walk away, Jake surprised me by saying, "Bubba, it's time we buried the hatchet. We stood on opposite sides of the grave when Sheila was buried. Let's move to the same side now. We loved her, you in your way, and me in mine. In her own way, she loved both of us, and I think she'd want us to be friends." He stuck out his hand toward Bubba.

Bubba looked at him, then reached toward Jake's hand. His first grasp seemed tentative, then he shook it vigorously. "Thanks, Jake," he said. "I've been sorry for a long time we hurt you. All I can say in my defense is I did love her, truly loved her."

"There're things I'll never forget—or forgive, but we can start new."

Maybe that was the first time I realized the power of love, and how badly Jake was hurt when he lost Sheila. I couldn't help but reflect that even with all his money and prestige, he'd lost the two women he loved. Love could bring down the most powerful, the richest among us.

I looked at Jake, then Bubba and saw the sadness in their faces. I knew I'd been right in not telling either of them what Joey told me about Sheila and Millener— about their love tryst.

We started toward the exit onto Second Street. I glanced back toward Terri's grave and saw Mr. Hart coming after us. My first impulse was to run. The last thing I wanted was a confrontation with Terri's dad at her graveside.

"Mr. Adams, do you have a moment?" he called.

Jake, Bubba and I stopped as Mr. Hart caught the three of us. He stuck out his hand toward Jake and said, "Mr. Adams, I had to thank you for helping us with Terri and Joey's funerals. The undertaker done a mighty fine job on both of them, but he went all out on Terri. Don'tcha think so?"

"Yes, she was very beautiful," Jake responded as Bubba and I stared at him, dumbfounded.

"Me and the missus could never have afforded to put'm away in style without your help. She's kinda upset right now, but I know as soon as she settles down, she's gonna want to thank you too."

"Think nothing of it, sir," Jake responded in an embarrassed tone. "Now, we have to go. Please give Ms. Hart my heartfelt condolences."

"Yore're a mighty fine man, Mr. Adams. Ah'm gonna tell ever'body what you done." Terri's father turned and headed toward the graves, but not before giving me a glare that would melt a glacier.

I stared at Jake and realized I was proud of him, proud to learn that his rich-guy layer was only a veneer. Inside, he still had small town values.

He caught me looking at him and shrugged. "What the hell's money for if not to assuage your own guilt?"

Since he was in a generous mood, I decided to test how far he'd go. "Hey, remember I told you the fire department needs a new utility vehicle. That old one—"

"Not to worry." Jake cut me off with a grin. "It's on order—a Jeep Cherokee with all the trimmings. That Chrysler dealer's getting rich off me."

Still the blasé rich guy.

That afternoon and evening, I re-discovered what makes living in a small town so personal, so wonderful. The Down Home was packed with people telling me how great Terri was, how sorry they were I'd lost her, and what a expert job I'd done in solving the case. All afternoon the faces changed, but the sincerity remained the same.

Sam Raleigh came in and apologized for giving me a bad time when I first came to town. He left me feeling proud when he said, "Hell, you're damn near as good as Mr. Adams bragged you to be. Come back anytime."

Sheriff Yardley showed up late in the afternoon. He wore his uniform with the hat I'd admired when it hung in his office. You remember, the tan department-issue, sweat-stained cowboy hat with character I saw in his office.

"Congratulations, Edwards. I don't know whether you're good or lucky. All the prints—gas cans, your motel, your house—were Joey's, especially the last set on your Beretta. Don't know how you did it, but you got it done. Of course, you made me look bad in my own backyard. You broke the case while my people spun their wheels. And me with an election coming up. I'd feel a whole lot better if I knowed you was leaving town and not coming back any time soon. And don'tcha ever think about running against me."

He stopped and glared at me before a smile split his face. "Other than that, I'm here to say you did one hellava job on this case, and I'm proud to have watched you play football when you wuz a kid. In spite of your years in the city, I guess you still got some Eastland County in you."

"I hope I never outgrow my roots here," I responded. "As for running for office, don't worry about me. You're the man this county needs. I got lucky and had the help of a good woman. You can be sure I'm on my way out of Eastland County. With Terri gone, I don't have anything to hang around for."

As he stood looking relieved, I added, "Did I do good enough for you to give me that great hat of yours?"

I plucked it off his head and headed for the door. First, he gave me a look that would melt glass, then threw back his head and laughed. "Edwards, you best not come back to Cisco. I might turn my head next time Sergeant Jones wants to have a private interview with you."

I walked out, climbed into the Chrysler and pointed it toward Dallas knowing all my ties to Cisco lay in Oakwood Cemetery—my mother, my father, and now, Terri Hart. I looked at the sheriff's hat on the passenger seat and tried to grin, but instead, tears trickled from my eyes.

\*       \*       \*

The next night I sat in my favorite position, kicked back in my recliner. I'd picked the boys up as soon as I got back to North Dallas. The concierge summoned a bellhop who carried them to my car. The boys had seemed unimpressed and glad to leave the cat hotel.

Striker lay in my lap, and Sweeper had ensconced himself on the arm of the chair, his private throne. They were content, purring happily, apparently glad to have me home. I stroked them and ran through the case.

As I finished, I said, "You're the hero, Sweeper. If you hadn't attacked Joey when he came to call, and ripped off his earring, I might have never caught on to him."

Sweeper yawned, then meowed, and gave me a look that seemed to say, "Hey, no big deal."

As soon as I was convinced he didn't care, he stood, stretched, and pranced up and down the arm of the chair a couple of times. After he'd performed his heroic march, he jumped onto the floor and scooted across the room. I figured he was headed for the food dish but instead, he ran to the sofa and flattened onto his belly. He reached under the sofa and I could see he strained to reach something.

I moved Striker to the arm of the chair and walked to Sweeper. "What is it, old boy? Did you lose one of Ms. Jacobs' kitty treats under there? Or maybe, your favorite toy, your love-toy?"

As I said it, realization dealt me a serious blow. I pulled the sofa from the wall and Sweeper raced by me and grabbed his miniature soccer ball, his favorite toy, his love-toy. He dribbled it around the room a couple of times then fired an accurate shot into the corner.

While he played, I stood and stared, remembering his performance when I'd come home after my first trip to Cisco. Love-toy. Could he have known? Nah, no way!

261

I sat back in my chair and Striker again took possession of my lap. Sweeper jumped back onto the arm of the chair, then stepped into my lap, nudging Striker to make space for himself.

Striker had stopped purring during Sweeper's performance, and now moved to allow Sweeper to settle. As Sweeper curled himself into position, Striker licked my hand with his sandpaper tongue. Sweeper nodded agreement. Both purred again.

"Now boys, let me tell you about Terri Hart. She was almost your step-mom."

They looked at me as if they'd prefer to return to the cat hotel than listen to another of my stories.

I told them anyway.

**CASE CLOSED**

Printed in the United States
17491LVS00001B/11